Love.V2

Julia Fisher

Julia Fisher

Cover design and illustration by Rebecca Driedger

Edited by Desert Ink Editorial

www.juliafisherwrites.com

For everyone just trying to keep their heads above water and hold on to a little happiness along the way.

This sh*t is hard.

Prologue

Tess

The porch light was flickering and something smelled alarmingly like vomit. This was probably not the best idea, but I shoved aside the worried feeling in my gut. It hadn't served me well up to this point in life, anyway.

"I'm fine," I said. A suspiciously familiar-looking rubber hose poked out of the unkempt shrubs. "I only wanted you to know where I was."

"Just stay where you are. Let me throw some jeans on and I'll..." Vanna's voice devolved into a hacking cough on the other side of the phone. Only two weeks into our first semester at Western Tennessee University and my roomie had caught some virus that was going around. "You don't even know anyone there," she reminded me weakly when her coughing subsided.

"I know Dylan." I bit my lip, willing myself to suppress the flush crawling up my cheeks in the beat of silence that followed.

Attending a college where I didn't know a single person was as freeing as it was terrifying. Thankfully, I'd won the roommate lottery with Vanna. One look at my shy, quiet self and she'd taken me under her wing. Her brash, outgoing personality meant she'd never met a stranger, and though I enjoyed how she'd kept an eye on me the last couple of weeks, I didn't want a mother hen tonight.

"Dylan's not a bad guy," she hedged. Like Vanna, he already seemed to fit in perfectly at WTU. People gave him fist bumps on the sidewalk. Even our English teacher called on him more often than everyone else. "But you don't really know him, Tess. It's dangerous to be at a college party by yourself."

Alright, so I didn't technically *know* him. We'd only spoken once, two days ago, when he'd invited Vanna to this party and said, "Bring your friend, too. Tess, right?"

My stomach still fluttered thinking about it. He knew my name. God, it was pathetic.

I'd spent the last two weeks pining after Dylan Morris like a middle schooler in heat, and he'd invited me (however indirectly) to his house for a party. It was the kind of opportunity I'd promised myself I wouldn't pass up.

"I'm going in," I announced, already walking up the sidewalk.

"Don't you dare go in there, Theresa Lynn Livingston, or I swear to God—" She erupted in a spasm of rattling coughs, which I used to my advantage.

"Lay back down before you choke on your own tongue. I'll be safe. Don't wait up, bye!" I practically yelled as I hung up. She was probably right, and this was a bad idea, but I'd made up my mind. I was going to my first ever college party. Tonight.

It wasn't anything like I'd seen in the movies. The little house on the edge of campus looked rundown. Paint peeled from the drooping siding, but a faint thrum of bass met my ears as I made my way to the front door. It swung open before I could knock, three girls leaving with angry looks on their faces.

"What a bust," one of them grumbled, barely glancing at me as they passed. "What kind of frat dudes don't know how to tap a keg?"

They muttered, teetering across the pavement in heels and flirty, ruffly skirts.

I glanced down at my Toms and thrifted lace tank top. Was I supposed to be wearing heels? I should have asked Vanna, but that would have meant telling her where I was going. She'd never have let me out the door if she'd known.

A few more people trickled past, all complaining and shaking their heads. I stood frozen on the front stoop, making myself as small as possible as they walked away. The party was a bust? And what was this about a keg?

I glanced around, locating that suspicious rubber hose I'd noticed earlier. A bubble of anxiety crept up from my belly as I examined my shoes. I probably shouldn't be here. What was I thinking, crashing the party of a guy who very likely didn't remember I existed? Just because his eyes were like dark chocolate, and he made my body feel like a toasted marshmallow—all gooey and hot.

I blew out a breath, straightening my spine and picturing my list in my head, specifically the first line: "Go to a normal college party. Have fun."

I plucked the rubber hose from the bushes and opened the door.

***

Dylan

"I'm telling you, it's not here," Derrick insisted.

"The dude said it came with the keg!" Mac yelled in Derrick's face, brandishing a receipt. Derrick bared his teeth.

"People are already leaving, guys. If we fuck this up..." another one of my brothers, Michael, muttered, his eyes darting around before landing on me. He didn't need to finish that sentence. Having the new pledges throw a party to kick off the school year was a time-honored Epsilon tradition. If it tanked, we'd have hell to pay.

"Alright, um..." I looked around the kitchen again, hoping a miracle would appear.

"Are you guys looking for this?" I could barely hear her soft voice over all the noise, but when I looked up, there she was. Tess Livingston. She had come. And she was holding the beer tap.

Mac raised his fists in the air, bellowing, "BEER ANGEL!!" Tess winced at the raucous chorus of cheers that followed, the crowd pushing her forward into the kitchen, chanting "beer angel!"

"Give her some space, guys. Back up." I glared at a dude who was getting too close, and he stumbled backwards, probably already a few drinks deep. I reached for Tess's elbow, guiding her through the packed bodies in the living room. The kitchen wasn't much better, but at least it was just my brothers in there, and I could trust them not to trample her.

Her skin was silky under my fingertips, and I wanted to stroke her. I was pathetic. Two weeks ago, I'd sat behind her in English class and noticed an incredible sketch of the quad poking out of her notebook. I'd leaned over to compliment the work and stopped dead in my tracks.

She was the most beautiful girl I'd ever seen. Her light blonde hair, big blue eyes, and delicate features made her look like an actual angel, or a fairy, or something. That she was beautiful and possessed an incredible artistic talent was pretty much all I knew about her.

She was quiet, shy even. I'd resorted to befriending her roommate to get a little closer to her. And holy shit, the far-fetched plan had worked. Here she was in our frat house kitchen, clutching a keg tap like a lifeline.

"You're a hero." I gently squeezed her arm.

"Hardly. I just found this in the bushes out front. Figured you might need it." She shoved the tap into my hands without meeting my eyes.

A pink blush spread across her peaches-and-cream cheeks, probably from all the attention. She hated being called on in class, curling up in her chair whenever our professor was about to ask a question. I always tried to answer before he could get to her. I was on track to receive a stellar participation grade in English.

"Beer Angel," Mac whispered again, reaching over to grab the tap. The party surged closer at the promise of alcohol, pushing Tess into me. I dropped her arm to reach around her waist, pulling her out of the way of another party dude, glaring at him for good measure.

"Oh, um, excuse me," Tess whispered, rigid.

"Sorry, it's a little crazy in here. Don't want you to get run over."

"Thanks." She finally looked up, her round, ocean eyes meeting mine like a clap of thunder. The corner of her pink lips curled upwards, and I realized I was staring.

"It won't explode, right?" Michael's uneasiness thankfully gave me something to look at other than her.

We all stared at the keg for a beat of silence. I was ninety-nine percent sure it wouldn't explode, but I'd never tapped a keg before. Our older fraternity brothers usually did the honors.

"You guys don't know how...?" Tess trailed off when we all looked at her. Her blush deepened. It would be weird to tell them all to look away, right? *Yes.* Right.

"I mean, we could probably figure it out?" Derrick looked about as confident as he sounded.

"I don't know, man. *Will* it explode?" Mac asked Tess, like she had the answer. She paused, looking around, before sighing and reaching her hand out for the tap.

"Line the threads up here. Make sure this is released." She did something with a lever, pointing to the top of the keg. After a quick twist, she straightened. "Done."

I stared. We *all* stared. Then Mac's guttural cry of "*BEER ANGEL-LLLLLLL!*" rang out with ear-splitting volume. The rest of the party followed suit, flying into a frenzy with Tess at the center. When her shoulders hunched over, I gave into my baser instincts and pulled her closer.

"Here." I took the red plastic cup from Mac's hand when it was half-full. "You deserve the first cup."

"FIRST CUP TO THE BEER ANGEL!" Mac roared.

"Alright." I gave him a quelling look, which he read in the blink of an eye, turning to scream. "And next cup to someone else!"

Everyone's focus shifted in an instant as my brothers rushed to hand out cups. Someone cranked up the volume on the speakers in the living room, and I felt a lifetime's worth of pressure lift off my shoulders. We'd done it. Party in full swing. And it was all thanks to the Beer Angel in front of me.

She was staring at the cup in her hands, looking uneasy.

"Too much foam?"

"I have a confession," she whispered, long lashes lowering.

"Your secret will be safe with me," I whispered back, taking a half-step toward her and enjoying when she didn't step away. In fact, she only craned closer, rising to her tip-toes and cupping her hand around my ear. Goosebumps erupted down my neck. *Pitiful.*

"I hate beer."

Between my body's ridiculous reaction to her closeness and the din of the kitchen, it took me a moment to understand what she'd just said. "You know how to tap a keg, but you don't drink beer?"

She shrugged. "Is that weird?"

"Not weird," I drawled, taking the plastic cup from her hands. In a way, it fit what I knew of her. Beautiful girl who recoiled from attention. Quiet student who created the most intricate and colorful art I'd ever seen. She seemed sheltered, naïve almost, but she rolled with Vanna, the most outspoken person in class. "Intriguing."

"Oh, um...thank you." Her neck flushed. Cute.

"Let me get you something else. What do you want?" She surveyed our offerings before settling on a rum and Coke. I let her open the mini herself.

"Very fancy with the individual cocktails," she observed while I poured. I popped a straw in the cup before handing it over.

"We take our reputation seriously. We want everyone to know they're safe with us. No communal hunch punch, no roofies."

She choked on her first sip. "Roofies? Does that actually happen at WTU?"

"I won't lie, sometimes, yeah. It's awful. But Eps don't get into stuff like that."

"Well, that's good to hear. Guess I picked the right party to come to alone." She smiled into her drink, but her words locked me up.

"You're here alone? Where's Vanna?"

"Sick," Tess replied, looking around the room casually, like she hadn't just dropped a bomb in my kitchen. I scratched my neck.

"She let you come alone?" I wasn't close with Vanna, but she and I would have words the next time our paths crossed. My brothers and I might have been on the up and up, but a frat party was no place for Bambi to be by herself.

"Oh, she freaked when she found out I was coming. But, you know..." Tess trailed off, straightening when she finally met my eyes. She could probably see the alarm coursing through me.

"Do I know?" I had no clue what could have possessed her to do something so reckless. I could only thank my lucky stars I was the one she'd ended up with tonight. Sure, I was interested as hell in her, but only under the most consensual circumstances.

"Well, it's one of the first parties of the semester, and you invited me..." Her eyes darted around my face like she was trying to read me.

She took another gulp of her drink. "It was on my list!" she blurted, sounding overwhelmed.

"Your list?"

She cursed, eyes dropping again. "Um, yeah. I made a list of experiences to accomplish in college. Oh, God, this sounds so stupid now that I say it out loud."

"No, no." I couldn't help the smile that stretched across my mouth. I tugged her hand away from where it shielded her face. "Now you have to tell me about this list."

I also couldn't help the slow circle my thumb made over her wrist. The movement drew her eyes. Was she feeling this, too? The same crazy pull I felt towards her? I was a magnet, and she was pure iron ore.

"It's stupid," she insisted.

"It's not stupid," I insisted back, using my grip to pull her a little closer, away from the crowd. I didn't want to share a single word that came out of her mouth.

"I, well, I grew up in this teeny town, right? And there are a lot of experiences you miss out on. So, when I came to college I...made a list."

"Of things you want to do?" I prompted when she stalled out, her gaze flickering away from mine. I wanted it back. I wanted that lightning hit in my bloodstream.

"Yes."

"Tell me some of them," I pleaded, completely ignoring the party around us. Tess and her list, and the hint of her bra strap peeking out of her lace tank top, had captured every ounce of my attention.

"They're stupid," she said again, glaring at me now. I just kept smiling, waiting. Finally, she rolled her eyes and took another drink. "So, alright. Go to a college party."

"Check that one off." I toasted her, and she rewarded me with a reluctant smile.

"Eat sushi. Get really, really drunk, but without being stupid about it. Make friends I wouldn't have made in my hometown. Ask a guy out. Enter one of my drawings in an art competition." She ticked them off her fingers, but I fixated on one.

"Ask a guy out?"

She grimaced before straightening her shoulders. "Yes. I've never done it before, and it seems like it'd be liberating." Her eyebrows arched, like she was preemptively scolding me for making fun of her list. "It's perfectly acceptable for women to ask men out."

I held up my hands. "I never said it wasn't. I'm just admiring the set of brass balls you got over there."

"Excuse me?"

"You heard me. Brass. Fucking. Balls. I'd never have the nerve to roll up to a party where I didn't know anyone and then steal the show."

"I didn't steal the show," she sputtered, but my smile widened into an out-and-out grin.

"You're the Beer Angel now. Tell me that's not going to follow you around campus. And you're talking about trying new things and putting yourself out there? That's fucking vulnerable. Ballsy as hell."

"I-I mean maybe," she stuttered. "I guess I'd never thought of it like that before. The list...I mean, it just seems like experiences I need to have."

"That's badass."

She clutched her drink with both hands and stared at me like I'd said something perfect. I wanted her to look at me like that forever.

"Mac," I yelled without tearing my eyes away from her. I wasn't sure I could. Her irises sparkled, sunlight on water.

"Yeah, boss?"

I nodded at Tess. "Meet your Beer Angel. She's an artist." Tess's eyes widened at the descriptor, but I barreled on before she could try to correct me. "Tess, Mac is my pledge brother. He's also the lead in the University's all-male a cappella choir. Voice like an angel, himself."

Her eyes widened. "You're in a choir?"

"You can draw? I'm thinking about getting a tattoo. Could you mock one up?"

"Maybe?" Tess's eyes flickered between me and Mac, looking cute and bewildered and excited all at once.

"What do you know about Dungeons and Dragons?"

With Tess's attention occupied by my brother, I could stare at her without it being weird. That glossy blonde hair had to be natural. If Tinker Bell was a co-ed, this is what she would look like. That is, if Tinker Bell secretly had a spine of steel.

She was an enigma wrapped in silky skin and fairy dust. Every second I spent with her made me more interested.

Finally, Mac put Tess's number in his phone to talk about "the tattoo shit," then pulled me in for a bro hug, one hand pounding my back. "You got dibs on the Beer Angel?" he muttered into my ear.

"Mine," I answered, pounding him harder. He slipped out of the kitchen without a second glance. I fucking loved my brothers.

"So, you met a nerdy frat-dude-choir-boy. Bet you don't have any-one like him hanging around your hometown. Check." I mimed checking something off her list, soaking in the smile that split her face.

"Oh, my God, he's amazing. You are amazing!"

"Well, at least now you know someone else at this party. Don't do that again, by the way." I pointed at her, joking, but not. I couldn't imagine her on her own anywhere else but here, where I could keep an eye on her.

"Hey, I knew you!" she corrected, leaning in closer.

"You could know me better," I challenged, stepping into her space. She didn't back away. "You *should* know me better. Ask me out."

"Ask you—"

"I swear I'll say yes," I interrupted, already seeing the denial on her lips. But she'd handed me a golden opportunity, and I was going to take it. "I know a sushi restaurant that sells dollar rolls after ten on Fridays. We'll have sushi, then come back here to a party. Bring Vanna, get shit faced. It'll be totally safe."

"You can't...I have other things on that list! We can't check them all off in one go." Her chin had one of those little dimples in the middle. I wanted to lick it.

"Try me. What else is on your list, Angel?"

I wasn't sure if it was the nickname that got her or what, but she arched her eyebrow, taking the bait.

"Skinny dipping," she said, like it was a challenge. A gauntlet thrown. I couldn't wait to pick it up.

"I can make that happen, too," I murmured, low enough for only her to hear. She shivered. I watched her lick her lips, the blue of her eyes intensifying as we stared at one another.

She broke first, glancing down at her almost-empty drink. "We can't finish my whole list in the first few weeks of classes. Then what will I do?"

She smelled like candy, something sweet and light. "Oh, Angel, that's easy." I waited until her eyes were on me again. Lightning struck. "We make another list."

Twelve years later
Dylan

The empty hallway greeted me, shiny gray-veined marble as far as the eye could see. Pristine white walls. Vacuum lines still on the carpet from when the cleaners were here a few days ago.

It was good to be home.

I abandoned my beat-up carry-on somewhere near the island, and as my laptop bag thumped onto the counter, it dislodged a piece of paper that had been laying there.

"Congratulations, son. Hell of a deal."

"It'll bring in about ten million to start." I cradled the phone between my head and shoulder, digging into the depths of the freezer for a lasagna. Desperate times called for desperate measures and all that. My flight from Tokyo had been delayed twice, and that was after the entire fucking trip had been extended three different times. What was meant to be a quick two-day visit to seal the deal of the year had drawn out into ten full days.

Now, after nearly thirty hours of travel, I wanted to eat something that wasn't airport food, throw my arms around Tess, and sleep for the next week.

"That's my boy." The pride in my dad's voice seeped through the phone, making me smile. "One step closer, huh? When are you finally gonna start running that place?"

Just like that, the happy feeling tanked. "I just won a multi-million dollar contract. Let me take the win before you complain I haven't gotten promoted yet."

"You know what I mean. You should be proud of yourself. But you can use this as leverage. Finally start taking the next step we've been working towards."

I bit my tongue as I popped the tray into the oven. I could remind him I was already well on my way up the corporate ladder, but we'd had that conversation before and it clearly hadn't stuck. Sometimes it seemed like no matter what I did, Dad still wouldn't be satisfied until I got to the next level. Then the level after that.

"Yeah, sorry." I pinched the bridge of my nose. "Just a long travel day. I'm getting there, but it's a lot of work. That Aruba trip with Tess in a few months can't come soon enough."

Even before my ridiculously extended trip to Japan, I felt like I hadn't seen her in weeks. I glanced around the condo. Where was she? Maybe still upstairs.

"Now's not the time to take your foot off the gas, Dylan. You close a client this big, you need to be around to see it through. Show leadership you're committed."

I bristled. "Henry knows I'm committed." I had years of late nights and closed deals behind me. Henry Worther, CEO and founder of one of the world's biggest media and advertising conglomerates, had personally taken a chance on a college grad with zero business experience, and taught me to be the best at what I did: Seal deals with some of the biggest companies in the world.

Now, I was the youngest VP in the company's history with only one place to go from here: C-suite.

"He also knows I deserve a break, and Tess has been on me about working too much again." I jogged up the stairs, padding across the carpet to our bedroom. Huh. The bed was made, with towels folded on the end. The maids left it like this when they came to clean every week, but Tess would have put the towels away and mussed up the covers by now.

"Tess doesn't know what it takes to support a family," Dad grumbled. I could feel my jaw clench as I checked the other rooms upstairs, only finding more of the same.

Where was Tess?

A beep sounded in my ear. Probably her. Maybe she had gone to stay with Lexi and Mac, or something.

The thought made me smile. She spent too much time holed up at home these days. It would be good to see her get out and do something with our friends.

"Dad, I gotta go. Tess is on the other line. Talk later, okay?"

"Remember what I said about leverage, son!"

I hung up without responding, frowning at the name on my screen.

"Henry?" I answered my boss's call, jogging back down the stairs. The more time I spent in the house, the emptier it felt. I could practically hear my voice echo down the hall. *Where was Tess?*

"Morris! The man of the hour!" Henry's voice boomed. I pulled the phone away from my ear as I stuck my head into the garage. Her BMW was sitting in its usual spot, keys hanging by the door. "Impeccable work in Tokyo. I told Randy we'd have lost it if anyone other than you had been in the room."

I let out a breath, the smile my dad had scared off growing once more.

"Thank you. They put some tricky stipulations in the contract, but we can make it work. I talked them down on a few things."

"I know you put together a bang-up deal. I wanted to say congratulations to Tess, too. Is she there?"

My steps slowed as I turned a full 360 in the living room.

"Tess?"

"Yes! Her big promotion! Put her on."

"Promotion?" My search ground to a halt at the threshold of the open-concept kitchen. Tess had gotten a promotion? I hadn't even known she was up for one. She complained about her work in the creative department at Worther so much, I wasn't sure she'd even take a promotion if it was offered to her.

"You don't know yet? Oh, damn, I bet she was waiting to tell you once you got home from Tokyo. Don't tell her I said anything."

I turned, trying to take in the news and the state of my house at the same time. Unease pricked across my skull. "Tess got promoted?" Maybe she was out celebrating?

"Long overdue, if you ask me. Jinx couldn't ask for a better creative director."

A pit lodged in my stomach as I surveyed the living room. White designer couches arranged beneath intricate iron chandeliers and recessed lights. The massive, antique coffee table was free of its usual clutter—Tess's books or my workout bag. The flowers she liked to buy at the farmers' market weren't there either. "Tess got the Jinx job?" I hadn't even known she was applying for that. She'd been excited when our company acquired the infamous little boutique agency based in Chicago, but she hadn't told me she wanted to work there.

"Ah, shit, me and my big mouth. I'm gonna hop off the phone before I ruin anything else. Act surprised when she tells you! Great work in Japan, Dylan. Keep it up." He ended the call.

I stared around for another beat. "Tess?" Only silence answered. "Tess?" I tried again, looking into my home office and even jogging to her paint studio above the garage. Her easel was empty, paints lined up in a precise row. A lump rose in my throat. Tess was never that neat when she painted.

I paced, scrolling through my phone to find our last messages.

Had it really been four days since I'd texted her? When I was out of town, I usually tried to check in once a day, but the Tokyo meetings had gotten intense fast. I'd barely had time to plug my phone in at night before collapsing on my hotel bed. In our last exchange, I'd told her the trip was being extended again. She'd just replied, "Be safe." The messages before that were equally transactional.

I tapped her name, but her phone went straight to voicemail. I shot her a text, immediately receiving an "Undeliverable" error message.

The oven pre-heat alert beeped, drawing my attention back into the kitchen where I'd dropped my laptop bag. There. I skidded on the slick marble tiles as I bent to retrieve the paper I'd dislodged earlier.

At the sight of Tess's handwriting, the sharp clenching in my gut eased. There was an answer for why she wasn't here. A reason.

But any relief I felt plummeted as I scanned the words.

Dylan,

We both know this is long overdue. I'm sorry it had to happen like this, but the truth is, I wasn't sure I could do this if I had to say it to your face. By the time you get back to Nashville, I'll be gone.

Please don't try to contact me. It's for the best that we both just move on.

- Tess

Bile rose in my throat as I re-read the words, brain spinning in a million directions at once. What was overdue? What did she mean, "gone?"

How the fuck did such an earth-shattering, life-altering, seismic shift in my life boil down to a few sentences? Tess was gone?

I looked around the house as if the white walls would give me any answers. Distantly, I felt a harsh shiver through my chest, like something had cracked open.

Tess was gone?

The paper fluttered from my numb fingers, once more the only thing out of place in the pristine white room.

Tess was gone.

Chapter 1

Tess

Six months later - Chicago

"Scale of one to ten, how much are you freaking out right now?"

Two thousand? I hummed, hands shaking as I downed the rest of my coffee. Black with a little milk. I usually preferred something sweet and flavored, but I was out of creamer and my anxiety had eaten me alive yesterday. Going to the store had seemed like an insurmountable task. "Probably like an eight?"

"Liar. It's at least fifteen," Vanna accused.

"Yeah, that's probably more accurate," I admitted, relieved she'd lowballed it. Fifteen was high, but it was no two thousand.

"Just remember, today is like any other day. The sun rises, you go to work, you go home," she coached. I could hear the soft cooing of a baby in the background.

I'd told myself I was going to stop using Vanna as an emotional crutch. With everything going on in her life, I shouldn't have bugged her, but today was an exception.

"It's just a presentation. You've given hundreds of presentations throughout your very prestigious career, young lady." She was lecturing now, and to be honest, it kind of helped. I desperately needed a distraction and some external validation.

Unlike college, my most recent dramatic life upheaval didn't come with a pre-assigned dorm buddy. No study hall or group assignments to force me a little further out of my shell. Most days, this 2.0 version of my adult life was just me, my teeny apartment, and the job I still wasn't sure I was qualified for.

No friends...no Dylan. Just Vanna on the other side of the world. I really needed to find some people in my own zip code.

"Right. It's just a presentation," I repeated. *Where I have to report my first six months' progress at my new job. In front of my ex.*

I took a deep breath—in for four, out for four—and told myself it was okay to be nervous. Under my leadership, the creative department at Jinx had done some great work, but we'd also lost a few deals, and I wasn't excited to rehash that.

I'd worked on proposals all the time at Worther. I knew the drill: you won some; you lost some. Now, though, I was *in charge* of those pitches, and Jinx, the boutique creative agency I worked for, was a smaller shop. *Much* smaller. I didn't know a ton about the business side of things, but I assumed the missed opportunities would eventually start to add up.

I wasn't sure how many losses were acceptable, or at what point Jinx's CEO, Eric, would realize I didn't know what I was doing and send me packing.

"It's just a video meeting, right? And a bunch of other people are presenting, too. Just ignore the screen," Vanna said, but I heard her unspoken advice: ignore *him.*

Dylan. My other half for over a decade.

When I'd found out the Worther executive team was going to virtually sit in on Jinx's annual Town Hall, I'd spiraled into the spiral of all spirals. I didn't feel great about my job most of the time, anyway. Yes, it was fun and challenging, but I hadn't really gotten the hang of it yet. Having to admit defeat in front of my former bosses was demoralizing. And facing Dylan? I wasn't ready for that. Even if it was just through a screen.

I rubbed at my chest. I'd thought I'd gotten used to the sinking, caving in feeling in my ribcage that had followed me all the way to Chicago, but today, the thought of seeing him again exacerbated the symptoms of my heartbreak, making it hard to breathe.

In for four, out for four. I shoved a strand of lavender hair behind my ears. Ditching my natural blonde had felt like a fresh start. I'd always wanted to dye it, and over the last few months, I'd experimented with emerald green, then a bright teal, before settling on this softer, more muted shade. It was a choice I made for me, and me alone, and I loved it every time I looked in the mirror. Now, though, I wondered what Dylan would think, and if it would look like some desperate, clichéd post-breakup move.

Oh, God. Was it?

"So, just pick a spot somewhere on the wall, focus on that for an hour or so, then go about your life. How bad could it be? Unless, wait. Is the twat going to be there?"

I snorted a laugh before it devolved into a groan. "Yes."

My co-worker Victoria, who Vanna dubbed 'the twat', had unfortunately been integral in pulling my slides together. Since I hadn't been at Jinx a full year, I'd needed Victoria to fill in the blank on the months I wasn't there. And boy, had she been glad to fill in those blanks.

I wasn't sure why she hated me. All I knew was since the day I started, she'd done everything she could to undermine my position. Hijacking presentations, redirecting designers to work on something other than what I'd assigned, and blatantly ignoring my direction. It was an issue, and one I didn't know how to deal with on the best of days.

I hadn't had a best of days in what felt like years.

"Well, fuck her. And while we're at it? Fuck Dylan, too," Vanna railed.

"Hey, feisty, that baby needs to go back to sleep soon. Don't get her all riled up," I warned, smiling at the image of my spunky, loud-mouthed college roommate cradling an infant.

I would have sworn Vanna would never settle down, but when she met Adrianna, everything had changed. Now, she was living her best life in Singapore, raising adopted twins, and yelling at people in two different languages in international courtrooms. I was so happy for her, even though thinking about her perfect life seemed to shine a spotlight on my lonely, broken one.

"Eff them. I'm serious. Icky Vicky has been nothing but evil to you for months, and Dylan was with you for *twelve years*, totally lost himself in work, and ignored you most of the time."

"You don't have to remind me of what happened with Dylan," I croaked, surveying my apartment. Along with my second-hand rug, bright prints on the walls made the miniscule square footage seem homey. The mountain of dishes in the sink ruined the effect, though.

I could handle those tonight. Maybe. If I had the energy and mental *anything* left after today.

"Dylan's the one who messed this up. It should be him freaking out right now. You're going to walk into that conference room and show them why you, out of all the people who applied to work there, are the right person to lead the creative department at Jinx. Right?"

"Right," I muttered, grabbing my work bag and slipping out the door.

"Right?!" Vanna demanded loudly, just as my elderly neighbor stepped outside her door.

"Um...right," I repeated, slightly more enthusiastically as I waved to the neighbor without making eye contact. I hadn't caught her name when I'd moved in, and now it felt like too much time had gone by to introduce myself.

"Theresa, don't make me put this baby down and yell at you. I. Can't. Hear. You!"

I cleared my throat, throwing my shoulders back. "Right. Right!" I repeated, gaining some volume as I smiled. "I can do this!"

"Fuck yeah! Kick ass today, Tessie." A baby's soft cry drowned out the last of her words. As soon as the call ended, my smile slid off my face.

After six long, miserable months, I was going to see him again. My heart jumped in my chest, squeezing and flipping at the same time.

That was the thing I couldn't tell Vanna. My best friend had hated Dylan fully and completely the moment our relationship had imploded.

She'd never understand how mortified and nervous and terrified I was to face him. And at the same time, I had been looking forward to this day ever since I learned I'd get a chance to see him again.

My anxiety spiked at the thought.

In for four, out for four.

***

"...see some of the fantastic feedback our clients provided at the end of the campaign. We've already signed with them for another project in the coming months. Of course, they can't all be winners. Tess, you want to take these?"

Victoria grinned at me with pointy vampire teeth, chestnut hair slicked back in a perfect corporate bun. The baby blue color of her blouse deepened the olive hue of her skin, making her hazel eyes stand out, shrewd and predatory, in the overly bright conference room light.

She looked sharp and polished, and she'd neatly commandeered my slides, no matter how many times I'd tried to interject myself and take back control. Somehow, she'd ended up with the clicker to advance the presentation, and every time I jumped in, she moved along like *she* had been the one poring over the deck for weeks, not me.

I gulped, glancing quickly around the table, feeling sloppy and unprepared. Noel, a designer on my team, shot me a sympathetic smile. Carl, one of the production artists, gave me a thumbs up. I appreciated the support, but it came too late. Victoria had done a great job explaining our team's biggest wins over the last year, and now I was stuck talking about clients we'd lost and proposals that hadn't quite hit the mark.

I should have been angrier, but mostly, I just felt relieved. I smiled at the faces on the video screen.

"Of course. Our team does incredible work, but occasionally, we have a project that falls short. We have a few learnings from the last twelve months that we'll bring with us on future pitches."

After walking through my lonely, miserable "losses" slide, the sales team hopped in to recap their year. I blew out a breath, trying not to make eye contact with my team.

All around me, the Jinx staff, forty people strong, lounged in an assortment of chairs dragged from around the office. Our little conference room was packed and getting stuffier by the minute, which didn't help my flaming cheeks, still prickling from Victoria's coup.

If Dylan had been there, I would have passed out.

But he wasn't. *He's not here. Dylan's not here,* I repeated in my head as the meeting rambled on around me. Was he sick? Traveling? Maybe he'd decided to do the decent thing and not crash my work meeting six months after I'd fled into the night like a burglar?

Whatever the case, I shouldn't have been surprised.

How many times had he canceled a date night or shown up an hour late to a party because "something came up at work"?

I was used to it...I *should* have been used to it. But maybe six months away from him had softened my tough skin. I was mad about bombing this presentation, relieved he had missed it, and simultaneously disappointed he wasn't there.

After all the buildup in my head, my nervous energy buzzed and fizzled as the adrenaline left my system.

All I felt was...empty.

"I love the enthusiasm, everyone." Eric clapped the nearest sales staffer on the back. "On top of all this great work you've accomplished, last year we were bought by the largest media conglomerate in the world. Jinx is their smallest portfolio company, and that might not seem like something to brag about, but it's because of everyone in this room that we caught the eye of a Goliath like Worther." He paused to scan the room. Smiles erupted as he searched our faces.

"We've done well this year, no doubt about it, but we have to tighten things up." Eric gestured to the screen where the Worther executives sat in a row, one empty chair at the end. "These guys know we have something special here. They gave us a year to settle in, and now we need to show them what we really got. We're gonna win more of those deals, right, Tess?"

I chuckled along with the rest of the room, even as my face heated again. "Absolutely!"

Eric winked. "Our parent company knows we're solid, but now it's time to take it to the next level. We're talking bigger clients, more national brands we can take on because we have the Worther network at our backs. Ah, here we go. Fresh from Nashville, just the man to help us get there."

Eric grinned as the glass conference room door swung open.

My stomach pitched. Whatever calm I'd collected seized up, spasmed, and disintegrated into dust on the conference room floor.

Dylan stepped into the room.

My body jerked like I'd touched a live wire. Six months without him hadn't been long enough. Just one look and I was going through withdrawals.

What was he doing here?

He was dressed for the Chicago summer, his favorite green Oxford shirt hugging his lean, muscled frame. The top two buttons were undone, sleeves rolled to his elbows. Dark wash jeans and a pair of polished leather loafers finished the look. And he looked...incredible.

Tall and tan. His dark hair was long enough for his curls to riot, pushed back from his face like he'd run his hands through it this morning and it had just stayed there, frozen in tousled perfection by the grace of God. He had shaved recently, the sharp cut of his jaw smooth and flawless.

Oh, God. Oh God, oh God. In for... something...out for...

My breathing failed me. I couldn't remember what oxygen was. Eric grasped Dylan's hand and said something I didn't catch. My gravitational pull was inverting. Dylan looked around the room with warm brown eyes, smiling.

And then those eyes met mine.

He paused, something flickering across his face at the same time my lungs squeezed, halting the breath in my throat. Oh, God. *He was here. He was here and...*

And in an instant, it was gone. He continued his casual survey of the table, as if I'd imagined the split-second of choking recognition between us. Maybe I had imagined it? I stayed locked in place, pulse pounding, staring.

"Worther has gotten us a chance at some bigger projects, and Dylan here came all the way from the big office in Tennessee to help us out." Eric's words finally filtered into my brain. I blinked, staring down at the table. My hands. Anything other than *him.*

"He will be here for the next several weeks, working with us on a few proposals and helping us find ways to scale our work and stay efficient. He's a big dog up at Worther. We're lucky they'll let us have him."

My mouth went dry. Did he say weeks?

"I know what you're thinking," Dylan said, a confident, controlled smile stealing across his mouth. His eyes flickered to mine and for another instant, that hot, suffocating pressure built in my chest. He glanced away. "But I'm not the corporate watchdog here to cramp your style. Worther sees great value in what you do. You're known for thinking outside of the box and pushing the envelope when no one else will take the chance. I'm just here to see if I can help take you to the next level, and maybe even figure out some of your secret sauce so we can take it back to our other agencies."

"Hey, that secret sauce recipe is mine!"

Laughter broke out at Eric's joke. More talking, more laughter. It all melted into a buzz of background noise. I focused on the ragged cuticles I'd picked bloody over the last week.

I'd barely been prepared to see Dylan on screen for a few hours. Now, he was going to be here in person? For days—no, weeks? My insides were liquefying. Or petrifying. Both? Simultaneously?

A flurry of activity made me realize Eric had dismissed the meeting. I lurched forward on shaky legs. If I could just make it to my office, I could lock the door and hide until...October.

"Tess?"

My head snapped up at Eric's voice. I'd already gathered my laptop and notebook, mentally sprinting down the hallway.

"Can you spare a few minutes to chat in my office?"

Maybe I was imagining it, but I felt the weight of eyes on me. I stared hard at my CEO, vowing I wouldn't look a few feet to his right. At the only man I'd ever known who could make me feel it when he looked at me. "Of course?"

Eric didn't seem fazed by my hesitant response. "Great. I'm going to go grab a coffee and I'll meet you there."

I nodded, blindly following my co-workers as we all spilled out of the conference room. The cool air of the hallway felt icy against my overheated skin, blowing over the spot I could swear I still felt a steady gaze following me.

"Um, did you see that Worther guy? When he came in here, I thought I was going to faint. Like, am I crazy, or does he look like if Henry Cavill and Adam Levine had a baby?" Meery, Eric's administrative assistant and the first person in the office to befriend me, appeared at my elbow and pretended to fan herself. Her bright, floral dress fluttered around her knees as she walked, her hair flowing in thick, black curls down her back.

"Henry Cavill and Adam Brody," I answered without thinking. I was shaking so badly, I'd lost my filter and good sense somewhere on the orange- and gray-striped industrial carpet behind me.

She grinned with perfectly plum lips. As usual, her makeup was Instagram-worthy, making her dark skin look glowy and poreless in a way I could never dream of achieving. "Damn, you're totally right. Nailed it."

She didn't have to tell me. I'd spent more than enough of my lifetime analyzing Dylan Morris's face. I knew exactly what he looked like, down to the almost indiscernible freckle underneath his left earlobe.

And he was *here*. For *weeks*.

"Hey, you okay? You look freaked out." Meery's hand hovered around my arm, like I was about to pass out. For a split-second, I considered it. Surely a quick fainting spell would get me out of this meeting with Eric. I needed to regroup. Or hide under the covers and try to convince myself this had never happened.

But fainting would only draw attention. What would Dylan think? I shook off the crazy, intrusive thought. "I'm fine. Presentation didn't go super well, and now Eric wants me in his office."

Meery nodded. "I know he's working out some plans for a big client pitch. Could be fun. Give you a chance to show us your stuff. You're the only one who's worked with the big national brands. Time to shine, girl!" Meery's hip bumped mine, and I gave her a weak smile.

She split off for her desk while I kept walking. Just a few more steps. I'd have this meeting, and it would be over. Maybe he'd give me a big new project, maybe he'd tell me I'd blown it and I needed to hand over my key card.

As the door swung closed, pressure tightened my chest. I sank into one of Eric's extra chairs, willing myself not to cry. In for four, out for four.

He was *here*. I could practically feel him through the walls. And he'd looked at me like...well, he hadn't looked at me. He hadn't even cared.

I was used to that, I reminded myself. He hadn't cared for a long time.

A teardrop splattered on my notebook.

Chapter 2

Tess

I glanced around the messy room frantically, trying to use the techniques I'd learned from my years of sporadic therapy. Steady breathing. Find three orange things in the room. Three books.

Focusing outside of my body was grounding, but it also helped me think about something other than the fact that I was in my boss's office hyperventilating, that Dylan had strolled into the conference room and had hardly given me a second look.

My head dropped into my hands. Twelve years, *twelve years*, and his gaze had passed over me like I was a piece of furniture.

I bit my lip, wiping a stray tear off my cheek. I needed to get a hold of myself.

The door opened with a waft of stale office air. *Too late*.

Dylan stood in the doorway, framed by the fluorescent lights behind him.

Of course he would walk in right at that moment, when I was at my weakest. Unlike earlier in the conference room, I was the only one here. Our eyes met and that same familiar, gasping tightness closed in around me.

I was going to cry. Oh, no. Oh no oh no oh no.

I shoved to my feet, pacing to look out the window, hoping the sunlight might dry the tears pooling behind my eyelids. But I wasn't fast enough. I'd seen it all: The way his eyes had widened. The flash of emotion that passed across his face. Pity?

"Tess."

The sound of my name coming out of his mouth was torture. I shook my head once, holding up a hand to stop him from coming any closer.

He stayed where he was, but I could feel him studying me. Was he remembering our life together like I was? All the good, the bad, and the ugly? Was he, like me, wondering where the hell it had all gone wrong and led us *here*?

I swiped under my eyes with shaking hands. I would not cry. I would *not cry*. But it was hard to hang onto that conviction as the thrum of the air conditioning system and a decade's worth of regrets filled the air between us.

The silence stretched and solidified, dragging the weight in my stomach down, down, down. There was nothing to say, no way to break this horrible, heavy silence without—

"I like your hair."

"What?" His opener was so unexpected, so stilted, it surprised a full sentence out of me. "No, you don't."

In the dim reflection of the window, I saw his outline shift, hands shoved into pockets. "It suits you."

Hot, resentful flames flooded my throat so fast, I nearly choked. I half-turned, glaring at him from the corner of my eye. "You hate dyed hair. You told me once you thought it looked trashy."

Did he think I wouldn't remember? Was this his way of hurting me? Barging into my workplace and calling me—

"I don't remember saying that," he said, hesitant, like he really was wracking his brain. "I'm sorry if I—obviously, I was wrong. Before. Sorry."

The Dylan in the window pinched the bridge of his nose, a move he only made when he was stressed or failing at something, as rare as that was. Seeing it smothered the fire of irritation in me as quickly as it had flared to life.

This was dangerous. There were a thousand emotions spinning inside me, all of them battling for dominance, and I wasn't sure which would win.

"Tess," he started. My muscles clenched. He sounded so small. Soft and sad and he somehow made my name seem like a question I didn't know the answer to.

"Dylan! You sure you don't want a coffee before we get started?" Eric's cheerful voice cut through the moment, and the world came rushing back into focus. My co-workers outside the office door. The beeping of computer notifications. The soft music Meery liked to play over the speakers.

Dylan responded, but I was too focused on my breathing to hear. I felt the resonance of his voice all the way to my bones, though. I knew what he sounded like in the mornings before he'd had his coffee. Late at night after a party, whispering in my ear when he'd had more wine than usual.

I knew what he sounded like when he couldn't be bothered to speak at all.

I bit the inside of my cheek, still lost in the tangle of emotions sucking me down into the carpet. I scrambled to think of something to hold off the tears. What had Vanna said this morning?

Eff him. He was the one who had ruined what we had together. He was walking in on *my* life. I swallowed, steeling myself and gathering my resolve. I could do this. I could be strong.

"Tess, great job today. Everything we do here is a team effort, but I know you did most of the work on those slides. Good stuff."

I tipped my head up to look at Eric. My vision was clearer, the tears gone for now. I could do this. "Thank you."

If my voice sounded weak or watery, he didn't comment on it, instead settling down on the neon green sofa while I sank into a chair. No boring conference table or corporate furniture for Jinx's founder. His office was a direct reflection of Jinx's bright, counter-cultural reputation. It was like Nickelodeon had exploded in here.

"Listen, I'll cut straight to it. I know there are *some people* in the office who are less than excited that Worther attended our annual meeting today." He gave me a dry look. We both knew he was referring to Victoria, who had practically thrown a fit when we'd learned the Worther team would be "spying" on our internal meeting, as she put it. She'd railed at anyone who would listen about how the larger company was going to take over and squash our creative process.

I'd been too busy reeling at the news for different reasons to give her a second thought. Dylan shifted where he sat next to Eric.

"That's why I kept it quiet that Dylan was coming today. I didn't want it to seem like it was a coup. But...some things are about to change around here."

Something about the way he said it, paired with the announcement of Dylan's extended stay, sent a shiver of worry down my spine. A new addition to the teeming feelings bubbling in my stomach, making me dizzy. This was all wrong. I wanted out of here.

Eric continued, unaware that I'd been diminished to a wobbling pile of anxiety masquerading as a conscious person.

"I know we've had a few misses recently on new business proposals. You've only been here for six months, and you've been doing a great job, Tess, but I won't lie. Worther is putting pressure on us to close more business. We've been under the Worther brand for a year now. Our honeymoon period is over."

I nodded, clasping my hands to keep from picking at my cuticles or breaking into sobs. *In for four...hold it together, Tess.*

"They're hoping we can take that 'secret sauce' Dylan mentioned earlier and expand it to bigger clients and larger deals. If we want to play with the big dogs, we have to stretch. Right?"

"So, what does this mean for Jinx? I know you said you didn't want it to look like a coup, but..." I trailed off, attempting to push the rising panic down. I couldn't go back to working like I had at Worther. There was a difference between churning out mediocre ads and the type of magic we created at Jinx. Worther's hyper-focus on profit choked out a lot of creativity. Here, I felt like I could breathe.

These last six months had been hard, but for the first time in my life, I actually liked my job. Really, I loved it.

"I've built this company into something I'm proud of. It's important we keep our culture intact," Eric assured, but his usually smiling face turned serious. Unease slithered through me again. "But we are under pressure to grow. And all of this is coming at an awkward time."

"Awkward?" I knew about awkward. Dylan sat mere feet away while I held back tears, actively searching for some sense of up or down in the emotions tossing me around like a tornado.

"Tess, I'm hoping for your discretion. We brought you on because I was the sole executive here, and I needed the help. Now, six months later, I realize I'm more than just burned out." A softness came over Eric's face that I didn't like. "My time at Jinx has come to an end."

A gasp left my mouth, and my racing thoughts went quiet for a split-second. Of all the awful, unexpected things that had happened in the last hour, this one came out of nowhere. "I thought Jinx was your baby?"

"Of course Jinx is my baby. But babies grow up, don't they? And I've grown, too. It's time to move on to the next thing. If you stay in one place for too long, trying to hold on to the way things were instead of the way things are, you'll be stuck and unhappy forever. I deserve more, and Jinx does, too."

"I don't know what to say." Eric *was* Jinx. The thought of him leaving was overwhelming. I could feel Dylan's burning stare, but determinedly avoided his gaze.

Eric smiled. "You've been doing great work to figure out your place here. Now, though, Tess, I'm going to need you to do a bit more."

I shoved down the threat of tears before it could overtake me again. "I know some of the recent proposals weren't ideal. I can do better, Eric, I promise."

"I know you can, but I'm not just talking about pitches." Eric leaned back, including Dylan in the conversation. "You get this place, in and out, but you also understand how Worther wants us to work. I'm hoping you can be the bridge between the two, helping Jinx keep its identity without getting lost in Worther's corporate machine. Especially as Dylan replaces me."

My heart thunked, recognizing the impact of his announcement before the rest of me did. His words didn't compute. Something in my brain felt mushy, gone soft with the flood of news and Dylan and awfulness of this day.

"Dylan," His name burned in my throat, but I forced myself to keep talking. To ask the question. To clarify, because surely he didn't mean... "replaces you?"

Eric clapped Dylan on the shoulder, beaming. "Meet your new CEO."

In the wake of his declaration, my brain checked out and a decade's worth of habit took over my body. I looked at Dylan.

He was looking right back, completely unreadable except for the slight divot between his brows. *CEO?* He was supposed to become CEO at Worther. Why would he throw that away to come here?

For me? I squashed the thought before it had time to take root in my brain. Of course he hadn't come here for me. I'd never taken precedence over his corporate ladder-climbing before; why would that change now?

"We're keeping it under wraps for now, of course." Eric smiled and rambled on, oblivious to the tension thrumming between me and Dylan. It hurt to look at him, and yet, I couldn't tear my eyes away.

"A leadership transition is a delicate thing. The plan is to bring him on for a few of the bigger proposals coming up, get him integrated. If it's a good fit, we'll announce the transition when everyone's more comfortable with him. We don't want it to seem like Worther is coming in and changing everything up. Right?"

"Right," Dylan responded. I'd lost track of the conversation, but he was following perfectly well, despite staring at me steadily. I didn't know what to do with that.

Finally, I looked away, trying to ignore the feeling of his eyes on me.

"Dylan, I know you brought a new proposal for us. Big national account, lots of feel-good stuff. I'd like you to work on it, just the two of you. Get your feet wet, so to speak..." Eric trailed off, looking between us. "Actually, it just occurred to me. You were both at Worther. Have you worked together before?"

"No!" I blurted before Dylan could answer. "No, we never worked closely together."

We'd filed taxes jointly, but that hadn't been the question. Dylan and I had always been in separate departments. Some of our work might overlap, but we'd never worked together, directly.

And for some reason, my mushy, sluggish brain believed it was imperative to keep my history with Dylan a secret. Back at Worther, almost everyone knew me as "Dylan's girlfriend." Did I really want to be "Dylan's ex" here?

My heart lurched. This was all too much. I had too many questions and feelings, and I needed to get out of here.

"I have a meeting in a bit, but if you two would like to hash the proposal out and get started on planning, I'm sure we can—"

"Actually, Eric, I'm sorry, but I have somewhere to be." Like, in bed, hyperventilating. I stood, and the two men rose as well. "I'd love to know more about the project if you could send it over." *Lie.* "I'll take a look and start thinking about it tonight." *Lie number two.*

Eric looked surprised, either because I'd never interrupted him before, ever, or because I had only left the office early once, for a dentist appointment.

"Of course. Do what you need." Eric turned to Dylan while I gathered my things. "You two can find some time to discuss in the next few days. Usually, Tess is the first in and the last out. Worker bee, this one."

"Really?"

Surprise dripped from Dylan's words. I'd never been the "worker bee" before, but things changed when you actually liked your job and didn't have a life outside of your office.

I aimed a strained smile in their direction and pulled the door closed behind me. I didn't want to hear anything else from Dylan. I didn't want anything else to do with this day.

I was so, so done. And even when I crawled into bed with Netflix and a trusty pint of Ben & Jerry's after leaving a voicemail on Vanna's phone, the same thought kept cycling through my head.

Dylan's here. What do I do now?

Eleven years ago

Tess

"Tickets?"

And just like that, I was out of time.

"It's only a few months," I told Dylan, repeating the same words I'd used like a mantra for weeks. His hum vibrated through my chest where we were pressed together. Even after two semesters with him, I felt like I'd never get enough of this feeling. Safe. Happy. *Loved*.

I'd never told anyone aside from my immediate family I loved them. Now, I told Dylan so often, it was like I was trying to wear the words out. But they didn't feel worn. Months later, saying it out loud still felt like the plummeting drop of a roller coaster—scary and exhilarating all at the same time.

I took a deep breath, inhaling his clean, piney scent, trying to focus on that instead of the gasoline fumes permeating the bus station around us.

"This sucks," Dylan finally rumbled, pulling back to look down at my face. He looked as tortured as I felt.

"It's only for a couple of months," I repeated, swallowing down the lump in my throat.

Dylan smoothed his fingers across my forehead, pushing a few strands of hair behind my ear. "I just don't feel like we're meant to be apart, Angel."

I burrowed my face against his t-shirt, unsure how to respond to that, because I felt it, too. Everything about this felt wrong—leaving him, leaving my home state, all of it.

"And I hate that you have to go off like this by yourself, to a place you've never been, where you don't know anyone."

His nose rubbed across the top of my head. I sighed. He'd voiced these concerns before. I'd never even been outside the borders of Tennessee. But an art camp near Indianapolis had agreed to hire me for the summer and compensate me in room and board instead of weekly checks. It had been a blessing. I didn't have to worry about having a roof over my head or where my next meal was coming from. Roughing it a little in the woods of Indiana was a sweet deal compared to some places I'd slept in my life.

Besides, Mom's new boyfriend had made it clear I wasn't welcome back home over the summer. I had a strained relationship with my mom to begin with, and this new guy was a walking red flag, so at least I wouldn't have to deal with all that.

"I've done this before. Recently, if you'll remember." I tried to sound braver than I felt. After all, I'd figured out how to get myself to college and showed up on day one without knowing a single soul.

"Sure, but that was before you had me."

I shrugged, finally pulling out of his arms and hefting my duffel bag over my shoulder. Standing around moping wasn't helping anything.

I couldn't afford to miss my bus. Literally. "It's fine. I got this. I'll see you in a few weeks."

I wasn't going to see him until August, when camps were over and the fall semester started back up again. I couldn't afford another bus ticket, and he wasn't allowed to stay on camp premises if he came to visit.

But I could lie to myself, and him, and pretend it was only weeks, not months, that we'd be apart. I could tell myself whatever I had to as long as it got me on that bus, because if I didn't, I was S.O.L.

"What if I come with you?"

It had been hard to look at him, but now I tipped my head back to roll my eyes. "You're going to tell your dad you're not working for him this summer? Follow me to an art camp and what? Get in touch with your creative side?"

A thoughtful frown creased his brow, the same familiar expression he wore when he was working on tricky homework or trying to solve an issue with his fraternity brothers.

"No, but I can at least get you there. I don't have to be at work until Monday. I can buy a ticket, sit with you 'till Indianapolis. Help you unpack, then catch the next bus out four hours later."

"Dylan—"

"I'll be back early Monday morning. I can make it."

"Early Monday?" I turned to stare at the schedule he was eyeing. "You'll get back into Nashville at two a.m. You'll hardly have time to sleep."

"It's my first day. Dad will go easy on me."

I wasn't so sure. I hadn't met Dylan's dad yet, but from the stories he told me, his father took the concept of "tough love" to a whole new level.

"We'll have a few more hours together on the bus. I can meet some of the other counselors, so they'll believe you when you tell them about your devastatingly handsome boyfriend back home." His mouth curved up. I could practically feel his resolve settling into place.

"Obviously, I want to spend more time with you, but I can't ask you to sit on a smelly bus with me for six hours, just to turn around and do it all again the night before you start your new job."

He cupped my cheek, tipping my face up. "You're not asking me. I'm offering." His eyes darted between mine, searching and warm. "You don't have to do this alone, Tess."

I blinked back the tears welling in my eyes. I'd been on my own for a long, long time. In some ways, maybe I'd been on my own for forever. I didn't know what to do with someone who loved me enough to offer something so selfless.

"I love you," I told him, because it seemed like the only thing *to* say. "I don't deserve you."

"You do." His mouth brushed against mine.

I grinned like a maniac when we bought his ticket and found our bus. His hand landed on my thigh the second we'd settled on the scratchy seats.

"Alright, Theresa Lynn. Let's get down to business here." He rifled around my backpack for a moment while I crinkled my nose at him.

"So serious."

"Oh, this is serious. You, young lady, need to start your list." He placed a pen and one of my sketchbooks in my hands. "I know you've been avoiding it."

I only hesitated a second before launching myself at him. His lips tasted like his smile. The pads of his fingers swept up into my hair, tongue spearing between my lips the instant I opened them.

A soft grunt sounded from his throat, and I cupped my hands around his neck. I wanted to feel everything about him, even his sounds.

"I love you," I murmured, pressing my mouth against his so many times that all the kisses melted into one long, feverish one. I shivered when his palm swept up the skin of my back, underneath my tank top.

"I love you, too." He stole another kiss, squeezing my waist. "But unless you want to get kicked off this bus, you're going to have to get back in your own seat."

I grinned while I climbed back to my side, running my hands down his chest while he glowered at me, the warning look ruined by his smiling, kiss-swollen lips.

As the bus lurched away from the station, I considered the blank paper in front of me. Truthfully, I'd been avoiding making this list because I hadn't wanted to think too hard about being away from Dylan. Now, though, with his warm hand on my leg and the smell of him drowning out the funk of the bus, the concept didn't seem so scary. My pen moved.

1. Write a letter to Dylan every day.

"Oh, I like that one." His fingers stroked the skin just below the hem of my denim shorts. "What else?"

2. See a waterfall.

"You've never seen a waterfall before?" His question wasn't judgmental. Just curious.

"Nope."

"There's a great hike about an hour away from campus. Beautiful falls. We should go when you get back. We could go camping."

"Camping?" Growing up with a family that couldn't always afford rent, the concept of *choosing* to sleep outside was bizarre to me. Even this art camp had cabins. But Dylan's eyes turned fiery as he scanned the length of my legs.

"Oh, yeah. You ever had sex in the woods, Angel?"

"You know I haven't." Dylan had been my first in many ways. His cocky smirk told me he was pleased to be reminded of that fact. Or pleased to remind me. I glanced at him through my lashes, asking oh-so-innocently, "Should I add it to the Indianapolis list?"

"No, no." Dylan's brow furrowed as he gripped my wrist to stop me from writing it down. A tickle of laughter simmered in my chest. "Maybe we need to start two lists. One for the summer and one when you get back..."

I had been dreading this bus ride for so long, so sure I'd be alone, miserable, and already missing him. Now, though, as he tore off a new piece of paper and labeled it "Dylan and Tess's August List," I didn't feel sad at all.

I felt like I couldn't wait to get started on a new list with him. To get started on our future together.

Chapter 3

Dylan

The baby's face was half-covered by a pink knitted hat. Its skin was squishy and looked a little orange.

"She's gorgeous," I whispered, looking at the little blob on my phone. I couldn't have picked her out of a lineup, but she was my best friend's kid and therefore flawless. That's just how it went.

Mac pulled the phone out of his new daughter's face, grinning at me with tired eyes. "Put her mama through the ringer. Twenty-seven hours of labor, man. It was brutal."

Ever since we'd met in college, Mac had been more than my best friend. He was family. There was something sappy and satisfying about watching him settle on the edge of the hospital bed where his wife, Lexi, cradled the newest member of their family.

"Couldn't tell. Lex, you look beautiful." She looked like she'd just pushed out a baby without sleeping for a whole day, but, again, it was just one of those things. Besides, they had this contented, quiet glow hanging around them. The three of them, sitting close together after all the frenzy that went into bringing a baby into the world.

I rubbed at my chest.

"Liar, I look like shit. Alright, enough about us. How's it going with Tess? Have you seen her yet?"

I paced across the orange Jinx carpet, letting out a grunt. "Yeah. I saw her."

"And? How did it go? How does she look?"

I peered out the window, looking at the Chicago skyline without really seeing it. How did she look? Perfect. Even totally petrified and avoiding my gaze, seeing her had made my gut clench up. Her blue eyes, soft cheeks, thin nose...The face of my favorite person in the world.

Then I remembered her expression when I'd walked into Eric's office. The tears. The bright anger. I winced. "She looked good. We didn't get a chance to talk."

She had run away. Again.

I tried not to blame her. I could tell from the second I'd walked into that conference room she hadn't been prepared to see me. That was all part of the plan, I reminded myself. Keep my visit to Jinx hush-hush so she didn't have time to bail before I even walked through the door. I'd told myself it was the right move.

But then I'd seen the shock splashed across her features. Maybe even a little panic, too, and I'd known I had to be careful, play it cool. I'd practically ignored her, which was ridiculous. I could be in a coma and still pinpoint exactly where she was in the room.

"Well, get on it, Morris. Auntie Tess needs to come meet her new niece," Lexi huffed. Since the day Mac had started dating Lexi, it was like she'd always been part of our group. They had mourned the loss of my relationship with Tess almost as much as I had, and I knew they were hurt by how she'd left—quietly, out of nowhere, without saying goodbye.

I'd heard there were five stages of grief, but there were only three when I lost Tess.

Desperation. Countless phone calls that always went to voicemail. Undeliverable texts. Half-formed prayers that this would all be some bizarre dream and life would go back to the way it was.

Anger. She was just going to throw our whole life away? Everything we'd built? I'd stopped calling.

Finally, the gut-wrenching realization that I'd have left me, too. Noticing just how much time I spent at the office. How little attention I gave to my family and the people I loved. One revelation snowballed into hundreds, and I had spent months in an avalanche of guilt and regrets. Until the only thing keeping my head above it all, keeping me sane, was the knowledge that I could be better. For her.

I could show her I'd changed, win her back. If only she'd let me.

"Dylan has a plan, babe. He always does," Mac said. "What's the play, man? Flowers? Groveling? Finally getting down on one knee?"

"I'm, uh, going to ambush her in her office." I glanced around the bookshelves, looking at the items so familiar they may as well have been mine. The brass frames that had once held pictures of us now held tiny watercolor prints. The ceramic pen cup she'd made in college. Her color theory books displayed in the same chromatic order they always had been.

It had taken about two days without Tess for me to realize those books had been the only splash of color in the whole house.

"That's the plan?" Mac sounded incredulous, which was fair.

"That's the plan." Granted, it wasn't romantic or over the top, but it was all I had at the moment. She'd practically sprinted out of

Eric's office after he'd told her I was going to be Jinx's CEO. Then she'd come down with a very convenient and unspecified illness and hadn't showed up at work for two days. I knew because I'd spent each morning in her office, pacing, staring at those frames, and waiting.

I'd do it again today, and the next day, and the next, if I had to. I wasn't letting her run away again. This morning, though, I had an extra ace up my sleeve.

"If you're sure..."

I wasn't sure of anything. All I knew was that six months without her was six months too long. Losing Tess had been the wake-up call of a lifetime, and I needed to show her I wasn't the man she'd left. Not anymore.

The door to her office opened and there she was. Her eyes widened, mouth popping open into a lush, surprised "o" when she saw me standing there. Our eyes connected. Lightning struck.

I'd missed that.

"Hi," I said.

Her gaze darted around the room like she was looking for an escape route. I held out my phone before she could make a run for it. "Lex had her baby. It's a girl."

"She...a girl?" Tess stared down at our friends' faces. "Lexi?"

"Tess, look at my new baby!" Lex squealed, wrestling the phone away from Mac.

"Whoa, careful, babe, you just popped out a kid. Lay back down, Jesus." Mac sounded alarmed as Lexi flipped the camera to show the baby's little squishy face.

"Oh, Lex, you got your girl!" A breathless smile spread across Tess's face as she took the phone from my hands. Sparks danced across my palm where her fingers brushed. I peered at her, wondering if she felt it, too, but she was too enraptured by the baby.

"I know!" Lexi crowed. "Three boys and I'm finally done. When the nurse comes back in, I'm going to ask her to rip my uterus out."

Tess's laugh rippled through my veins. "Does this gorgeous, smart, strong little girl have a name?"

Mac pretended to scowl. "I tried to convince Lex to go for Beer Angel, after her aunt, but we compromised on Annabelle."

"Annabelle Beer Angel McCarthy. What a superstar," Tess whispered, beaming down at the camera. My heart lurched.

Being in the same room with her was bad enough, but watching Tess talk with our friends and coo over their baby was like pouring salt in a six-month-old wound that wouldn't close.

"She's amazing. Congratulations." Tess glanced up at me with a glowing smile that nearly knocked my feet out from under me. *When was the last time I'd seen her smile?*

I tried to reciprocate, but the instant her eyes met mine, she faltered, like she had only just remembered this wasn't part of her life anymore.

"Sorry to hijack your call. Um, give those kiddos a squeeze when you see them, alright?" She passed the phone back without waiting to hear what they replied.

"Dylan?" On the screen, Lexi and Mac wore matching expressions of confusion. Hurt.

"Yeah, listen, I have to go. Tell that baby girl to give her brothers hell. Text me when you're out of the hospital." We exchanged goodbyes that

I barely paid attention to, my focus squarely on the woman slipping into the office chair behind her desk, rubbing at her chest like it ached.

"They don't say it out loud, but they miss you," I said, sinking into the chair across from her, watching her shoulders bunch up to her ears. She probably wanted to curl up under her desk and hide.

"Save the guilt trip, please. I miss them, too, but…" Her soft voice trailed as her gaze shifted around the room. She fidgeted. "It just is what it is."

"I don't get a say in what it is?"

She practically deflated. "If you're here to yell at me over how I left…"

"I'm not here to yell, Tess. I understand why you left, and even why you did it the way you did." At least I thought I did. I perpetually hoped the reason she'd disappeared without a word was because, deep down, she still loved me. And that last shred of faith was sometimes all I had to hang onto these days.

Because if she still loved me, even a little, maybe I still had a chance.

"What are you doing here?" She sounded so small, staring down at her Jinx mouse pad, I wanted to gather her up in my arms. I folded my hands in my lap, instead.

"I'm here to talk with you."

A breath caught in her throat. The smallest scoff known to man. "I mean here in Chicago."

"I'm here to talk. With you."

Her chest rose and fell as she stared blankly down at her desk some more. Her brow furrowed and finally, she glanced up at me. "You gave up a nearly guaranteed CEO position at Worther, picked up your life, and moved to Chicago to work at Jinx just to talk?"

"Yes."

Her face didn't change, but I was the world's leading expert on deciphering her silent, blank stares. She didn't believe me. I reached into the bag I'd brought in, pulling a cup from the drink holder inside, along with a paper-wrapped bundle. "Here. I know me being here is a lot, and you don't eat when you're anxious."

Her head shook. "I can't do this. Whatever...this is." She stared at my offering like she'd never seen a latte before. "This is where I work, and you being here is a lot and...and I have a meeting with Eric in a few minutes, anyway."

There she went, running again. Avoiding this, as if I'd magically disappear if she dodged my gaze for long enough. But she was going to have to be a little more intentional if she wanted me to leave for good.

"I asked Meery to put a meeting on your calendar." I nudged the cup closer. "It's half-caf. Lavender."

Lavender, like the dark skin under her eyes that told me she'd probably been sleeping as well as I had. Lavender, like her hair.

My sister had removed Tess from all my social media accounts, claiming it was for my own good. I hadn't laid eyes on her since the day I'd left for that God-awful trip to Japan. Her hair had been the first thing I noticed, and I hadn't lied back in Eric's office. It suited her, making her ocean-blue eyes look huge.

She looked good; stronger. There was definition in her shoulders under her silk blouse and in the curve of her calves. I had no right, but

I wanted to trace all the ways her body had changed since we'd been apart.

Because even though she wasn't mine anymore, I still knew her. Knew her like you knew your next breath was coming. Without having to think about it.

"You put a fake meeting on my calendar?" She demanded, the smallest spark igniting under her hollow words. I nearly grinned.

"I did what I had to do. Just like coming here was something I had to do."

"Dylan...I don't know what you're trying to prove, but you need to just go back to Nashville and we can..." Her eyes darted around the ceiling, looking for the right words and avoiding looking at me. "Pretend this—us—never happened."

My jaw tightened. Did she really think so little of me? That I'd just move on after losing the only woman I ever wanted to love? Keep living without her, as if she'd been *optional*?

She wasn't optional. She was oxygen.

"I can't do that. I can't just erase the last twelve years of my life." *I can't just erase you.* "Look, I know I screwed up. A lot. I got lost in work and I lost sight of you, and us. But I'm only asking to talk. You just left, Tess, out of the blue. You didn't give me a chance to fix what I'd broken."

"It wasn't out of the blue," she whispered, voice so soft I barely heard. Something hot and angry spiked in my veins. I shoved it back down. Yes, she'd left me without a word, but I was to blame. I couldn't be angry with her when I was the one who'd fucked everything up so badly.

I took a breath, calmed my thrumming pulse. "You're right. I should have realized how unhappy you were. I was too focused on things that didn't matter. My work, the promotion, it means nothing if you're not there to share it with. So yes, I left Nashville, because you're here and that's what matters. I can be better for you, Tess. Just give me a chance to show you."

She'd found something fascinating to stare at on her desk. It held her attention for a long time before she spoke again. "I don't know if I can do that. I...I left for a reason. You hurt me so much. And now you're here and it still hurts. It took me months to feel okay again after I left."

A single tear dripped from her eye, dragging my heart along with it.

"Do you feel okay now?" It was the million-dollar question. The one I'd abandoned everything to fly across the country and ask her. Because if she was fine without me, if this was really, truly what she wanted, I'd walk away. The thought made me want to ram my head into the nearest lime-green wall, but I would.

But if she didn't feel anything for me, this wouldn't hurt, right? If it was over, she'd be able to look at me. She was treating me like I was the sun, glancing everywhere but directly at my face.

"Because I don't feel okay. Not since you left, and not a long time before that. I know we weren't in a good place, Tess, and we never talked about it. Give me a chance, just to talk. Don't you think we owe it to ourselves?"

Her face twisted, unconvinced. My attention snagged on the brass frames on the wall behind her. The ones that used to hold us.

"Don't you think we owe it to them?"

She stiffened, like she knew exactly what I was looking at. We had built entire universes together, she and I, and now they were gone. While we were here, sitting in the ruins, didn't our life together deserve some sort of recognition?

Her fingers fidgeted in her lap, picking at her cuticles. I waited, but she didn't say anything.

"I have been miserable since the minute I realized you were gone, and probably a long time before that, too. But if you're happier here, if you can look me in the eye and tell me there isn't a part of you, however small, that wonders what would have happened if you'd stuck around, I'll walk out this door right now." She'd sunk so low in her chair, I had to lean forward to try and look into her eyes. "But if there's a shred of a chance that part of your heart is still mine, I'll fight for it. Tooth and nail. If you give me the opportunity, I can show you how much better I can be for you."

"I can't do this right now." Another tear, hastily wiped away by raw, ragged fingertips. I stared at the sheen it left behind on her cheekbone.

"We don't have to do this now, but...another time? Will you talk with me?"

Her teeth sank into her lip. "I'm on thin ice at Jinx, and with Eric wanting to expand to bigger proposals, it's too much. I...don't have the space for all this."

Oh, the irony. Her telling me she needed to focus on work. It still wasn't an answer, and I could practically hear her brain scrambling for an excuse; a way to get me out of the room as she reeled.

"Tess." Maybe her name on my lips snagged her attention, or the gentle way I said it. Blue eyes lifted to mine, and I saw all our universes there. Our past, our present. Grief and shame and hurt and...a little bit of hope. My heart leapt into my throat. "Are you done with me? For good? Tell me now and I'll walk out that door. Forever this time, I promise."

Her eyes shut on more tears. They spilled over, two identical tracks running down her face.

"But if you can't give me an answer, I'm blindly, maybe stupidly, going to believe I still have a shot. Do I?"

"I...I don't know." Her lips formed the words, but I barely heard them. Her fingers twisted in her lap.

"You don't have to have an answer right now." I could let her avoid it all for a little longer. I had waited this long, months to work out the logistics and deals with Henry just so I could stand here today. I could wait a little longer on the off chance that maybe, just maybe...

"This is just a lot. You being here, *working* here. It hurts to even be in the same room with you. How are we supposed to work together with all this...I don't know." Her hands flailed at her computer monitor.

"Let's take it one day at a time. I didn't come here to run you out of your dream job. We can get through this first project together and figure out what happens then, alright? Take your time. Think it over. In the meantime, we can be...professional." I nearly choked on the words. I'd rather chew off my own arm than be relegated to Tess's colleague. But for now, if that's what I had to do, that's what I'd do.

"I need to think about it."

"Then think about it." I pushed the latte and breakfast sandwich across her desk. "Take your time, Theresa Lynn. I'm not going anywhere."

Chapter 4

Dylan

I gave her as long as I could. Easy to do, since she avoided me like the plague. When she couldn't squirm out of a meeting we had together, she avoided my eyes just as purposefully.

But after two days, all it took was one innocuous question from Eric to force her hand. "How's the National Canine Rescue project going?"

One question, and I was back in her office watching her sit ramrod straight in her chair.

"It's not poisoned." I nudged the latte closer. She'd been staring at it since I'd placed it on her desk a few minutes ago.

"I know," she whispered, still looking like she'd never seen a go-cup before. She cleared her throat, straightening her shoulders and sounding stronger when she tried again. "I know. Thank you."

I had so many questions. Had she thought about what I'd said? Was she considering giving me a chance? Had she texted Lexi about the baby? But she looked so brittle, I felt like I could crack her with the wrong word, and I settled for: "Have you read the brief Eric sent?"

My brief, more accurately, carefully prepared on the plane earlier this week. The national dog rescue organization badly needed a new brand facelift, but hesitated to work with a big corporate machine like

Worther. Yes, the campaign would be worth millions, but it was the ideal project for a company like Jinx. Smaller, with a more wholesome, human-centric image.

At least, that's what I'd told Henry when I'd poached the project to bring up here. I was still thanking my lucky stars he'd agreed.

Otherwise, I wouldn't have been sitting here, across from Tess, watching her contemplate her coffee like it held the secrets of the universe.

Her breath blew the little wisps of hair away from her face. She'd left half of it down, falling in gentle waves down her back. Was it still soft as silk now that it was purple?

"Right." Her fingers danced across her keyboard, pulling up the document, as well as a presentation deck I'd never seen before. She paused to take a tentative sip of her coffee.

It felt like a win, a concession of some sort, and I wanted to ask her right then and there if she had an answer for me yet. If we could ditch this whole charade and go somewhere and *talk* so I could tell her everything I'd been thinking for the last six months. Everything I'd learned about myself and what I missed about her and the person I wanted to be for her.

Her eyes flashed up once, and I could have sworn the word *professional* floated in the air between us like a ghost.

"Right. So. National Canine Rescue." I sipped my coffee.

"I looked over the brief yesterday. Compiling the information on Jinx's capabilities and creative process will be easy." She flicked through a few preliminary slides she'd pulled together. I frowned at the screen.

Technically, Tess was right when she'd told Eric we hadn't worked closely together. I was high-up in Worther's echelon and I didn't work directly with designers.

I knew working there hadn't fit with her creative style or what she wanted to achieve in her career, but I hadn't realized Worther had also been holding her back.

As she took me through the slides, voice getting stronger with every minute, memory after memory washed through my mind. Searching. I didn't recall her ever having this easy grasp on business strategy, but maybe it was a newfound talent.

The thought didn't sit right. I'd overlooked something, or she'd developed new skills without me. Either way left me feeling empty. And unnecessary.

"You don't need me for this at all." Dual feelings of pride and devastation twisted through me. She was so incredible. And I was an idiot.

"It's pretty standard. I'm not completely sure it will do the trick to advance us to the next round of the business pitch." Tess frowned at the screen a little too hard, still trying not to look at me, even though she'd loosened up over the last half-hour. "They've done the agency thing before, and they're looking for something different. I'm not sure I have it yet. I hit a wall last night and had to step away."

She stared at the slides as if they'd magically produce the answers for her. I couldn't help but think about the Tess I'd known who had dreaded Monday mornings and logged off her computer as soon as she could at five p.m.

"You really do love it here."

"Yes, I do." She sounded uncomfortable, and maybe a little defensive, as she navigated through a few more slides, jotting some notes down on a rainbow notepad in front of her.

"Why?" I was dying to know. Why this place? Why now? What made her light up when everything in Nashville had seemed to grind her down?

She frowned, picking at her nails. "We don't have to get this...personal. We can just go through the slides and be done with it."

"It's for the presentation." I'd never told a bigger lie in my life. "To pitch the company, I need to know how it stands out. Tell me what you like about it."

She leaned back, considering, as I took another sip of coffee. She was quiet for so long, I wasn't sure she'd answer.

"I like that we're encouraged to fail here. We're not expected to be little robots churning out Facebook ads all the time, you know?"

"You once told me the Worther campaigns didn't have any soul."

She blinked in surprise, glancing at me for a too-brief moment. "Yeah. I probably said that. Here, though, people are passionate about what they do. Other corporate design jobs have burned most of us out. Jinx feels like a safe space." Her mouth hitched to the side as she surveyed the bright furniture and big windows in her office. "It feels like we...like we..."

Frowning again, she looked up at me. She'd been avoiding my gaze for so long the extended, unfiltered eye contact caught me off guard. My heart jumped.

She grinned when she spoke, and that jerked my feet from under me, too.

"I have an idea for the pitch."

Just a couple of hours later, and we did, in fact, have one helluva proposal coming together nicely.

"This is going to blow them away next week." I stood, grabbing my stuff, fighting to keep a smile off my face. I liked our pitch, the approach. I liked working with her. *I liked her*, and I'd missed her so damn much.

"You think?" She was still clicking around on her computer, looking at a few of NCR's competitors we'd been stalking. "I'm wondering if we shouldn't pull a few loose designs together to give them an idea—oh. You're leaving?" She'd finally looked up to see me standing, jacket and laptop in hand, just listening to her talk.

"I'm told people usually go home around five. It's been a refreshing change of pace."

She stared at me like I'd grown a third head.

"I mean it when I say I'm not the same man you left in Nashville, Angel. Maybe I'll tell you about it when we talk."

I waited for a few more seconds, but she just held still, rigid in the frosty silence that suddenly permeated the air.

"Goodnight, Tess. Don't work too hard." That, at least, got a reaction. The dry, disbelieving look she shot me made me grin, and the smile held until I walked into the hall.

What would Tess do after work tonight? Where would she go home to? Did she have people she was meeting? Friends? Someone...

I scrubbed my hand over my face, trying to smother that thought into nothingness. I had too many questions—about Tess, and us, and her life.

Soon, maybe, I'd get a chance to ask them. For now, I could be happy with the progress I'd made this afternoon. An empty coffee cup, a few smiles she hadn't been able to bottle up, and just a bit less stiffness than she'd had towards me a few hours ago.

I was good with that. Happy, even. And I would take those positive feelings with me all the way to my crappy long-term-stay hotel room, where I'd get more work done because I had nothing better to do this weekend.

"Jesus," I sighed. I'd thought just passing evenings alone in a strange town was bad, but what was I going to do about an entire weekend? I'd already checked out a few restaurants in the little neighborhood I was staying in, but there were only so many times a person could eat.

"That didn't sound good. You okay?" Meery, Eric's assistant, smiled from her desk as I passed.

"Yeah, I'm—Actually...." I paused. Meery was nice, friendly. And she knew Chicago better than I did. "You know of a good gym around here?"

Chapter 5

Tess

I'd spent the week exhausted, unable to sleep because of the buzzing anxiety thrumming through my veins, then expelling too much emotional energy during the day, trying to stay cool as Dylan practically glued himself to my hip.

After a Saturday of restorative hyperfixating, I'd resolved to do more of the same for the rest of the weekend, until an SOS text from my friend Lainey changed my plans.

I'd met Lainey the first time I'd ever gone to my gym, R^3, and she'd made me feel so welcome, I'd kept coming back. She and Jasmine, the wife of one of the gym's owners, had hung out with me once or twice, including a notable girl's night when I'd consumed way too much wine and babbled about Dylan for an hour, but they hadn't held that against me.

They were both smart and kind, and I really, really wanted to be their friend. I just didn't push them to hang out very often.

Lainey was usually busy with her work as a cardiothoracic surgeon, and Jas had her own career, a family, and another baby on the way. My life and its problems seemed small compared to their priorities, so I held back. But when Lainey reached out, I'd immediately agreed to meet.

Probably for the best. My wallowing had reached a pathetic point, and I needed to muster as much strength as possible before I walked into work on Monday.

I tried not to think about Dylan as I crunched across the parking lot, utterly failing like I had been all day, and yesterday, too. And all the other days this week.

In the last six months, I'd indulged in my fair share of late-night fantasies of Dylan busting in and confessing how he'd made the mistake of his life and wanted to be a better man. In those fictional scenarios, holding on to my righteous indignation and remembering how he always prioritized his work over me, it was easy to come up with a scathing response to his fictional groveling.

But in all my imaginings, I hadn't accounted for his face when he told me he wanted another chance. There was a reason I'd left without saying goodbye. One look at him, and I crumbled.

Because no matter how many times I told myself we'd been unhappy, that he'd hurt me beyond repair, there was a part of me that still loved him. That would always love him.

Now, after months without him and what felt like years of him slipping away, he was just there all the time. Lavender lattes, my favorite salads, pastries, and organic smoothies magically appeared in my office throughout the day.

It was hard to hang on to my resolve to be mad at him when suddenly he was here—for me—giving me the attention and consideration I'd been missing for a long time. For crying out loud, he had left his whole life in Nashville behind just for a chance to talk. None of it seemed like the actions of the man I'd left in that cold house in Tennessee.

Every day I softened a bit more toward him, and that seemed dangerous. It had been so long since I felt like he cared, and he was wearing me down.

Did I owe it to myself to hear him out? To hash out our history and where everything went wrong? Probably. But the possibility terrified me. I wasn't sure which outcome would be worse: if we decided our relationship was really dead, or if we tried to give it another shot, and I ended up hurt again.

I grappled with it, going back and forth and back and forth. I knew I had every right to tell him I was done and had nothing more to say to him and that he needed to catch the next flight home. But he'd asked me if I was happier here, and I wasn't. I should probably talk to him. Or maybe the will-they-won't-they stuff was messing up what little peace I'd recovered over the last few months, and I needed to tell him to take a hike.

I was stumped and desperately hoped a workout and a talk with a friend might help me decide. It wasn't something I could bring to Vanna. If she found out I was thinking of giving him another chance, I'd be in for the lecture of a lifetime. In her mind, he had hurt me, so we hated him. End of story.

The reality was more complicated, and I needed to get some distance from it all. As I opened R³'s door, I resolved to do just that: try and put Dylan out of my head and gain some much-needed perspective.

Except the man himself was standing in front of the desk talking to my trainer, Will, and my stomach bottomed out. A grin lit Will's face when he saw me.

"Livingston! I was gonna send out a search party. Haven't seen you all week."

"Uh, yeah. Lots going on. You know how it is." I attempted a weak smile that felt as shaky as the rest of me, but my eyes were snagged on Dylan. He held up his hands, speaking before I could.

"I didn't know you'd be here, I swear."

"How...what are you even doing here?" The panicked, happy, hopeful feeling of seeing him was becoming more familiar. At least I wasn't fully hyperventilating, which was an improvement over earlier this week.

"Meery said this place was good. She mentioned you came here sometimes, but only in the mornings." The pained sincerity on his face told me he was telling the truth. That, and seeing him in a familiar, ratty WTU shirt, was a sledgehammer to the walls I'd been carefully keeping up. He looked surprised. Flustered. Out of his element, which was endearing, somehow. "I really didn't think you'd be here."

"You guys good?" Will addressed both of us, but he was staring at me, the question clear on his face. *Is this guy bothering you?*

"No. I mean, yes, we're good. We're...Dylan is a friend of mine. I'm just surprised to see him, is all," I assured Will, shuffling a little closer. My relationship with Dylan was complicated, but he wasn't dangerous. To me or anyone else.

"I can just go. I don't want to butt into your personal life. Work is enough, don't you think?" Dylan's mouth hooked in an unsteady smile that didn't reach his eyes. It wasn't a good joke. Only a painful reminder of the not-so-distant past when he'd been the cornerstone of my personal life.

Now, we were strangers. I didn't even know what he'd been doing this week in Chicago. I assumed it was bleak. Alone in a strange city, probably in some mediocre hotel room, filling his time with work and wondering if I was going to tell him to scram. The thought hurt.

I left *him.* I'd reminded myself of that often over the last few days. But something about the visual of him going back to his cold hotel room, probably with a crappy gym in the basement, without even getting a workout in, was too much for me to take.

"It's okay. We're professionals at work. We can handle a workout class."

Dylan paused on his way out the door, just inches from me. "You sure?" It was the hope in his voice, so soft and hesitant, that sealed the deal. I met his eyes. Warm chocolate with too many emotions layered behind them.

I cleared my throat. "Yeah. Will puts on the best class. I know it's full, but do you have room?" I asked my trainer.

He was still eyeing the two of us, but more relaxed now. "Obviously." The warm-up mats were already teeming with bodies, but Will didn't seem concerned. "I always save a few spots for my favorite regulars."

"Don't let Lainey hear you say that. You know she considers herself your most favorite," I joked, trying to break some of the tension, only to realize my mistake. Lainey had just broken up with Will's brother, Sam, hence her SOS text today. She wasn't doing well with the split. Will's wince told me Sam wasn't, either. "Sorry..."

"Yeah." Will waved me off. "I hope those two crazy kids can make it work. I'm Will, by the way."

"Dylan." The two men reached across the check-in desk to grasp hands. They held on for a beat too long before Dylan pulled back. "You have a water fountain?"

"Sure man, right there." Will pointed across the room. I watched him walk away, an unexpected and unwelcome flutter of attraction tickling my belly when I noticed just how well that old t-shirt molded to his body. I shook my head to snap myself out of it. When I turned back to the counter, Will's face was wary. "Isn't your ex's name Dylan?"

"Yeah? How'd you know that?"

"Jas likes to gossip while she's working the front desk. You say the word and he's out of here."

Will was usually the definition of casual and charming, so it took me a second to realize he was serious. "Dylan?"

"Yeah. That guy." He tipped his head to where Dylan filled his bottle. "If you're not comfortable with him here, or he followed you or something, game over. He's out."

I was speechless. I had only joined this gym a few months ago, and even though I'd struck up a friendship with Jasmine and Lainey, I wasn't as close to Will.

He read the surprise on my face. "What kind of person would I be if I didn't speak up when I thought something might be wrong? Besides, you're a regular. Lainey and Jas would kill me if something happened to you."

I swallowed past the sudden lump in my throat. When I was a kid, there hadn't been enough money or resources or love to go around. It was hard and gritty and even years after escaping Johnson County, it was easy to forget that good people existed in the world.

"Thank you," I finally spoke, touching Will's hand where it rested on the counter. "You're a good guy, Will."

"Anyone else would do the same." He shrugged like it wasn't a big deal, but a light flush appeared across his cheekbones. "You didn't answer my question, though. In or out?" He looked to where Dylan was strolling back across the mats, eyes zeroed in on where my fingers still rested against Will's skin.

I snatched my hand back. "In. It's...complicated right now. But he's a good guy, too. I promise," I added when Will sized him up one last time, just as Dylan joined me at the front desk.

"You let me know if that changes, alright?" Will looked so serious, that lump formed in my throat again. I only nodded.

"Cool. Paperwork, bro, then we'll give you the R^3 welcome."

***

I trudged across the parking lot, gulping water and trying to extinguish the flame of lust flickering inside me.

It had been easy to keep my emotional distance at work. I was so preoccupied with the feelings and confusion of having him around, I hadn't realized how much I still wanted Dylan physically. Him staring at me in the mirrors, amidst the exertion and sweat and my pumping heart, sparked an intense heat that worked its way through my bloodstream, along with a good dose of pheromones.

We'd spent the entire class eyeing each other and pretending not to. I'd nearly dropped a kettlebell on my foot.

"She okay?" Dylan asked, leaning against a sleek black car I'd never seen before. Soft cotton clung to his biceps, plastered to his abs. I wasn't the only one who'd been working out while we'd been apart.

This doesn't change anything, I reminded myself. I'd always been attracted to Dylan. It was nothing new. A little more of my resolve crumbled. Or maybe melted was a better word.

I tore my eyes away from a bead of sweat working its way down his neck to look at Lainey's car as it drove away. "She's going through a tough breakup right now. Her ex-boyfriend did something pretty crappy, but for the right reasons. I think she's still on the fence about what to do."

"Well, you're an expert on exes doing shitty shit." I didn't return his self-deprecating smile. "I don't know the whole story, but I think she should give him another chance."

And just like that, we were in risky territory. We weren't talking about Lainey anymore. Gravel crunched as I shifted my weight under his heavy gaze.

"Dylan..." This wasn't a good time to talk about us. Not when I wanted to ask him very politely to please take his shirt off.

"I know. But I need you to understand, even if you don't want to talk to me after this project, even if you need more time, I'll be here waiting. Call me in a year, Tess, ten years, I'll say yes."

A sigh gusted from my lips. I watched as a few cars backed out of their spots and drove away. "Ten years is a long time to wait around for a conversation," I argued. He was being ridiculous and hyperbolic, and I was feeling all hot and steamy. I needed to go home and take a lukewarm shower and try to think about anything other than him. He ducked his head to catch my eye again.

"Ten? Fifty? Tell me there's a chance, no matter how small, and I'll be waiting by my phone." His sincerity seared the sensitive, ragged parts of my heart that had once belonged to him. My teeth sank into my bottom lip. I wanted to say yes almost as much as I was terrified to say yes.

Growing up, creating defense mechanisms was a matter of life and death. I instinctively shied away from the things that hurt me, getting quiet and small, waiting for it to blow over. *Just leave*, a voice inside me urged, *turn around and escape the pain he's caused you this week and all the weeks before.* I'd already tried that once, though, and it had just delayed what felt now like an inevitable reckoning.

I was quiet for a few beats too long. Dylan's shoulders fell. "You still haven't told me you're over me, and it's the single shred of hope I've been holding onto." He took a breath, looking up at the sky. "But if you're truly done, I'll get out of your hair and you won't have to deal with this, with me, again."

"That'll be pretty difficult when you're my boss." It was another sticking point I'd tried not to think too much about. If I was spinning out with him being around for only a few days, what would happen when we were together every day for the foreseeable future? Being around him all the time, watching him date and get on with his life, would be more than I could bear. There was a reason I'd moved so far away. If Dylan wasn't living his life with me, then I didn't want to see it. I'd have to leave.

His gaze collided with mine again. Everything got more serious.

"Not if you don't want me to. I told you. Say the word and I'll leave this city. The company. All of it." He clutched at his chest like he was in pain. Something painful echoed in me, too. "You are always a yes for me, Tess. Always. I know I haven't done a good job of showing you that in the past. As much as I *hate* the thought of living without you, I can't stand the thought of hurting you even more than I already have."

I stared at him as if I'd never seen him before; his declaration more impactful than the coffees and food and everything else from the last week. The Dylan from before would have done anything to keep his job, to get to the next promotion or bonus check. Had he really been serious about giving up his role at Jinx? Maybe even his job at Worther? It didn't quite compute, but the look on his face told me he meant every word.

"How do I know this will last? What if we get back together and after a while it just goes back to the way it was?" Faced with his sincerity, my own deepest fear came bubbling out to the surface. The real reason I hadn't given him an answer yet. Because I couldn't get hurt again. I'd barely survived the first time.

"Give me some time, Tess." Dylan lifted his hands between us, pleading. "We're taking a few months to see if I'm a good fit at Jinx. Let me show you I'm still a good fit for you. A few months to prove I can do this, then if you're still not convinced..."

His hands fell back to his sides. He didn't need to speak the rest. If I still had doubts, he'd go back to Nashville and stay as far away from me as possible.

I tried to imagine going back to my life the way it had been before he showed up in Chicago. Driving to the office, returning to my shoebox apartment. Going to the gym. Instead, my brain just kept serving me memories.

Thoughts of us from years ago—dancing in the kitchen, getting tipsy and making love on the couch, holding each other under the covers as rain tapped on the bedroom window—melded with the present. I could see us in Chicago, holding hands on the Riverwalk. Exploring the galleries and public art installations. Going to Jinx together in the morning and coming home to cook dinner.

The memories and maybes clashed until my heart didn't know which was reality. But it lifted at the thought of trying again. I had been so alone before I met him, and lonely ever since I'd left. I missed him, and the feeling that there was someone in the world who knew me better than anyone else and still chose me.

"Okay."

My answer was a whisper, a scrap of fluttering gossamer hope, swirling in the air around us.

"Yes?" He sounded desperate, eyes wild.

"Yes." I nodded, cautious even when my heart beat so hard it felt like it would fly right out of my chest. "After this project is over, let's talk. Let's...see what happens."

He shuddered a breath, and his hands lifted again as if he wanted to hold me, but he stopped short, raking them through his hair instead. "Okay. Thank you. *Thank you,* Tess."

My name sounded like a prayer in his mouth. It echoed the same, urgent rhythm now flooding my veins, every beat of my racing heart pounding out his name. *Dyl-an. Dyl-an. Dyl-an.*

It raced faster, and I wasn't sure if it was from fear or anticipation. Or both.

Chapter 6

Tess

"To the agency strays!" Eric cheered. Our team filled the back of Willy's, a bar near the office, as we raised our glasses.

In the middle of the peeling, fake leather seats, sticky floor, and dingy dart boards, I was riding on a high. National Canine Rescue had loved our pitch so much, they'd signed a contract on the spot. No next round. No other agencies to consider.

I was floating on a cloud.

"It was all Tess," Dylan said, beaming. I wondered if anyone else noticed how his eyes turned soft whenever they looked at me, or was it just my imagination?

"You did your fair share of the work," I told him, tucking my hair behind my ears. Seeing Dylan still sent a lurch of dizzying emotions through me, but it had gotten easier to handle. In reality, working with him over the past week had been fine...more than fine. We were a good team, and every day being around him became just a bit more comfortable.

"Well, you nailed it. I mean, look at Carl!" Noel picked up one of the slides Eric had printed. It featured an image of a Bernese Mountain Dog with a barrel around its neck. Noel read the text. "Carl. Strong, calm, the one you call if your project needs a rescue."

"It's true, man!" Aaron, a designer, clapped a blushing Carl on the back. "You're the go-to when it's crunch time." He blushed.

"I'm dying over Victoria's," Meery squealed. Dylan and I traded a glance over the heads of the Jinx team. Icky Vicky's had been the hardest to come up with, mostly because I'd struggled to find anything nice to say. In the end, we'd landed on a picture of a manicured poodle. "Alert, active, won't rest until every detail is just right!"

The little seed of my idea—describing Jinx as its own sort of "creative designer rescue"—had flourished once I'd explained it to Dylan. Together, we'd developed a presentation that didn't just focus on Jinx's offerings or pricing, but on the heart of the agency: its people. Just like the dogs at NCR, we all had our own backgrounds and talents, just waiting to be picked by the right owner...or in this case, client.

"Glass of red?" a server asked behind me.

"Here." Dylan reached back to take the wine, setting it in front of me and smoothly swapping it for the beer Eric had poured for me. No one else seemed to notice, but my whole body flushed. It was such a Dylan thing to do. He knew I didn't like beer, but wouldn't refuse a drink someone handed me. For most of our relationship, he'd been exceptionally good at taking care of me, and making sure I had what I needed.

I'd forgotten that about him.

"Thank you," I murmured, looking away. Now that I'd committed to talking about our past, it was like all the anger and resentment inside me had begun to evaporate. My feelings were shifting, unearthing things I'd forgotten. Like how much I wanted him.

Before, I'd been too hurt to feel attracted to him. Now, opening the door to our relationship had unlocked the possibility of other things. Hot, illicit things I hadn't realized I'd been missing.

"Of course." I could feel where Dylan's attention lingered on my skin. His arm brushed against mine, making the hair on the back of my neck stand up. What was wrong with me? It had been a long time since I'd been touched by anyone. Even before I'd left, Dylan and I hadn't been intimate in months.

Weren't there studies that showed physical isolation was bad for your health? Maybe that was why all day today, I hadn't been able to stop staring at his mouth, or the veins in his neck. Yes, that must be it.

"So, Dylan, how do you like Chicago so far?" Victoria leaned across the sticky table, closer than necessary. Her teeth looked exceptionally pointy, hazel eyes narrow as she studied him. Had she seen him slide the drink in my direction? That wasn't incriminating, was it? I gulped a sip of the wine without tasting it.

"I like it a lot. I've been here before for work, but never stayed an extended amount of time. It's nice to explore a bit."

"Mmhmm." She rested her chin on her hand, sizing him up. "And how long are you planning on staying? We've never had someone from corporate up here before. I thought you were only supposed to be here for a few days?"

I gulped more wine and pretended to listen to a story Eric was telling at the other end of the table. Dylan's promotion to Jinx's CEO was still a secret. Eric had reiterated multiple times that he wanted to ease the team in, make sure they trusted Dylan before making the announcement.

"Like I said before, Worther is interested in the work you're doing here. We want to see what kind of gold mine we're sitting on." Dylan sounded so sure of himself, nonchalant. I could practically feel Victoria simpering. I stared harder at the other end of the table.

"Well, a lot of that has to do with the original staff of the company. We built this place from the ground up. Did you know I was only the third hire Eric ever made?"

I nearly rolled my eyes. She loved to flaunt her tenure at Jinx, like it was a Nobel Peace Prize or something.

"I think you're right. Jinx operates differently from other agencies within our portfolio. There must be a reason." I nearly jumped when I felt his fingers nudge mine under the table. When I turned to look at him, lines crinkled at the corners of his eyes. "Probably the same reason Jinx hired our best designer right from under our noses."

My lips tilted up in a reaction I couldn't stop. In the past, he'd liked to brag about my artistic talent, mainly when I dabbled with watercolors, or when he wanted to dominate our friends in Pictionary. But he'd never complimented me on my work before.

I hadn't thought anything of it since our paths hardly crossed at Worther. He was always out wining and dining clients, and I was on the back end eagle-eyeing the kerning. But now, he was practically my shadow around the office, in the trenches for most of my meetings and project updates. Apparently, he liked what he saw.

I didn't know what to say, aside from a muttered thanks. His eyes dipped, watching my mouth move. I bit my lip, and he followed that, too.

Dylan chatted with Victoria for a few more minutes before engaging Noel about her recent house search.

He had always excelled at socializing. He listened and asked great follow-up questions in a way I'd never really gotten the hang of. My colleagues were drawn to him like moths to a flame, captivated by his ability to make them feel important, valued.

There was a time, not so long ago, when I'd been proud to call him mine. I loved watching him in his element, working a room and dazzling everyone in the vicinity. It was bittersweet to watch it up close and personal again, knowing these people didn't know who we were to each other. Knowing the truth: right now, we were nothing to each other.

"Oh, sure, I'm familiar with that company. Tess, weren't you in charge of the creative when Worther worked on that new software launch? The blue with the cartoon stuff?" Dylan turned back to me and oh, crap, he was *doing it to me*. Including me in the conversation, making me feel important.

"Yessss…" I drawled, fiddling with my wineglass. The first had emptied a while ago, and another one had magically appeared in front of me. "How do you even remember that?"

It was the first campaign I'd been completely in charge of at Worther, over two years ago. I'd gotten the opportunity about the same time Dylan had nosedived face-first into his next promotion. I didn't realize he'd ever even seen it, or known it was mine.

His smile was just slightly off, brown eyes searching, like he was willing me to hear him, and believe him, when he said: "It might not seem like it, but I'm always paying attention to the good stuff."

***

"I knew there was some magic going on here." Eric clapped Dylan and me on the back. He was the last of our group to leave the bar, everyone else heading home for dinner or out for another drink somewhere else. "This is going to work. I can feel it. Can you feel it?"

I swallowed, trying my hardest not to think about how Dylan had shifted closer to me a few minutes ago and hadn't moved back. His leg pressed up against mine. It had been fine when the table was full. Now, it was just us, but I couldn't bring myself to move away.

Yeah, I could feel it.

"Absolutely." Dylan grinned in a way that told me he wasn't inclined to move, either.

"New leadership, new ideas. Everyone already loves having you around." Eric squeezed Dylan's shoulder. "Tab's still open at the bar. Use it! Get to know each other a little more. The future leaders of Jinx Creative."

I watched him stroll out the door, achingly aware that suddenly it was just me and Dylan and the warmth radiating between our bodies.

I traced old condensation rings on the table, considering my next move. We'd said we would find time to talk when the rescue pitch was over. Was that time now? Did I really want to do this here, in a bar on a random Friday night?

"I can close out if you have somewhere else to be," Dylan offered. When I glanced up, the intense look on his face broke. He gave me a charming smile that didn't fool me for a second. "I'm going to stick around and finish my drink. Might as well, if it's going on the company's tab. You can head out if you want."

"Hmm," I hummed, studying him. He didn't squirm, just met my eyes with that steady, cocky smile. I saw through him, of course. He was giving me an out, in case I wasn't ready to do this tonight. He was so...so nice. How had I forgotten how nice he was?

In the last week, as the cloudy lens of resentment and bitterness I'd carried back in Nashville started to fall away, it had felt amazing and agonizing.

Amazing because he *was* amazing, and he still wanted me. Agonizing because he was amazing, and he still wanted me, and I wasn't sure what to do with that. He might have been on his best behavior now, but how long until he reverted to his old ways, leaving me feeling invisible and unimportant again?

I picked up my half-full glass, weighing my options. It would probably be best for me to call it a night. My thoughts about him were still too muddled and confused. I should leave my wine unfinished on the table and say goodnight.

Right.

"I can stick around to finish this." I nodded to my drink, betraying every ounce of logic in my brain. "It's on the company, after all."

The sides of Dylan's eyes crinkled, and he placed his elbow on the table, eating up the distance between us. He was close enough for me to see the scar on his hairline from the time he'd fallen off his four-wheeler in high school.

"Thank God, because no one back in Nashville watches Palm Springs Matchmaker, and I have to talk to someone about Vince."

"Oh, my *God*," I gasped, clutching my hand to my chest. "He's such a sleazeball! I don't know what Ariana sees in him."

"When he walked out after the dinner party, I had to turn the TV off," Dylan confided. I felt like my cheeks would crack from the massive grin stretching across my face. I had started watching the reality TV show years ago, and somehow Dylan had picked it up, too. I'd had no idea he'd keep watching if I wasn't around to turn it on.

I took a sip. "We have to talk about the dinner party. Raquel?"

Dylan's hand sliced through the air. "Absolute shitshow." He was grinning now, too, the air between us popping and fizzing like the carbonation in his beer. I rocked my glass back and forth on the table, my mind warring with my heart. There were a lot of reasons I shouldn't even be here right now.

But he was so handsome it hurt, and he was looking at me like I was the only thing he wanted to look at for the rest of his life.

"We should probably get another round. This could take a while."

Dylan's hand raised, flagging down the server before I'd even finished speaking.

Chapter 7

Tess

"Dylan," I moaned. His only response was to shove his tongue further into my mouth, like he would die if he wasn't inside me.

If he didn't get inside me soon, I *was* going to die.

His hips rocked against mine, hands squeezing my ass. The whole stumbling trip up the three stories of my walk-up apartment had been like this. Grabbing, desperate, choking on each other's air in an attempt to devour.

I'd known I had missed Dylan. Seeing him, talking to him, being around him every day, had just sharpened that longing into a blade that cut something open between us. Everything was heat, light, *more, please, please, more.*

He grunted when my fingers wrapped in his hair and tugged. "Tess...Angel, if you don't open this door right now, I'm going to fuck you against it," he growled, leaving a trail of sucking kisses across my neck.

I shuddered, fumbling in my purse for my keys right as he licked up the length of my throat. My bag dropped to the floor. I drew his face to mine again, lips crashing together.

"Door it is, then," he whispered. A sweet, searing ache consumed my heart as I felt his lips lifting against mine. Smiling as we kissed.

Only years of experience could have made him move as quickly as he did, fingers diving underneath the hem of my pencil skirt.

My whimper and his groan blended together when he met the stretchy barrier of my sheer pantyhose.

"You're kidding me," he growled, pulling back to meet my eyes. The same molten urgency I felt was reflected in his blown pupils. "Since when do you wear tights?"

"Hose are professional. We had a client meeting today," I whined, hips churning against his, straining for his hand. The tension in the tights was keeping his fingers off me.

Rrriiiip.

The sound of the fabric tearing at the apex of my thighs made me gasp. He crowded me further against the door, claiming my mouth with his as he shoved my underwear aside. Fingers brushed hot, slick skin.

"Dylan!"

I had a handful of brain cells active enough to keep me from screaming his name in the public stairwell. I only had one neighbor on the other side, that older woman, and she seemed nice enough, but she probably didn't want to come out and see me writhing against my front door, my ex-boyfriend's hand working literal magic between my legs.

I was hot and desperate, and he felt so good, moving in that way he knew drove me wild every time. Pure bliss.

"You're so wet. Have you been this wet since the bar?" His breath steamed on the side of my neck, lips nipping and sucking.

I bit my lip, nodding. If I opened my mouth, I'd scream. It had been too long since I'd had him. Even longer since I'd had him *like this*. In the last few years, the sex had been fine. Good.

But this reminded me of sophomore year in college when Dylan had missed a whole midterm because we hadn't been able to keep our hands off each other.

He pumped another finger inside, and a cry finally worked its way up my throat. His mouth covered mine. "I want you to scream for me, Tess. Just not here."

I mumbled something in response, gripping the collar of his shirt tighter. My legs were shaking, pleasure shooting through my body as his fingers played and pumped, unhurried and purposeful. Despite his words, he wasn't making any moves to open the door.

Was he so desperate for me he'd take me up against my front door like this? In public? Was I so desperate I'd let him?

I suspected the answer was yes, but he stumbled away from me before I could find out.

He looked disheveled and hot, hair wild from my hands, mouth red and swollen. Chest heaving.

"Keys, Tess," he demanded, sucking his fingers in his mouth, tasting me while I watched. I nearly slid to the floor.

"Bag," I managed to stutter, pointing helplessly.

In seconds, my bag and keys were in his hand. He pulled me in, arm wrapping around my back like he couldn't stand to be apart, like he had to be close and touching me. Metal rasped against metal. Then nothing.

"You have to jiggle it…" I whispered, too busy skimming my finger-tips along the side of his jaw to help. The stubble scraped against my skin. I had a brief second to register the wicked, silly smile that cracked across his face before he lifted me with his arm, shaking me up and down.

My door swung open as my laughter split through the air, louder than my previous cries.

Dylan clicked the lock behind us, then hauled me against him again, his lips on mine. "I missed that laugh. Missed you so much."

"Dylan," I sighed, arms around his neck. He couldn't be close enough. "Bed. I need you."

We stumbled across the tiny studio apartment, the table lurching to the side as we passed. A tray of watercolors teetered before smashing to the ground. Pigment scattered.

"I'll replace it," he promised, peeling off my tank top. Clothes trailed behind us in haphazard piles. He pulled back the edge of my bra to take my nipple in his mouth. "I'll buy you ten more. A hundred. Just don't stop."

I worked his zipper down, his cock jerking when it touched my palm.

We tipped onto the bed together. The air whooshed out of my lungs, but his weight on top of me was perfect. Everything I'd been missing for months.

I laughed more when he cursed up a storm, shoving my hose halfway down my legs before ripping them the rest of the way. "I will not buy you more of those," he muttered, mouth everywhere, fingers everywhere.

I found him again, pushing his pants down with one hand, stroking with the other.

"Fuck, I'm going to come. Let me…inside you, Tess, please. I swear I'll make it good. Fuck, it's so good…"

He wasn't speaking in full sentences, but I understood every word out of his mouth. Every inhale, sigh, and curse. Being with him was like rediscovering a language I spoke fluently, but had forgotten until now.

"Yes," I whispered, pulling him closer.

Then, he was right where I needed him. The head of his penis easily slid up and down, preparing to push inside where I craved him most.

We'd done this so many times, but now it felt new, exciting. Maybe because we'd been apart, or maybe because something had changed. Him or me or both of us?

I wondered what it would feel like to have sex with him again for the first time. If I was just some random girl he'd brought home from the bar, would it be this hot? This natural?

The thought, and the feel of him sliding closer to where no one else had ever been, made me freeze.

Had he done this with some random girl from a bar? We'd been apart for half a year. Just because I hadn't dated or had a random hookup, didn't mean he hadn't. The thought was a splash of ice water on my libido, and I instantly hated myself for it.

I was the one who'd left. I couldn't complain if he had moved on, or had a fling or, or, or touched some other woman the way he was touching me now. Gripping her skin as if he wanted to imprint himself on her.

"Wait." The image was painful enough to give me pause, even though I didn't want us to stop. But...I needed to be sure. And safe. "Should we...do we need a condom?" I panted, my hips churning against his, reacting to the feel of him even while my mind raced.

I was here, in bed with him, but I was also imagining the worst-case scenario: Dylan, back at the condo in Nashville, making some other girl gasp and moan. I was back at the bar with Meery, months ago.

"You've only had sex with one guy? Ever?!" She'd gasped, seeming both delighted and horrified by the admission. "Well, whenever you're ready to get your groove back, you need to be careful. HPV is rampant these days. *Rampant.*"

Dylan's head lifted. The question in his gaze clouded some of the lust in his eyes. "A condom?"

He sounded bewildered, and the implications of those two words swept around us, like a breeze we couldn't feel, but we knew was there.

"I...should we?" I parroted the question back to him. I was clean and safe, but was he?

He stared at me like I had just asked him to solve an advanced mathematical equation.

"I mean...yes. Yes, sure, if that's what you want." All at once, we were two strangers, speaking different tongues. That common language began to disintegrate. I couldn't read his face, he couldn't understand my question.

I hesitated for a second, heart pounding now with uncertainty. "Sorry, I know it's—"

"No, no...we can...yes, that's a good idea," he panted, lips planting again and again against mine. Even as his brow crinkled.

I reached into my nightstand, fumbling in the drawer to hand him a box of condoms. He rolled to his knees.

It was weird, watching him do this. I'd been on birth control for years, and we'd been faithful. Seeing the box in his hand stole several more degrees of heat from the air in my lungs.

He must have felt it, too, pausing the second he looked down. I gulped, scooching up on the bed, putting some space between our bodies.

"This..." he trailed off, staring at it for a beat. "This is open." His brow furrowed.

A slick, cold feeling trickled down my spine. I knew exactly what he was thinking. "I didn't use any," I blurted, too quickly and frantically to sound sincere. His eyes flickered to mine, then back down at the box.

"O-okayyy..."

"I swear. Meery got them for me and then grabbed some because she had a date that night. I...it's...I'd told her I was just getting out of a long-term relationship, and she wanted to be sure I was safe."

Dylan sat back on his heels as I babbled, unable to tear his eyes away from the gold foil packages. "*Very* safe." I thought he was attempting a joke, but his voice was off, hollow.

Yes, Meery had gotten me a value pack. I had cringed when she presented it to me, but I completely recoiled now, feet drawing up, legs folding me into a little ball.

Dylan's hand whipped out, snaking around my ankle to hold me in place. My movements seemed to break some sort of spell, and he finally looked at me, his expression carefully blank.

"That's good. That you have a friend like that..." He broke off, blinking down at me, naked and splayed against my pillows. A little line appeared between his brows. "Sorry, I...sorry."

"Are you alright? I promise I didn't use—"

"I believe you," he interrupted, glancing back at the box before setting it aside. It was ridiculous, of course, to feel so guilty about owning a box of condoms. I was an adult. A *single adult*.

But that was the problem, wasn't it? These last couple of weeks, it had been easy to re-introduce small pieces of him back into my heart. His laugh, his smile. That hopeful look in his eyes when he handed me my coffee every morning.

Like tiny pieces of porcelain had pulled together one by one after shattering, reforming a pattern my heart knew like a beat.

Tonight, I'd sipped from the cup I thought was whole again, getting drunk off the knowledge that I could have him if I wanted. But we hadn't been whole.

Everything we'd circled around over the last few weeks was just smoke, and icy regret pooled low in my belly, extinguishing what was left of the lust swirling inside me.

I pulled the sheet with me as I sat up, covering my chilled skin.

"I'm sorry," he repeated, watching me pull away from him. "I'm fine. This is fine...of course..." He glanced at his lap, and my attention followed his. Apparently, his desire had fled as quickly as mine did. I drew the sheet tighter around me as he scrambled off the bed to locate his pants, babbling as he pulled them on.

"You are perfectly...I mean, obviously you don't need permission to..."

I'd never in my life seen Dylan babble, and any other time, it would have been funny. For now, though, it was just a reminder that things were different.

Dylan babbled, and I kept condoms in my bedside drawer.

"I'm sorry if—"

"Don't apologize. You have done nothing wrong. I'm the one..." Abruptly, he knelt on the bed, hands skimming down my arms. His fingers felt cold. "We weren't together. You...can...sleep with whoever...I mean, you could have...you *should* have..."

"I *should have?*"

He pinched his nose, rocking back onto his heels once more. "That's not what I meant."

"No?"

"No!" His denial was sharp and immediate. He looked slightly ill. "But, I mean, we weren't together, and if you chose to...do that, then I would have no place to comment on that. Or...judge. Obviously."

"Right." I wanted to ask if he'd been with anyone else since I left, but it felt weird to talk about this. I had never worried about losing him to another woman before. Just a corporation.

"Everything is fine. I just need a minute here...just a minute." He was repeating himself, shoving his hands through his hair and glancing wildly around my apartment, searching for something I wasn't sure he'd be able to find. I only had to look at the foil packets on my bed to know everything was *not* fine.

I curled my knees tighter into my chest. "If you need to leave, you can." My voice sounded small. I *felt* small, and I hated that. Logically, I knew I had done nothing wrong. The unapologetic feminist in my brain screamed, holding a big *"my body, my condoms"* sign, telling me he could fuck off if he had an issue with me exploring my sexuality as a single person.

But I knew the condoms weren't the problem. It was what they represented.

"Leave?" Backlit by the dim lights over my oven, I couldn't see his face well, but he sounded lost. My hands fidgeted in my lap.

"Maybe."

He knelt in silence for a few more seconds. I couldn't see his eyes. Couldn't see what he saw. Me? The condoms? The dingy, dinky apartment I'd run away to? Possibly to have sex with other people?

Slowly, like the stomach-lurching start of a roller coaster, he shook his head back and forth, gaining momentum. "No, Tess. I don't want to leave."

Eight Years Ago

Dylan

"No, I told you to *go* left, so you need to *cut* right!" Tess dragged frustrated hands through her ponytail. This morning, when we'd loaded everything into the U-Haul for the hours-long trek to our new Nashville apartment, I'd thought she looked gorgeous. Cut-off jeans and a tank top, perfect for moving day—the day after graduation, when every possibility seemed like it could be ours.

Now, though...

"Use the right terminology, otherwise this will never work," I hollered, so frustrated there was probably steam coming out of my ears, adding to the blistering heat in the truck.

She threw her hands in the air. "It's never going to work because we've somehow gotten ourselves squeezed into an impossible spot and if you move three inches to the left, you're going to hit that dumpster, and any further to the right, you're going to take out that car."

"Funny how *we've* gotten into an impossible spot when *you* were the one in charge of directing me."

Half an hour ago, it had seemed easy to back this truck into the gated parking lot of our apartment building. The good news, our truck was at least inside the fence. The bad news, something had gone horribly wrong. The back door was too close to a wall, so we couldn't unload and, for some inexplicable reason, the damn truck was incapable of moving more than two inches in either direction without hitting something.

"Hey, this is a team sport, dude! You're not listening. I told you backing it up more was a bad idea," she shot back.

"You're right," I called, jerking the key out of the ignition and tossing it out the open window at her feet. "If you're so fucking smart, why don't you figure it out?"

Her shoulders rose and fell sharply before she picked up the keys. "Fine. I fucking will."

"Great!" My eyes narrowed as she turned on her heel to walk away, toward the security gate.

"The truck is over here!"

"Yeah, and you're in the truck, and I don't want to look at your face for at least five minutes," she yelled without looking back.

I gaped as she walked away, so pissed off I was shaking. "Theresa!"

"Do not follow me!" she yelled over her shoulder, every muscle rigid.

"You're in an unfamiliar neighborhood. You can't just leave by yourself!" I fumbled my seatbelt, reaching for the door only to realize I would never in a million years open it wide enough to get out. I rolled the window down more. Maybe if I jumped on top of the truck next to me, I could get to her before she—

The gate slammed shut behind her, clanging like my nerves. I was still halfway out the window with no hope of wiggling free.

"Goddammit," I muttered, grabbing my phone from the seat and stabbing at the screen to call her. The familiar, bouncy ringtone sounded beside me. I glanced down to see her purse on the floorboard. "Fuck."

By the time I'd escaped out the other door and run to the gate, she was nowhere to be seen. No phone, no money.

"*Fuck.*"

I spent a moment glaring out at the street as if she'd magically reappear before I looked back at the truck. It was unlocked, but it wasn't like anyone could have gotten to our stuff, anyway. We certainly couldn't.

I finally turned, punching in the code the front-desk woman had given us earlier. I had hoped the first time we walked into our new apartment would be *together*, but I'd had to take a piss for the last hour, and I couldn't hunt Tess down if my bladder was about to explode.

Outside our scuffed front door, the parquet flooring felt sticky under my tennis shoes. As it opened, squeaking hinges revealed a unit that looked nothing like the photos online. I should have known something was wrong when I'd seen the barbed wire topping the fence around the parking lot.

As I passed through the space to the single bathroom, it didn't get any better. The floors were warped, making me feel like I was listing from side to side. There was a long crack in the bathroom mirror, matching the chipped shower tiles, and an orange-ish ring circled the inside of the toilet bowl.

I stomped through the apartment again, bee-lining to the kitchen sink. It sputtered when I turned it on. That and the musty smell of the unit made me question just how long this place had gone un-occupied. I cupped my hands to take a drink. I was sweaty and tired and thirsty and I hadn't even started the hardest part of the move yet because our shit was still trapped in the truck.

I cast my gaze around the place again. The windows were tall, which should have been a good thing, but it just shed more light on the apartment's imperfections. Tess had wanted to come see it in person, but we'd been too busy cramming for finals and trying to get her interviews. My job in the sales department of an advertising agency started Monday, but she was still having some trouble getting her portfolio in front of the right people.

I'd told her not to worry about it. We'd specifically gotten a place I could afford on my own. She'd find work, and we'd move as soon as we had enough saved.

I'd hunted for a place while she'd focused on perfecting her cover letter and finishing classes. And this was what I'd come up with.

I pictured the little velvet box buried deep in one of my suitcases in the U-Haul. I couldn't ask her to start a life with me *here*. She deserved better. I could do better.

I whirled at the shriek of the door opening. I'd need to oil those hinges. Tess stepped in, laden with a massive, grease-stained paper bag and a box of hard lemonades.

I froze, unable to form words as I watched her mouth pop open. While she looked around, the silence stretched. When her eyes filled with tears, I broke.

"I know it's not like the photos they had on the website—"

"It's better," she whispered, gliding across the tilted floors to set her load on the kitchen counter. "Dylan, look at those windows!"

Years of ingrained habit compelled me to put my arms around her when she hugged me, even as my brain struggled to keep up. She *liked* this pit?

"They are"—I cleared my throat—"good windows." What else could I do but agree? What else could I do but let her drag me across the floor as she rushed over to them?

"We have a little fire escape! Do you think we could see the stars at night?"

I blinked at the ferocity of her grin, craning my head to look up. "We are on the top floor. Maybe?"

She gathered me up again, squeezing. "Let's go out there with a blanket tonight and see!"

"You're...okay with this place?" My fingers rubbed the bare skin between her shoulder blades.

"Okay?" She pulled back to smile, her eyes still wet. "It's perfect! It's *ours.*"

A knock on the door broke us apart. Tess sprinted to open it and didn't even seem to notice the hellish screaming of the hinges. A tall man carrying two familiar boxes stood on the other side.

"Ezra. Look at my windows!" Tess gushed, stepping back to let him in.

"Niiice," he agreed, setting the boxes down and holding out his hand to me. "Ezra. Nice digs, congrats on the move, man."

"Um, Dylan. Hi." I blinked, nonplussed. A long whistle at the door made me turn to see another man walk in, single-handedly carrying my box spring.

"Damn, look at those windows!"

"I *know.*" Tess grinned at this guy, too, like he was supposed to be here, carrying our stuff.

"This is Nelly. He and Ezra own a moving business," Tess explained, correctly reading the confusion on my face.

"Your girl came up to us bold as brass at the gas station around the block and asked if we knew how to maneuver your truck. Got it out far enough to unload, by the way. Should be able to move it nice and easy tonight," Ezra called on his way out the door, presumably to go get more of our stuff.

"Tess, we can't pay them," I muttered, gripping her elbow, still trying to figure out what the hell was going on. Where had she been and how had she found these guys so quickly?

"Don't worry about that, bro! We were about to grab tacos for our lunch break. Y'all don't have much in there. It'll take us twenty minutes, tops."

"I told them I'd buy lunch if they could move the truck, but they insisted on helping unload."

"You sprang for the drinks, too! Only fair." Nelly patted the box of hard lemonade on his way out the door.

"I'm sorry I left. I was frustrated and needed a minute," Tess said, pulling me into her arms again. She hadn't grown up in a stable home. I hated when we fought, because we were usually so in sync, but also because I knew how much it ate her up, spiking her anxiety.

"I'm sorry, too. I shouldn't have yelled," I admitted while she melted against me. My fingers massaged the back of her neck. "I was mostly worried about you being in a strange city without your phone or your wallet."

She shrugged. "I only went down the street. And I had some cash in my pocket. Besides, I checked off items number two and seven on the Nashville list."

"Two *and* seven?" I didn't like how flippantly she approached running off in a new city, but we could talk about it later. I sometimes forgot about my girlfriend's secret spine of steel. She was so soft and gentle, most people underestimated her. I tried to remember often why I'd fallen in love with the Beer Angel. "Make friends in the neighborhood and find the best place to eat within walking distance of the apartment."

"Fuck yeah! The Quick-n-Stop has the best tacos in the city. You won't be disappointed. Your girl got enough to feed the whole building." Ezra was back with more boxes.

I lowered my head as he disappeared down the hallway to drop them in the bedroom. "I fucking love you." My lips met hers for a kiss that was too short before I pulled away to help the guys unload.

Chapter 8
Dylan

"No, Tess. I don't want to leave."

In all the months Tess had been gone, it had occurred to me, of course, that there might be someone else. I spent days and nights tormented by the thought of her with another man, one who would be home by five, and notice when she started withering away before his eyes.

A better man than me.

If that were the case, I told myself I'd deal with it. I could step aside and just be happy she was happy. Back in Nashville, when I'd had nothing to lose and my only plan was a lot of groveling and hoping she gave me half a chance, it all sounded so simple.

But there were variables I hadn't considered. Like how now, even though she hadn't been with anyone else, a glance at the box of condoms on the bed was enough to flatten me.

No, she hadn't been with anyone else, but she could have. Any single thing could have gone differently in the last six months, and I'd have lost her forever.

It was the adrenaline shock of almost rear-ending someone. The shaky, baffled breath after a near-death experience.

"Maybe it's for the best," Tess ventured, killing me. "This is a lot. Maybe we should take some time."

She was huddled in a little ball, pulling the sheet over herself. Looking at her cut me open. How did she see everything and still not understand how she could end me with a single look?

"Fuck, no."

Tess's head reared back, and I cleared my throat, as surprised as she was at my outburst. Aside from that first ambush in her office, I'd been so careful not to spook her.

"I mean," I began, weighing my next words. The Tess who had lived without me for six months was a wild animal. When I talked to her, it was soft. I sat slowly, carefully, across from her in the conference room. Even though I wanted to grab her and yell at her for leaving and beg her to come back until I was hoarse.

Now, it occurred to me it hadn't gotten me anywhere. Not for the past few weeks, when I'd been quietly courting her with caffeine, and not last year when I'd watched her go to bed alone, shoulders hunched, too many times without saying anything.

If I had, maybe we wouldn't be here.

"Actually, I did mean that. Fuck, no." I paced, hands on my hips. Her apartment only allowed for a few steps in each direction. "We've taken six months of time, Tess. I don't want more time away from you. I won't run away, and I won't stop fighting for us."

A sigh hissed out of her mouth as she searched for her clothes. When I saw how she kept the sheet clenched to her chest, I tossed a shirt from the end of the bed and turned my back. As if I didn't know her skin better than my own.

"This is too complicated, Dylan."

"It's not complicated at all, Angel. I still want you. Do you still want me?" The question had been living under my skin for weeks. That yes or no I'd been trying to drag out of her with every look, every exchange.

When I turned around, she stared at the box on her bed. "It *is* complicated." She sounded defeated. "We're freaking out over a box of condoms I've never even used before. It's...the definition of baggage."

"What you call baggage, I call the best years of my life." She looked away, biting her lip. I dropped to my knees, threading my fingers through hers. I'd always loved how delicate they were. Perfect for holding a brush or smoothing a precise line of charcoal. Now they felt cold.

"I'm freaking out because it's a reminder that I almost lost you. I almost screwed this up so badly that you could have moved on and had a completely different life without me. And I would have found a way to be okay with that because I'm the idiot who didn't hold on to you when I had the chance. But, there still is something here. You were willing to give this a shot earlier tonight."

Her brows snapped down over her eyes. A spark of something flashed there. Anger or regret. Whatever it was, I hadn't seen that light, that fight, in a long time. "Only because you were making it seem so easy! *Just talk to me; give me one chance.* Like we could somehow pick up where we left off. Obviously, it's harder than that. *Complicated.*"

She spat the word like it was poison, and I realized my approach to this had been all wrong. I'd treated her with kid gloves, scared she'd hiss and claw at me or, worse, run away. Now I realized I *wanted* her to scratch at me. Bite, maul, chew me up and spit me out. Anything but that blank apathy she'd given me for the last gasping months of our dying relationship.

Not many people had seen Tess mad before, but I had. No matter how quiet and agreeable she appeared on the outside, she felt just as strongly about things as everyone else. Maybe even more so. I wanted her to let it out all over me. To let me *in*.

"You're right. It was ridiculous to think we could just start at the same place we were and get a different result."

"Right." The spark died. Her gaze dropped to her hands, fingernails already picking at the skin of her thumb. I'd have to get her those colorful Band-Aids like I used to when she was stressed and picked her nails before exams. She thought I was giving up? I was only getting started.

"We have to start from the beginning."

Her fingers stilled. "What?" She was looking at me like I was crazy, and maybe I was, but she was right. We couldn't pretend the last six months had never happened. We couldn't build on a cracked foundation.

"Start over. From scratch. Isn't that what you're trying to do here, anyway?" I tilted my head to the walls around us. Her eyes floated across the room, taking in the multicolored prints and the wall full of little potted plants.

"I get it, Tess. Baggage. There are things I love about our baggage, but it started piling up towards the end there. What if we just wiped it away?"

"Like a fresh start?"

"Exactly like that," I agreed, as if I couldn't hear how incredulous she sounded. We hadn't been good at the end of our relationship, but we were fucking incredible at the beginning. "I'm a different person since you left. Hell, I'm a different person since I met you all those years ago. What if we tried again, right now? The people we are in this moment?"

Her face twisted in confusion, but it felt right as I said it. I loved Tess. What would I do to go back and fix the mistakes I'd made over the last few years?

Anything. I'd give everything up.

Except her.

But the longer she stared, the rightness, that conviction in my chest, wavered. Maybe it was a ridiculously stupid idea. But maybe, if we just tried to start over, we could get to a place where we could hash it out. Find a space where we were happy, and comfortable, and able to speak about our—my—mistakes.

"Tess?" She'd been quiet for too long. That confused look on her face had morphed slowly into something like stricken surprise. She blinked, eyes refocusing.

"I'm not going to some frat house to tap a keg."

I practically deflated in relief. My fingers squeezed hers. "We can go where someone else taps the keg."

"And what does it even mean, fresh start? Do we...pretend we don't know each other? What do we talk about?"

"Whatever people talk about on first dates." My pulse raced. She wasn't. Saying. No.

"I haven't been on a first date in about twelve years, I have no clue what people talk about. I'm going to have some very interesting questions for the AI search later," she mumbled, staring down at our hands. I laughed despite myself.

"Yes? Are you saying yes? Because I need to know there's still hope here. After everything—tonight, these last weeks, this last year. I need to hear it, Tess."

That little furrow re-appeared between her brows. Her nose scrunched the way it did when she was worried.

"Before we decide to start fresh, can I ask you one thing?"

"Of course." *Let me in. Let me in the way you haven't in so long.*

"I know I didn't...get with anyone these last few months." Her fingernails plucked at the raw skin again. Her shoulders curled inward, bracing for impact. "Did you?"

The air in my lungs escaped with a long sigh. "I thought you'd ask me a hard one." I ran a soft finger over her sharp chin, nestling my thumb in the indent there when she finally looked up at me. "I haven't looked at another woman since the day you walked into English Lit 102."

The smile hesitated as it crossed her face, eyes melting into a shining gaze I didn't feel like I deserved.

"Okay, then."

"Yes?"

"Yes."

***

"Gracie, I don't have long, I'm about to walk into a...meeting," I hedged, hesitant to reveal where I was really heading. My little sister was a romantic.

"You are literally always about to walk into a meeting. Every minute of your life is a meeting, even on Saturdays, apparently," my sister complained. I shifted the phone to my other ear as I shuffled past someone on the busy Chicago sidewalk. Guilt bit at my conscience.

I'd made a lot of changes since Tess had left me, but Gracie and Grant had their own stuff going on with school. They didn't see firsthand how much I'd changed.

It was hard for them to get used to the fact that I prioritized things other than work now. That they'd ever had to question where they stood on my list of priorities sank a rusty, clawing weight straight down my esophagus and into my stomach. It made me think uncomfortable thoughts about my relationship with our dad.

Screw playing it safe.

"If it makes you feel better, it's really a date."

Gracie's high-pitched squeal was loud enough to cause radio interference. I expected a plane to come plummeting out of the sky at any moment. "With *Tess?*"

"Who else would I go on a date with?" The thought burrowed that spiky weight further into my gut. A couple of months ago, Gracie had cautiously asked if I wanted to move on.

That had been the night I'd called Henry Worther and told him I was moving to Chicago whether he liked it or not.

"Oh, my God! Does this mean you're back together? Is she going to be around for Thanksgiving? I still haven't figured out that epic fishtail braid she did last year."

"It's just..." Just the beginning. Again. My mouth went dry from a simmering combination of nerves and anticipation. "...a date. Don't get your hopes up, alright?" I wasn't sure if that last bit of advice was aimed at my sister or myself. "Anyway, what's up, Gracie Lou? I know you didn't call to talk about my love life."

Gracie's forlorn sigh echoed across the miles between us. "I can't help but get my hopes up. It's you and Tess! A world without the two of you together doesn't make sense."

"Agreed."

She paused. "I'm proud of you, Dylan."

I nearly stumbled on my own feet. "You are?"

I'd been in middle school by the time Gracie and Grant had come along, and sometimes the twelve years between us felt more like thirty. By the time they were two, and my parents' marriage had officially ended, it had felt like it was just the three of us against the world. I kept vivid memories close to my heart of the nights when they were up with a fever, and I rocked them back to sleep. Or days when I was the only one home to tend to a scraped knee after school.

I was proud of *them*. They'd clung together through all that, forging their own way in the world. They were freshmen in college now, which blew my mind in the best and worst ways.

The fact that she was proud of me...I didn't know what to say.

"Of course. I know it's been hard. I can't imagine losing the person you thought you were going to spend the rest of your life with. But you didn't give up. That's beautiful."

All grown up and giving me pep talks. I blinked hard. "That..." I coughed, my throat too tight. "Thank you, Grace. I love you."

"I love you, too."

We paused in the rare moment of quiet affection. Too often, I was going one way, and the twins were going the other. Even in the last few years, when we'd lived in the same city, the times I'd seen them were few and far between.

I coughed again, spotting the sign for the restaurant where I was meeting Tess. "Okay, enough of that. What's up?"

"Oh." Grace grumbled. "Mom dropped her phone in a glacier."

"I thought she was in South America."

Gracie snorted. "She is, dummy. In the Patagonia Ice Fields. Doing oil painting or something to capture the ice before it melts."

I pinched my brow. At least I'd gotten the country right. When she'd told me weeks ago she was going backpacking through South America with an artist's collective, I assumed she meant something more like the rainforest.

"She's backpacking through a glacier?" I should have asked more questions before I paid for her plane ticket.

"I think it's more like a glamping situation? Like they stay in some campgrounds and then go out there during the day? When I talked to her last week, she was curling her hair, so it can't be totally dystopian."

"Okay, so she dropped her phone in a glacier." I was starting to get the picture, and already making a mental checklist of the things I'd have to ask my mother before I bankrolled another one of her artist retreats.

"I can't get ahold of her now, and my sorority payment is overdue, so I can't go to the formal next weekend, and I'm legitimately freaking out." Gracie sucked in a breath. "And Grant has to pay the deposit on his summer mini-mester trip for the photography internship thing?"

My eyes squeezed shut. I could see where this was heading. "And Dad said no." It wasn't a guess so much as a fact.

"Technically, Dad said we were in school to learn, not to party. But, yeah, it was a no. And he was pretty brutal about it, too."

Yeah, that sounded like our father. I loved my dad, but his worldview left little room for anything other than work and golf. My free-spirited, artistic siblings definitely didn't check those boxes. Despite my attempts to shield them as much as possible, they still bore the brunt of his rigidity too often.

"Are you alright? Did he say anything out of line?"

"Just the normal stuff. You know, we need to apply ourselves to our studies, and we're a waste of breath or whatever."

"Grace."

"I'm joking! He was just normal. It was fine. He even asked how my geology class was going."

"Alright." I nodded to myself, adding another mental to-do item to call my dad and get him off the twins' backs. Juggling absentee parents and navigating college life was challenging enough for them, especially now that I wasn't close by. They didn't need the pressure he put on them to succeed. He could reroute that to me. "I'll go into the sorority accounts and put some in there. Tell Grant to text me how much he needs for his deposit."

"You promise?" Gracie urged. "The formal is *next weekend*, Dylan, and I'm going with Owen Marshall and if I have to tell him it's canceled because I'm poor, I will literally die of shame."

"First of all, yes, I promise it'll be there later tonight. Second, who the hell is Owen Marshall?"

"Her boooyfrieeend!" Grant sang in the background in a high-pitched falsetto before he cut off with an "oof."

"Gracie, don't hit your brother," I warned.

"It was just a throw pillow, *Dad*. Thank you for the money, weloveyoubye!"

She hung up, deftly avoiding any further questions about this Owen character. I'd have to press Grant for details later. Now that she was in college, I didn't keep such a close eye on who she went out with, but if she was getting serious with some guy, I wanted to know about it.

Another item for the to-do list. But later, I told myself as I walked into the restaurant Tess had picked. It was cozy. Shining, warm wooden floors. Brass lamps and soft jazz playing low in the speakers. But none of that interested me.

The second I walked through the doors, all I saw was her.

She was sitting at the bar, her lavender hair twisted up into a curling bun, loose strands fluttering around her face and down her bare back. Her silky black shirt clung to all the right places on her body. My fingers tingled. I remembered that shirt, and my hands did, too.

My nerves, the anticipation, all faded into the background as I made my way across the room. This was Tess. My Tess. It didn't matter what had happened before—ten years ago or ten months ago. All that mattered was now.

She'd said yes. She was giving me a shot.

I was grabbing it with both hands.

Chapter 9

Tess

"You come here often?"

There were a lot of things I'd missed about Dylan, and his voice was easily top three. I'd always loved it. The underlying rumble of laughter, a foundational warmth that drew people to him and made them want to stay awhile.

I probably missed it the most because that's what I lost first. Sentences trailed off as his eyes darted over his phone screen. Nearly silent dinners when he sat, visibly exhausted, across the table, picking at his food. Early mornings alone in the giant house he'd supposedly bought for us, but spent no time in.

Even as I turned, his corny line making me smile, it was those thoughts that poked a pinprick of worry in the fragile hope I'd been carrying around all day.

To say Dylan was reluctant to leave my apartment last night was an understatement. He'd made me choose a restaurant right then and there. "Somewhere you've wanted to go but haven't had a chance to yet," he'd practically begged. After he'd booked a table, he'd forwarded three different calendar invites and email confirmations.

"You'll be there, right? Tomorrow?" His eyes had pleaded as he'd left, spooked by the awkward moment with the condoms and everything after. His concern was tinged with a wild sort of happiness like he couldn't believe I'd actually agreed to his crazy "start from scratch" scheme.

I couldn't believe it, either. Could we really start over? He'd said it wasn't complicated, but it was. All the memories of our first years together and our bitter ending clashed with the tingling anticipation swirling in my chest.

But one thought of those dark, pleading eyes last night made me want to try.

"First time. How about you?" I spun on the barstool and nearly teetered off of it. He looked good. Deliciously, remarkably good. I had griped at myself all afternoon as I pinned up my hair and tried on three different shades of lipstick until I'd settled on the one I wore now. *It's just Dylan*, I'd whispered, adding another layer of blush to my cheeks. But he'd said it was a first date, so I'd prepared accordingly.

He had, too. His crisp white shirt peeked out from the sharp lines of his blazer. His jaw was shaved clean, and I caught a whiff of the light, spicy aftershave I loved. The one he only wore for special occasions.

My teeth dug into my bottom lip. *I was a special occasion.*

"My first time, too, if you can believe it."

I drew back in a gasp. "No. What are the odds?"

"Fate." He was grinning like a lunatic, but then again, so was I. "I'm Dylan."

My eyebrows raised at his offered hand. When he'd said we were starting from scratch, I'd figured we'd go more for first date territory than a complete do-over. But apparently he'd bought into the "pretend we don't know each other" angle. His eyes sparkled with mischief and interest in a way he hadn't looked at me in so long. I was dying for more of it.

"Tess." My palm slid into his. An eruption of butterflies in my stomach. He gazed at where our skin touched. Was he thinking about last night, too? Not the condoms, but...before that?

"Would you believe, Tess, that I just happen to have a reservation for two and no one to dine with tonight?"

"Wow, it really must be fate."

"Must be." His soft words were still teasing, but they sounded like something else, too. When I looked up to see his gaze roaming my face, the butterflies transformed into flashing drones, sending urgent signals through my veins.

Dylan Morris is looking at you like he wants to eat you.

As he pulled my chair out after the hostess showed us to our table, when his fingers brushed lightly down my arms, I wondered if this starting over business just might work.

***

"Creative director at an advertising agency. Impressive."

I admired his commitment to the bit, but as our salads were placed in front of us, I had to wonder just how far he'd take it. The whole night? Into next week? What happened when we saw each other at the office on Monday? Did we lead secret double-lives now, pretending to be strangers?

I hummed, scooping a black olive over to the side of my plate. "It's fulfilling. I never loved a job until this one."

"That's incredible." I tried to ignore the pride shining out of him. That wasn't first date stuff, but it still made me feel warm inside. "Everyone deserves to love what they do. Being miserable at a job can wear you down."

I cleared my throat, thrilled and cautious about the opening he'd given me.

"Do you? Love your job?" *What exactly is going on with your career, Dylan?*

It skirted the rules. A normal first-date question, layered with so many pieces of history and hurt, the subtext felt like it had stepped onto the table and started doing a striptease.

Dylan took a sip of water, a small line between his brows. "I used to. There are still things I like about it. I've realized recently that work isn't everything. I'm in the process of re-prioritizing."

My throat went dry. The next first date question, the follow-up, would have been something like, *"What are you trying to prioritize more of?"*

The answer, of course, echoed in Dylan's face. Determination flashed across his features, then vanished. *Me.*

"Work-life balance is important." A cop out. A cliché that kept us floating on the surface of the conversation, ignoring the twelve-year-old chasm underneath us. His eyes tightened at the corners, but in an instant, they smoothed. A slow smile unfurled.

"I agree. What else do you do, Tess? Outside of being a very important and talented creative professional?"

"You can hardly call me talented. You've never seen my work." A bite of salad gave me a moment to think, to escape the close call of the conversational sand trap we'd almost fallen into.

"I think you'll find I'm an uncanny judge of character."

"Oh, yes, I'm sure you know more about me than I could ever imagine."

His eyes creased for real this time. "Not nearly as much as I'd like. You mentioned your gym earlier." His words were a purr, curling across the table towards me. "What else do you do for *fun*, Tess?"

The way he said it made his question seem indecent. Now I was *definitely* thinking about last night. The feel of his hands on me. What could have happened if things had gone differently.

"I, um..." My mind blanked, and it took another few seconds of stuttering and searching for an answer before I realized...I didn't have an answer. "Um..."

My routine consisted solely of the gym, my apartment, and work. I hardly even watched any new TV, opting to loop all my bingey comfort shows on rewind.

"You said you moved to the city a few months ago. What have you explored since you got here? Parks? Museums? As a recent transplant, myself, you have to tell me where the action is." He stole the olives from the edge of my plate as he threw me a bone.

Could he see the dawning realization on my face as I discovered in real-time that I was the most boring person in the world?

"I haven't..." That couldn't be right, could it? I'd been here for *six months* and I hadn't been to a single museum? There were days I'd literally begged Dylan to go to a new exhibit with me in Nashville, only to miss it when he, inevitably, backed out or couldn't make time.

"You're an artist, right? Working on anything in particular these days?" He was so nice. I was drowning, and he was tossing these conversation starters at me like life preservers. And I couldn't grab them.

As they had been since last night, his words replayed through my mind. *I'm a different person since I met you all those years ago.*

I'd been tipping them around in my brain, tumbling them like river rocks over and over, thinking. Abruptly, the stark contrast between that first night at the frat house and this night hit me like a ton of bricks.

He wasn't the only one who had changed.

"Tess?"

"I'm sorry. I've just realized I'm...I think I'm boring." I could barely meet his eyes, but I saw enough of his face to see the quirk of his mouth.

"That's impossible. You're the least boring person I know."

"I used to be." I watched the people on the sidewalk pass the restaurant, painfully aware that they probably all had rich and meaningful lives, and I had...work. How depressing. I'd sworn to never get caught up in a relationship where I'd be second to someone's job again. Only to realize now, I'd been putting myself second to my own. "I don't know what happened. I work, go to the gym, and...that's it. Even my TV shows are boring."

"You *are* still new to the city. I'm sure it's an adjustment..." Dylan trailed off as I shook my head. God, he was so *nice*, giving me chance after chance, excuse after excuse. Reasons to justify why my tiny, inconsequential life was as tiny and inconsequential as I'd let it become.

My mind cast back to those last years in Nashville. Had I been this lifeless then, too? I'd dragged myself to yoga every once in a while. Lexi had usually invited me for drinks every few weeks.

I'd told myself I needed to get out of town, that Dylan was the one weighing me down. He'd walled himself off in his corner office, and I'd beat my head against the door too many times. When I left, I'd thought I'd be happy again. Light and free.

Six months later, I was neither.

It was *me*. I blinked hard, eyes unfocused on my salad. I was the problem.

Cue Taylor Swift.

"Hey." Dylan could certainly feel me spinning out across the table. I looked up into his familiar brown eyes. "Don't beat yourself up. I've been doing a lot of soul-searching over the last few months, and I realized work has become my whole personality. Like for years."

"I think...I think I used to be fun, though."

"Me too. I think."

He had been. *We* had been. We looked at each other for a moment. All that light, airy first date energy evaporated like champagne bubbles. Like our life. All that fizzy potential had popped somewhere along the way, and now we were just staring at each other. Flat.

"I'm about to break your starting over fresh rules," I warned.

"I think we passed that boundary a few minutes ago, anyway."

"What *happened* to us?"

Dylan propped his elbow on the table, hands massaging his brow. "Angel, it's the question I've asked myself every day since you left."

We blinked at each other, and all the carefree artifice that had gotten us to this moment stripped away. We weren't going on a first date. We were two people who had once been deeply in love and gotten inextricably sidelined by life. I didn't know what to say.

Dylan leaned closer. "All I can think about right now is that night in Austin, when you wanted to cross 'riding a mechanical bull' off your list."

The weight sinking in my chest couldn't stop the spread of an automatic grin. "And we ended up getting a ride back to the hotel with that clown."

"He was a rodeo clown. There's a difference."

"I'm not sure he was, and I'm not sure there is."

There was a lot I remembered about that night, and also a lot I didn't. Like, I didn't remember falling head-over-ass off the mechanical bull, but I remembered Dylan's warm, familiar face, laughing as he held me close and bought me a mezcal margarita to make up for my epic failure.

I hadn't been afraid to fall back then.

"Right." Dylan rapped his knuckles on the table, glancing around and waving our server over. I didn't know how long I'd been staring down at the sad dregs of salad on my plate. "You have mezcal? Think your bartender can whip up some margaritas?"

My eyes widened. "I don't care what you say or how many margaritas you buy me tonight, I'm not breaking into a hotel pool to go skinny dipping."

Dylan's eyes darkened, flicking down to my lips before climbing back up my face. "I'd forgotten about that. The B&E, I mean. Not you naked in a rooftop pool. That's...ingrained."

It didn't matter that we were having some sort of existential crisis together. When he looked at me like that, heat spread through me, nerves tingling.

"No, we are still those people. And if we want to get to know each other again, we'll need to have something to talk about."

The certainty in his voice calmed the increasingly anxious pitch of my thoughts. He had a plan. Dylan always had a plan. "Okay," I allowed, intrigued.

He grinned up at the server who dropped off our drinks, then pulled his phone from his coat pocket, tapping through some apps. "We're going to make a new list."

It took a second for his meaning to settle in. "A list? Like...one of my old lists of stuff I had to do?"

"Not had to. Wanted to. And your lists have led to some of the best experiences of our lives."

"It's been a long time since I did one of those." I'd started one the week I'd moved to Chicago, but between getting used to Jinx and wallowing over Dylan, I'd never gotten around to filling it out. "Besides, I feel like I'm a pro at sushi these days."

Dylan shook his head. I itched to brush away the lock of wavy brown hair that fell onto his forehead. "Not anything that prescriptive. I want to know...I don't know. I want to know who you are now. Who *I* am now. What would we do if we had to do something we've always wanted?"

"Something I've always wanted," I repeated, my brain spinning in a million overwhelming directions. A trip? A hobby? A new flavor of ice cream? "What would yours be?" I asked. I needed a touchstone. A parameter. Otherwise, the choice was going to flood me into paralysis.

Dylan took a sip, looking at me with eyes too knowing to be comfortable. "I need to think about it. I'm tired of...I don't know. Sitting around and being miserable and missing you and then only breaking any of that up with work."

His words cut too close, booming and echoing in my head.

"Yeah." My unsteady hand made the margarita ice swirl. "I know what you mean."

Another pause settled over the table, more comfortable this time. More like the quiet moments we used to have in our ratty old apartment, sitting around on a Saturday afternoon reading and painting.

"So, we do something we've always wanted to do, and then report back?"

"Yes." Dylan nodded. "We can grow the list, too. Maybe add things to it and keep checking back in with each other. Weekly?"

I liked the idea of having an excuse to see Dylan every week, just as much as I liked having someone to hold me accountable to do something other than sitting around my apartment. "This is a good idea, Morris."

"I think so, Livingston."

Our glasses clinked, the smoke and burn from the mezcal blending with the sweet feeling of anticipation swirling in my stomach. It didn't feel like earlier today, the buzzing expectation of being with him again. The weird déjà vu nerves of a first date.

No, this felt more like...the start of something.

"I've always wanted to join a club," I blurted, my mind still cycling through all the things that had appealed to me in my thirty years on this earth. There were bigger ones, scarier ones, but I wasn't quite ready to say those out loud yet.

"A club?" Dylan sounded surprised. It surprised me to say it out loud. Introvert artists weren't known for voluntarily meeting other people on a regular, pre-determined basis. My shoulders bounced in a self-conscious shrug.

"You always loved your fraternity. I'm jealous of your friendships with Mac and Adam." I traced a water ring on the table with my thumb. "I've always thought maybe it would be fun to do something like that."

Dylan was silent for a beat too long, and I glanced at him, not sure what to expect.

Interest, raw and unfiltered. He set down his glass, leaning onto his forearms. "Theresa Lynn. I have so many questions."

A warm heat radiated from my chest at his comment, at how he was looking at me like I was the only person in the room.

I knew what he meant. Because I had questions, too. About him and me, what I wanted. What we wanted together. And I wanted to ask them all.

Chapter 10

Tess

"—interested in what Tess has to say. She's the one who called this meeting, after all."

Even lost as I was in my haze of happiness, I didn't miss the snark in Victoria's voice. My eyes flickered to Dylan as heat rose in my face, but I forced my attention back to my computer. We'd both agreed to keep our relationship quiet around the office for now. It felt too new, too fragile, potentially complicating things when Eric announced Dylan was next in line to be CEO.

So far this morning, we'd kept things very cordial. Until he'd shared a document with me two minutes ago simply titled, "List."

The first bullet we'd written on our date was already in place:

1. Do something you've always wanted to do.

I'd stared at his blinking green cursor on the shared document for several seconds before it moved, watching in real-time as he wrote.

2. ??? (Your turn, Angel.)

Of course, that was the exact moment Victoria decided to relinquish her hold on my brainstorm and make it seem like I was the one who wasn't doing my job. Maybe she had some kind of radar that went off if anyone in her vicinity was happy, and she was duty-bound to her demon overlords to put an end to it immediately.

The second the thought crossed my mind, I blushed even harder. It was unkind and probably undeserved. Victoria was annoying, but she was passionate. Even if it seemed intrusive or aggressive, I couldn't fault her for working so hard for the company she obviously loved.

"Sorry, I was lost in some notes." I clicked out of the shared document, eyeing the whiteboard Victoria had been scribbling on for the last twenty minutes. There were a few ideas written, but nothing cohesive. I hadn't missed much.

"We're getting nowhere with this. Let's go with my idea. It's the strongest and most marketable. Steel. Classic metallics. It makes a powerful statement," Victoria pushed, circling (again) the central word on the board. Her long, sleek ponytail swished across her perfectly crisp, tailored shirt.

BOTTO, she'd written in big, bold letters, taking the time to sketch in some rivets and bolts.

The international robotics company was building new manufacturing facilities in the U.S., and wanted a big rebrand to kick-start its push into the states. And they wanted us to bid for the job.

"Botto's CMO said Jinx's history of unique campaigns impressed her, but she's equally excited by our position under Worther's agency umbrella. Essentially," Eric had drawled, giving us a conspiratorial look when he'd made the office-wide announcement, "they like that we work like a boutique with the firepower of the big guys." He'd nodded to Dylan, who was standing by his side. "This is exactly what we wanted when we joined Worther. Perfect opportunity to show them what we can really do, huh?"

We had two weeks to pull together an initial round of proposed concepts for their company-wide re-brand, and I hadn't wanted to waste a moment of it. I'd pulled everyone I could into the conference room to brainstorm. Victoria had grabbed a marker and stationed herself at the whiteboard before I'd even walked in, but I hadn't cared.

The Botto proposal would be the biggest work Jinx had ever bid for. To compete with the larger companies with lower costs and an army of interns at their disposal, I needed everyone's help.

Unfortunately, we'd been sitting there for almost half an hour, and all we had was rivets.

Before I'd zoned out, we'd had a few solid ideas floated. Maybe not fully baked, but the beginnings of something. Victoria had halfheartedly scribbled down a few words, but I didn't see any of the bigger concepts on the board.

Just...metal.

As I looked around the room, no one else looked back. It seemed I wasn't the only one distracted by my inbox. Or maybe Victoria's high-handed running of the meeting had squashed everyone's interest in collaboration.

Resignation set in as I considered my next move. Was there a way to salvage this without totally destroying the delicate dynamic Victoria and I teetered on?

"The creative brief requested something unconventional. I'm wondering if going with a metal and steel concept seems a little..." My brain scrambled to find a word that wouldn't insult her.

"Basic?" Leave it to Dylan to cut right to the heart of things. A few of my colleagues shifted around the table, and I caught more than one smirk.

Victoria would have glared if anyone else in the room had said it, but she chuckled like she and Dylan were in on some kind of joke together. "It takes a lot of brainpower to get to a final design, but often the most effective ideas are the most obvious."

Dylan shook his head, clearly unconvinced. That made two of us. "It's something the Worther team would come up with. Don't get me wrong, Worther has good talent, but we play it safe." He leaned forward, giving her a bland smile, lacking his normal charm. "Worther is too traditional. That's why we're counting on Jinx to do what you do best and win this business with something truly extraordinary. Like that tablet campaign you did two years ago. The mural one?" Dylan's attention shifted to me, and so did everyone else's.

"Um..."

"That was you?" Noel leaned into the table to look at me. "I bought that tablet because of that ad campaign."

"Well...good. It worked then." I laughed, weakly, but I could already see the curious glances exchanged around the room.

"Wait, the one that featured all those local artists in major cities?" Carl asked. Noel nodded, still staring at me, looking a little...impressed.

"They had all the artists design and plan the murals on the tablets, then put them up overnight. They paired it with this massive campaign to showcase the artists and their stories. It made some of their careers completely take off."

"Changed the brand narrative, too," Dylan added.

"I, uh, can't take credit for that part," I assured them, sinking lower in my chair. The campaign had been fun, and it had been a hit. We'd known the company wanted to break into more creative applications, so the brand had doubled down on our work, creating scholarships and artist residencies, too.

"But that's the power a rebrand can have." Dylan may have been addressing the entire room, but I could feel his eyes locked in on me.

To avoid his gaze, I looked around the rest of the table. Bad move.

Everyone was waiting for me to say something. After months of sitting in this back corner, Dylan had put a big ole spotlight on me. I could practically hear his voice in my head.

Come on, Angel. Show 'em what you got.

"Well, I," I began, toggling back to my notes from earlier in the brainstorm. Where were those sparks of ideas I'd written down that Victoria hadn't? I scanned them. Nothing. "That campaign was a true collaborative effort, you know. We had a lot of people with a lot of different backgrounds who worked to make that a reality."

When I looked up again, they were still waiting, watching like I was supposed to say something profound.

"We knew they wanted to break into a new market, so we stopped thinking about the product and started thinking about what they wanted it to do, you know?"

Out of the corner of my eye, Dylan cocked his head. It was enough encouragement that my thoughts shifted into a somewhat more pro-ductive pattern.

"What do we know about Botto? They've been traditionally in the manufacturing space, making robots for assembly lines, but they feel like the future is in food service. Fast-food places; robots that can cook food faster and more safely than humans." My brow furrowed, something tugging at my brain. I looked at Carl. "Didn't you used to work at one of the big regional burger brands?"

"Oh, yeah. Big budgets. Fun, but major burnout," he replied.

"What was the goal there? I mean, we want to get in with fast-food people. You infiltrated their inner circle." The very weak joke got a soft laugh from around the table.

"Big on humanizing the brand. Social media campaigns to get more reactive to trends, almost snarky. They want to seem like a person, instead of a soulless corporation, you know?"

"Personal," I murmured, considering. "Maybe that's it. Robots are so *im*personal. In-human, even. Maybe we play that up. Chassie, you create anime, right?"

Usually quiet, Chassie glanced up, their eyes widening at being addressed directly. They were younger and didn't have a huge role in creating the campaigns, but I'd insisted on everybody I could get my hands on for this meeting.

"I...dabble."

"How would you start creating a character if you were beginning a whole new series?"

Down the table, hands poised over keyboards. Noel was already jotting something in her notebook.

"Well, I, um, I would consider the storyline. The hero's journey. Their characteristics." Chassie continued, picking up steam as we nodded along. I grabbed my printout of the creative brief and slipped from my chair, picking up a marker on the way.

Our meeting ran over by an hour, but by the end, our board was filled with little cartoons and concepts for Botto, the aspiring chef robot our collective brains had created.

I was chatting with Noel about identifying a color palette when Meery popped in, handing Dylan a drink tray with two coffees.

"This just came for you, Dylan. Tess, we still good to meet at six? I can't wait to get my hands dirtyyyy," she sang, wiggling her perfectly manicured fingers.

"Absolutely," I confirmed, watching Noel rush out, still scribbling in her notebook. Victoria had bolted from the room the second everyone had started closing their laptops.

When the door shut behind Meery, it was just me and Dylan.

I glanced at the tray in his hands. "You have anything for me?" Brainstorming was thirsty work.

"That was incredible." He sounded a little breathless as he handed over my latte. I popped the top to blow on it, giving me something to look at aside from his eyes as they skimmed across every plane of my face.

"I feel like I just completed a task without putting it on the list to begin with. Will I still be able to check it off?"

"You were going to put 'be a creative badass' on our list?"

My face heated. "More like, 'do something you should have done a long time ago.'"

"Oh, yeah. We're gonna let you check that one off."

***

"How are you even doing that?" Meery scowled, mashing her fingers into the lump of clay in front of her. To her credit, she didn't seem to mind the gray mush as it smudged into her long nails and shiny bracelets. She looked sideways at the beginnings of my pinch pot mug like it had wronged her. "You've done this before."

"A little. I took a pottery elective in college." I'd adored the class, but it had been so different from my usual medium of pencils and paint-brushes, I'd been too scared to sign up for the intermediate course. Every time I walked by a pottery studio, I had to stifle a little voice inside me that said, *what if?*

It hadn't taken much thinking on my part to book a seat at an introductory class at a nearby pottery studio, Glazed.

"Well, next time you do an artsy thing, maybe bring someone who won't embarrass you." We both looked at the lumpy, uneven pot under her fingers.

I nudged her. "It's not that bad. Most of the artistic process is failure."

Meery hadn't been my first choice in pottery partners, but Jasmine had just recently given birth and Lainey was tied up starting a new job and making goo-goo heart eyes at Sam now that they'd gotten back together. We'd planned to hang out soon, but then our group chat went silent, and I wasn't sure how to revive it, or if that would be welcome.

While I enjoyed the occasional work lunch with Meery, our interests didn't always overlap, and I sometimes felt a little bored listening to her gush about the latest celebrity scandal, or whisper about some office drama. But she had been one of the first people to befriend me at Jinx, and had come with me to R³ that first time.

I'd thought about inviting Dylan, but that felt like breaking an unspoken rule of the list. We were supposed to be finding out who we were as individuals, not as a couple.

"You're a trained artist, though. I never even went to college." Meery sighed, now playing with her clay more than actively molding it. "Just out here living the dream, scraping by with a limited skill set."

Her nose wrinkled when she said it, like she was making a joke at her own expense, but I frowned. "I don't think anyone who's met you would say that. Jinx would fall apart without you."

"Yeah, we'd run out of coffee pods pretty fast. There'd be a revolt."

"No, I mean it." I put my muddy hand out to get her attention. I didn't like the rounded curve of her shoulders. "You aren't just Eric's assistant. You keep all the break room snacks and office supplies stocked. You run the office happy hours and onboarding stuff. Aren't you the one who pays all the company bills? Sounds to me like you're running office operations and HR and finances. *I* couldn't do that."

"When you say it like that...but I don't know. Sometimes I feel like I want to do more, you know? Like, is managing his calendar and the coffee deliveries really what will make me happy?"

"Hmm." I was surprised. My conversations with Meery mostly revolved around work, or chatting about lunch places to try. I'd assumed she was happy with her life and her role at Jinx. Her unfailingly bubbly personality gave her a bit of a ditzy vibe, and I was instantly ashamed I'd fallen for it. "What do you think you'd do?"

With a snort, she mashed her clay into the table. I realized she was uncomfortable. Self-conscious, even. "It's not like I can do much. All my friends and coworkers have these impressive degrees and internships."

"Degrees aren't everything. You're very organized, and you're kind. You have a big heart. That means something." On my first day at Jinx, I'd planned on eating lunch alone in my office, but Meery had insisted she take me out. When I'd mentioned I wanted to try a workout at R^3, but was too nervous, she'd said, *"Bump that, let's go together!"*, then showed up at 6 a.m. the next morning.

"A big heart can only get you so far. Sometimes it feels like I started out behind everyone else. We didn't have a lot of money growing up, not a lot of opportunities."

"Same."

Meery whipped around to stare in astonishment. "What?"

"Sure," I responded, rolling a little pillar of clay for my mug handle. I'd made my peace with my rough upbringing a long time ago. "There were times my family struggled to put food on the table. There were some days that I wasn't sure where I was going to sleep at night."

"Wow, Tess, I didn't realize. I guess you always look so put together and...aloof. Fancy."

A sound like a scoff mixed with a snort escaped my lips. A few people at the surrounding tables glanced over. "Meery, I'm a mess. I have anxiety up to my eyeballs, and the only reason I'm in Chicago is because I'm running full tilt away from a twelve-year-long relationship."

Her eyes narrowed. "Yeah, you still never gave me the deets on that."

"I...we're not done with you, yet." Meery was a kind person, and I had written her off as silly. She deserved me taking her seriously. "I'm the only person in my family with a college degree, and the only reason I got that far was because when I was young and stubborn, I found the thing I loved most and refused to settle for anything less. So...tell me. If you could do something else, *anything*, what would it be?"

Meery pursed her lips and scrunched her nose, like she was physically holding the words in. I glanced up at her every few seconds while I rolled my handle some more, quiet.

"I want to do social media," she blurted, clay squishing out the sides of her fingers.

"Cool. In what way?" When I didn't immediately laugh at her, or tell her she was ridiculous, her shoulders lowered a little from her ears.

"Well, I'm on there all the time. I see what's trending and what's working. I have a decent following on my personal pages, and I feel like I'd be good at doing that for other people."

I'd been surprised by the number of followers on Meery's pages when she'd friended me. Her content was good, and she always did the trends and dances before everyone else caught on.

"You know, Worther's social department has, like, ten staff members completely devoted to social trendspotting."

"What?" Her squeak was shrill. "That's a *thing*?"

"Sure. And you're right, I feel like you'd be good at that." I attached my handle, picking up a needle tool to draw some feathered lines across the surface of the mug. "We have a new social campaign we're doing for that bookstore chain. Maybe you can sit in on some of those meetings. If you want, you could take a first stab at writing some of the copy."

"Are you shitting me?" Meery's strangled shriek made more heads turn. We were making quite the impression at beginner's night.

"Of course. I can put a word in. Eric will probably be cool with it, as long as that's something you want to try."

"I want." I stilled my hand as her fingers wrapped around my wrist. She looked up at me with amazed, slightly glassy eyes. "Tess, you would...do that for me?"

My muddy hand topped hers, mixing and squishing together. It was messy, scary even. I wasn't used to getting so open and vulnerable with other people. But I shrugged. This felt right. "Like I said, you have a good heart. And a passion. Most of the time, that's all you need. You deserve to take a chance on yourself, Meery."

"Thank you."

"You're welcome." My cheeks heated, and I used the excuse of my mug to look somewhere else.

"Okay, enough about me. Tell me about Mr. Twelve Years. It's Dylan, isn't it?"

The tool slipped as I jerked, ruining the flowing line of the peacock feather I was freehanding. "What? How...how did you...?" I stammered, pulling my hands away from my work to stare at her.

She rested her hand on her cheek, unconcerned about the clay smudging her skin. "He buys you so much coffee. And treats. And sometimes when he looks at you, it's like he's trying to set you on fire with his eyes. Not like in a laser-y way, but like in a sexy way."

"Do you think anyone else has noticed?" Jinx didn't have a policy against interoffice dating, but Victoria would have a field day if it came out that Dylan and I were together.

"No one else does, trust me. They're not paying attention. So, it is him? You were with *Dylan* for twelve years?"

"Yes." I resigned myself to this conversation. If she could be candid with me, I would be with her, too. Besides, it might be nice to get a neutral third-party opinion. Vanna had exploded when I told her I was seeing him again, and I was still conflicted about it. Ecstatic that he was here and attentive and wanted to try again, but terrified we'd end up the same way we were before.

"And you two never got engaged or anything?"

"We talked about it, but the timing was never right." The words came out smoothly, with the practiced skill of a line repeated countless times.

"Hmm." I didn't look up from my mug, but I got the feeling Meery was narrowing her eyes, scowling. Maybe she was more perceptive than I'd given her credit for, too. I needed to re-think how I stereotyped people. "You left Nashville, and now he's here. He followed you, didn't he?" she asked with the same enthusiasm someone else might say, *"He gave you a million dollars, didn't he?"*

I felt my mouth curve into a smile before I could stop it. "He did."

"And how do you feel about that? It's not a stalking situation, is it? Because I will fuck him up."

My smile advanced into a full-out laugh. Even though Meery was five-foot-nothing, I had no doubt she'd throw down if she thought she needed to. "No, not like that. I feel...good about it. We're working on some things, and we haven't really told anyone yet, so could you keep it quiet?"

"Obviously, I'm the literal embodiment of low-key." She grinned, and then the smile slid off her face. She wrapped her hand around my wrist again. "You deserve to take a chance on yourself, too, Tess. I hope it works out, if this is something you want."

"I think it might be," I croaked around the lump in my throat. Maybe she hadn't been my first choice, but something told me inviting Meery to this pottery class was one of the best decisions I'd made all year.

Chapter 11

Tess

Dylan appropriately ooh-ed and ahh-ed when I presented him with my mug. It may have seemed silly, but the second the instructor had placed it on the rack to go into the kiln, I'd desperately wanted it to fire correctly. I needed tangible, physical proof that I had done something difficult. I could change, shift, like the glaze on a mug.

"Do I get to keep it?" Dylan asked, tracing the lines of the feathers where they criss-crossed the surface of the ceramic.

"It's a girly mug," I warned him, as if he couldn't see the neon peacock feathers for himself. "I mostly blame Meery for that. She's glaze-happy."

I would have been more restrained with the color palette, but I had to admit, the Lisa Frank/paint rave thing it had going on was fun. Plus, it made me think about giggling with Meery and talking about her first meeting with the social team. The mug wasn't perfect, but I was proud of it.

"It reminds me of your watercolors," Dylan murmured, tracing over the splotched handle, an echo of longing in his voice.

"Then you should keep it." Our eyes met across the table. "I signed up for a studio class membership, so there will be plenty more where that came from. Besides, it takes a man truly secure in his masculinity to rock a pink and purple peacock mug."

There was a part of me that wanted to keep it. But an equally powerful part remembered a time when all my mugs had lived in a cabinet beside his. Maybe I'd see it again.

"Thank you." His face lit up, like I'd given him a precious gift. He carefully tucked it back into the tissue paper I'd wrapped it in when I'd picked it up earlier today.

"What about you? How did you do on your assignment this week?"

"Very well, actually."

"Do tell." We'd been texting sporadically, and by a weird unspoken agreement, had avoided discussing almost anything about our list.

I got the feeling Dylan didn't want to invade my phone too quickly, and most of our conversations were succinct and to the point. But yesterday, he'd texted to let me know the coffee shop was out of lavender syrup, which led to an intense Q&A about my coffee preferences, if they'd changed, my stance on non-dairy milks, and if I thought American coffee culture was contributing to overconsumption and pollution.

I'd spent the whole morning glancing at my phone, giddy and waiting for his responses, my stomach a riot of butterflies.

We were just talking about coffee, but his questions had a way of making me curious about him, too. What was *his* stance on alternative milks and, like me, did he not care what anyone else drank, as long as I had good 'ole cow's milk in my cup? Had *his* preferences changed? Not just with coffee, but with anything? Did he still hate cottage cheese, or now that everyone was hyperfixating on protein, had he come around?

I wanted to know it all and more and couldn't be happier for the opportunity to ask.

"Well, you got me thinking last week about clubs. I did a little digging, and I found a silent book club I went to on Wednesday."

"A what?" I couldn't even begin to think what a silent book club entailed.

He laughed and leaned back so our server could place our pasta in front of us. "It's a club where we meet up somewhere like a coffee shop or a bar for an hour and all read quietly, then there's optional social time afterwards."

A club where I didn't have to actually talk to anyone? I perked up.

"Thought you'd be interested in that. It was fun. You should come with me to the next one."

"Would I like what the club is reading?"

"That's the beauty. It's silent, so you can read any book you want. I started a new sci-fi I'd had my eye on."

"I can only remember you reading business stuff." I was visualizing his bookshelf back in Nashville, filled with titles like, *Who Moved My Cheese?* and *The Power of Persuasion.*

"I read fantasy when I was a kid. Since then, I only read because I felt like I had to. It was nice to do something just for myself, without it feeling like an assignment."

He gestured, animated, as he told me about his new book. Our conversation meandered while we picked apart the food on our plates and chatted about anything we wanted, just for the fun of it. I realized how much that critical element had been missing from our relationship.

Fun. The simple pleasure of doing something just because you wanted to, not because you had to.

"I think the list is magic," I admitted later. He shook his head, grinning.

"And this is just week one. Imagine what next week will bring."

"Oh, trust me. Meery's already insisting we go do something *she's* good at. She's dragging me to a karaoke bar."

Dylan winced in sympathy, intrinsically understanding that a loud bar where I was expected to get on stage in front of people was the most cringe-inducing scenario I could imagine. It ranked up there with those horrifying dreams where you're back in high school, then suddenly all your clothes are missing. "Maybe I can come with you? I can sing a mean Elton John, if I have to."

I nearly snorted water out of my nose. "I remember." Who could forget the night he'd climbed onstage at that dueling pianos bar in Nashville? He and Mac had been hungover for days. I paused, not sure if he'd be mad about the next part. "I know we agreed not to tell anyone at work, but I told Meery about us. Really, she guessed, but she told me no one else suspects. I hope that's okay."

He shrugged. "It makes sense for us to be careful about this for personal reasons, but I'm not keeping you a secret, Tess."

My head bobbed. "Right. I know. Still, probably for the best if we don't go shouting it from the rooftops."

"You're worried about Victoria?"

His shockingly quick and accurate assessment threw me off, pushing my shoulders back in my chair. "How did you know?"

We hadn't spoken once about Victoria. I didn't enjoy thinking about her too much. Plus, I wasn't sure I wanted to know if he'd noticed her flirting with him. She was beautiful and assertive, like him, not shy and awkward, like me. I didn't want him to notice her. It was safer to simply avoid any conversation about her.

Dylan also sat back in his chair. "Everyone at Jinx loves you. She's the only one who would have something negative to say about our relationship. I don't like the way she talks to you."

"I know. She's difficult."

Dylan snorted, letting me know how much of an understatement he thought that was. A pressure eased from my shoulders. He wasn't attracted to her. The thought made me feel generous.

"She's actually good at her job when she's not trying to one-up me or make me look bad."

His eyebrow quirked, incredulous. "Is she?"

"I..." I stopped to consider the answer before I gave him a knee-jerk response. Yes, her designs leaned toward the safer side, but she worked well with clients, and I'd seen her create some seriously decent work. "I think she can be, if she focused on her job and not me."

"You can always fire her," Dylan offered, swirling his wine. I watched it spin inside the delicate glass. The thought had crossed my mind, but the concept of firing someone, being responsible for the loss of their livelihood...I wasn't the person who fired people. I couldn't be, not when I couldn't even correct a barista if they got my coffee order wrong.

"I want to give her a shot. She has potential, and maybe when I've been around for longer, she'll move on and make everyone's lives a little more bearable."

"Some might say you're too nice."

Dylan slid the wineglass back on the table, leaning forward on his elbows. I mirrored his pose, only a few inches and a fake candle danced between us.

"Some might say that." I swallowed, searching his face. "What do you say?"

His eyes crinkled at the corners, lips pursing as he swept his gaze across my face and lower. Goosebumps erupted on my skin as he took in the curve of my bare shoulder. The dip in my throat. The vee of my top that gave him just a peek of cleavage.

"I say"—his eyes returned to mine, fire lighting in their depths—"perfect."

***

Dylan insisted on parking on the street and walking me to my door. Very chivalrous. Very nerve-wracking.

On one hand, it reminded me of college, when he'd walk me as far into the girls' dorm as he could, then wait on the sidewalk for me to wave out my window.

On the other hand, it made me think about how we'd crashed and collided up these same stairs last week with our mouths fused together.

"I don't remember there being this many stairs," Dylan said, running his fingers across the handrail like it had appeared there by magic.

"Third floor walkup," I chimed, trying to sound light and breezy, when really I was thinking about how he'd ripped my tights open in the middle of the hallway.

"Yeah, well, I might have been distracted the last time I was here."

We topped the stairs, and our eyes fell to the wall beside my door. The ripping sound of sheer nylon still floated around the landing.

I looked at Dylan as he glanced at me. A wicked grin tilted his lips up.

He'd shaved earlier today, but now the shadow across his face made me want to reach out and feel it. I didn't mind if he was rough against me. My best memories with Dylan were the ones where he was a little unkempt. Relaxed and almost sloppy in a way he rarely allowed himself to be.

Dylan took a step closer. "Tess."

Every nerve in my body jumped at the sound of him saying my name. Like a question. Like an answer. I reminded myself again it was ridiculous to feel nervous. It wasn't like this was actually our second date. Or like I hadn't kissed him before.

Was he going to kiss me? Unbidden, my eyes darted to the wall again, like I had some sort of heat-seeking memory device in my brain that pinpointed the exact location of the last time I'd nearly combusted.

"You remember back in college?" I blurted, because my brain was desperately trying to reboot itself. "When you used to wait for me to wave at you when I got back to my dorm room?"

His face warmed, looking fond. "Of course."

"I always wondered what you thought would happen to me in between the lobby and my room."

"Nothing." He shrugged, taking another step closer. I backed away instinctively. After the nuclear detonation from the last time we'd stood here, I wasn't sure how to proceed. Should I invite him in? Leave him in the hall and ask myself for the rest of the night if I regretted going in alone?

Wait. "Nothing? You didn't ask me to wave at you because you wanted to make sure I got to my room safe?"

"Nah, it was a college dorm. Key card security." He took another step closer. My shoulder blades touched the scuffed drywall beside my door.

"Then why?"

His mouth hooked to the side as he slid the back of his fingers across my cheek. I shivered at the touch. "I just wanted to see your face one last time. You usually blew me a kiss, and I liked that, too."

His index finger traced my bottom lip, and it felt more intimate than when we were here the last time. My brain fried.

"I don't know if I should invite you in or not."

The pad of his thumb felt rough against my cheekbone, dragging. "On the second date? Scandalous."

"I'm serious. I don't know what the plan is here." My fingers wiggled in the inches between our bodies, as if that could encapsulate all the history and newness and familiarity swirling between us. Some people liked the butterflies in the stomach feeling of a first kiss. The 'will they lean in?' 'Is it going to happen now?'

Not me. I was awkward and anxious enough without adding attraction into the mix.

"You could grab me and plant one on me like the first time."

"I did not grab you," I argued, heat flushing my face. It had been our second date, Dylan hadn't kissed me yet, and we'd been walking across the parking lot after dinner. I was freaking out about whether he was going to kiss me when I got in the car, or back at the dorm, or...at all? I'd pulled him to a stop in the middle of the half-empty parking lot.

"We should kiss," I'd told him. He'd agreed. After a few seconds of a small eternity, I'd realized he was waiting for me. I'd rolled up to my toes and, well, planted one on him.

We'd made out in his car for nearly an hour after.

"I know a lot of things have changed since college, but I don't think I'm the sex on a second date kind of guy," he offered, stroking a stray piece of hair back from my face. The hum of anxiety quieted in my head at his admission. "I like getting to know you again. Seems like we should...wait. Right?"

"Right," I sighed, finally leaning into him. His arm wrapped around my waist, and my chin rested on his chest as my eyes slipped closed. "I like getting to know you again, too."

His answering hum rumbled through my body. "I would take a kiss, though, if you're willing to part with one."

My eyes blinked open, catching him looking at my face with a tenderness that made it hard to breathe. "Air kiss? Like college?" I tried to tease, but I sounded wispy.

"Real, if it's all the same to you."

His lips brushed against mine, feather-light, stroking back and forth. At the last second, his tongue darted to swipe into my mouth. The quickest taste, like he couldn't help himself.

A new sort of butterfly-tingling took over my body. It was a first kiss, but not. It was a millionth kiss, and in this moment, looking at him with new eyes, that made it feel like the only thing that mattered.

Chapter 12

Dylan

"Thanks for being flexible."

My dad stood from his seat to give me a brief, back-smacking hug. The sports bar a few miles from the airport wasn't the most convenient place to meet for dinner, but Dad had insisted on seeing me before his flight back home from his quick business meeting today.

"Would have been better if we'd stuck with dinner last night," he grumbled. I held in a sigh.

"I told you. Standing date with Tess. Couldn't reschedule it." More like, I didn't want to reschedule it. Three weeks into our regular check-ins and Fridays had quickly become my favorite day. I'd known something was missing in my life. I'd assumed it was Tess, but I gradually realized it wasn't just her I'd missed.

It was us. What we could be together. Me when I was with her, at my best.

Seeing her now, thoughtfully leading work meetings, going off to karaoke with Meery, and finding new excuses to meet up with friends from her gym, made me want to be that man.

It reminded me of the Tess that had been so attractive to me in college I hadn't been able to focus on anything else.

"Yeah," Dad grunted, sipping his beer. "How's *that* going?"

"Good." I motioned to the server for a glass of whatever my dad was having, choosing to ignore his flat tone. "Great, actually. We're getting to know each other again. Having fun. Last night we went to an omakase place and tried about seven different types of sushi I didn't even know existed." Tess's face when the chef had presented her with raw sea urchin, still nestled in its spiky shell, had been the highlight of my evening.

"Sounds pricey. You footing the bill for all this 'fun' you two are having?"

Jesus. "Dad, I'm not talking with you about Tess if you're going to be like this."

"Be like what? Concerned for my son when some girl makes him move across the country with no commitments? Makes you press pause on your dream job? What are you even doing over here? *Consulting?*" He said consulting like other people might say "drug lord." It had been easier to tell him I was trying out a temporary travel gig for Worther, instead of the truth: that I was leaving altogether. Just like with the Jinx employees, it would take time to ease him into that decision. He'd been pushing me to become Worther's CEO since the day I was hired.

"She's not just some girl." I couldn't stop myself from snapping. He had liked Tess at first, but his approval waned when we started getting more serious. He was worried she'd distract me from my post-grad plans, and after I'd graduated, his snide comments had only gotten more frequent. Tess leaving had just given him more ammo. "It's Tess, Dad. She's important. It's a miracle she's even giving me another chance."

He scoffed as the server slid a glass in front of me. "It's a miracle *you* are giving her another chance." He held his hand up when I opened my mouth to argue. "I remember what it was like, son. Watching you work so hard, and her not caring. All those eighty-hour weeks you put in? For her? For your future? And what was she doing? Some shit like a yoga class or painting? What kind of partner does that make her?"

A spike of anger heated my skin. An oily, nauseous feeling followed. The familiar sensation of the resentment I'd cultivated over years of working my ass off, and Tess not seeming to notice or care at all. I pushed it down. I'd gotten over that. I was the one who had screwed everything up and needed to make it right. I was *over that*.

"You don't know what Tess and I have been through," I started. His shaking head silenced me again.

"Same as me and your mom."

"Do not bring Mom into this."

He kept rolling as if I'd never spoken. "Pregnant with you so young, and the only job I could get was mopping the fucking floors at that manufacturing plant. But I did it for her, so she could stay in school and get her high school degree. How does she repay me? Doesn't give college a second look. Just starts fucking around with acrylic."

"Dad—"

"I scratched and clawed for every raise, every promotion, so you could have shoes. So your mom could stay home with you and work on her art. Janitor to CEO, Dylan. All for her. For my family. And how did she repay me? Fucking left the minute it didn't suit her anymore."

"Tess isn't Mom." I knew enough about both of my parents' failings to at least know I was right about that.

"Isn't she?"

His words woke a small, wounded piece of myself. In the first few days after Tess left, those same thoughts haunted me as I lay alone and angry in the bed that used to be ours.

"When you got that big house of yours? Million-dollar condo near downtown? Didn't you tell me she had nothing to do with buying that place? Barely looked at it? You did that for her, Dylan. That girl who grew up sleeping in a trailer park, if she was lucky. You gave her that home, and what did she do to repay you?"

I didn't respond. We both knew the answer. She'd left. She'd left without saying a word. Like none of it had ever mattered.

Like I hadn't mattered.

I stumbled to my feet, jostling the table. "I have to go."

"I'm just trying to look out for you, son. Learn from my mistakes, alright?"

"What do you think I'm trying to do?" I snapped. The server glanced over from where she was bussing another table. My eyes shut, head shaking, as I reached into my back pocket for my wallet. "All my life, you've told me the best thing to happen to you was when they made you CEO at the plant. The *best* thing."

I fished a twenty out of my wallet and threw it on the table.

"What about me, Dad? What about Grant and Gracie? What do you think it does to your kids to know we don't even come close to first place with you?" His eyebrows crumpled, but now it was my turn to barrel on. "Tess and I have both made mistakes, but I will not repeat yours. There is more to life than work. More than your all-holy, C-suite position that, by the way, they'd fill tomorrow if your plane fell out of the sky. *Learn from your mistakes*? All of this, *all of it*, is to prevent me from making the biggest mistake you ever made."

"Dylan—"

"Have a good flight. And lay the hell off the twins. They're kids, Dad. Let them be."

I turned and left before he could speak again.

***

"I thought you were the UberEats person!"

I'd driven like a bat out of hell, squeezing the steering wheel so tightly, my fingers were still numb. The image in front of me almost made it worth it. "You answer the door like this?" I bit my lip to hold in a laugh.

If Tess's face could have creased into a frown, it would have, but a layer of thick green goop froze it in place. A thorough sweep down her body got even more interesting. The fabric of her shirt was just shy of sheer, and she had on the world's smallest pair of sleep shorts.

If I recalled correctly, the silky outfit came as part of a matching set with a soft knit sweater she liked to wear around the house. I didn't know where the sweater was now, but when she stepped closer, I could almost see straight down her shirt. If I ever saw the sweater again, I'd burn it.

"Usually not, but you were beating the door down. I thought there was a delivery emergency or something."

Ah. I had been sort of pounding on her door, hadn't I? "Sorry about that. I, uh, just left dinner with my dad. Abruptly."

Her eyebrows drew down as much as they could. She stepped even closer, her front brushing against mine. I could definitely see down there now, but I kept my gaze on her face. She was mine, but she wasn't *mine* right now.

"Are you okay? Did he say something...?" She was too polite to ask outright if he'd been a dickhead, even though he had been, and she probably knew it. My dad wasn't her favorite person, so she'd avoided him as much as possible over the last few years.

I grimaced. I should have told him off sooner. Protected her from him more. Another failing.

Maybe you wanted her to hear that from someone. Someone who wasn't you.

I had to get a hold of that spiteful voice in my brain. I'd spent the entire ride over here trying to calm down, reminding myself that I wasn't in Chicago to point fingers, just fix my relationship. My life.

After forty-five minutes of traffic, I still wasn't very calm. I was angry at my dad, and myself, guilty for even thinking he might be right about what he'd said. The thought of going back to my hotel room alone had made me stir crazy.

"He was...Dad. I know I just saw you last night, but I wanted to see you again. If that's okay. I don't want to interrupt...whatever is going on here." Miraculously, when I waved a hand at her face, I cracked a smile. This was already better.

She swatted me away. "I'm checking the 'do something for yourself' item off our list tonight. Self-care and all that. Meery wanted to go out, but I needed to do laundry. Do you...want to come in?"

She cracked her door open the tiniest bit, but that was all I needed. The TV was paused, and a bowl of popcorn sat on her coffee table. Little nail polish bottles lined up like soldiers.

"Am I going to interrupt spa night or something?"

"Not at all. Though I *will* make you come with me to the creepy basement when I have to move my laundry along." She stepped aside to let me in and, I admit it, I snuck a glance down her shirt. I missed her tits so bad.

"These not up to snuff?" I tapped the stacked washer and dryer unit wedged into the area that seemed to serve as pantry, hall closet, and laundry room.

"They haven't worked since I moved in. The washing machine sprays water everywhere. I emailed my super, but it's not a priority, I guess. Oh!" Tess startled when a knock sounded on her door. Everything under the tank top jiggled delightfully. I lunged to intercept her, opening the door and blocking the view inside with my body.

"Thanks, man." I smiled at the guy standing in the hall. "Appreciate it."

I lifted the bag out of his hands, aromas of egg rolls and lo mein wafting out of it. I didn't regret leaving my dad back at that bar, but damn, I wish I'd eaten something before coming over here.

"The face mask isn't *that* bad," Tess griped, swiping the bag from me. Did she realize when she did things like grumble at me when she was so cordial and composed with everyone else, it made me want to melt at her feet? It reminded me I was one of the few people who got to see the real Tess. Not just the one she wanted people to see.

That beautiful girl, who's quiet and thoughtful, with paint under her fingernails? She has road rage like you wouldn't believe, and once she's got two glasses of wine under her belt, curses like a sailor.

That was my Tess. It was a privilege to see it.

"It's not the mask, trust me." My eyes traveled down her face, then down, down, across her throat, and down some more. It took her a second.

"Oh!" She jumped. I got another glimpse of a jiggle before her arms wrapped around her chest. "I forgot I wasn't wearing a bra. Oh, shit."

"Please." I laughed, watching her pivot on her heel to her bedroom, then turn back to the laundry hamper by the door, her cognitive dysfunction firing hard as she tried to find the closest acceptable underwear. "Please, *please*, don't cover up on my account."

She flicked a sports bra at me. I snatched it out of the air, still laughing.

"It's not funny! This shirt is practically see-through. What if I'd answered the door like this?" she demanded. Little cracks were forming in the clay on her face, which only made me laugh harder. She crossed her arms, hiding again. "I'm serious. I almost just flashed that guy."

"Good thing I'm here to save the day, then." I chuckled, coming down from my laughing fit.

"I guess," she mumbled, still glaring.

"Admit it." When I pulled her arms away from her body, they came easily, wrapping around my waist when I scooped her up. "I'm a hero. Surely that's worth at least one egg roll?"

"Oooh," she hummed. "You don't care about my boobs at all. You just want to pilfer my delivery order."

"Whoa, whoa, let's not be hasty." I gave her my most charming smile. "It can be both."

After finishing the egg rolls and settling in with old *Friends* episodes, we spontaneously added a new entry on our list. I proudly checked "do something you've never done before" off while Tess gave me a pedicure.

Getting my toes painted with bright red lacquer and daisies shouldn't have been erotic, but with Tess leaning over me in a see-through crop top, anything could be hot.

I helped fold her laundry, grinning when she strictly forbade me from touching her underwear.

I snagged a pair anyway, and the ensuing chase ended with Tess in my lap, groaning as she rocked her hips while I licked into her mouth. We took our time, nowhere to be but right here. Our agreement to wait to have sex slowed everything down—no pressure, just appreciation.

All her little sounds and movements. The sigh that flowed out of her throat as she tipped her head back. Her skin under my palms when I swept them under that almost-sheer top. Time took on a slow, languid stretch, and I didn't know how long we sat there, grinding together like teenagers.

"I don't want to go." The Netflix had gone dark some time ago, the polish was dried. Her laundry was neatly tucked into her dresser, and I'd run out of excuses to stay. The thought of leaving physically hurt.

She paused just long enough for me to realize how that might have sounded, especially since she was splayed out on my lap, lips puffy and chest red from where I'd tried to devour her. "I didn't mean it like—"

"I don't want you to leave either."

A relieved sigh gusted out of me. I pressed my lips to the crown of her head.

"We don't have to—"

"We can just slee—"

We grinned as we spoke and stopped at the exact same time. I pressed a grateful, careful kiss on her mouth.

It was that strange, unfamiliar mix of new and routine. She handed me one of my own shirts to sleep in—one that had gone missing about six months ago—but didn't make eye contact as she crawled into bed. Clothes remained on by unspoken agreement, and when I pulled her across the mattress and into my arms, every muscle in my body relaxed.

Home.

When I woke up in the morning, Tess's purple hair in my mouth and arm numb from where she laid on it, I'd never felt as happy as I was at that moment.

My dad was full of it. *This* was right. *This* was what everything was about.

I still had daisies on my toes when I went into the office on Monday.

Chapter 13

Tess

"You really don't need to keep bringing me these." I tried to sound serious, but it was hard when a silly smile danced across my face. Was I going to turn into a pile of giddy mush every time Dylan brought me something? Very likely.

Every latte or bouquet that showed up at my door was another thread woven back into the tapestry of our relationship. The one I'd thought had been ruined forever.

"You like them, though." Dylan's head cocked as I leaned against my desk, sipping the coffee he'd handed me. I felt his eyes travel along the length of my neck as I swallowed. It wasn't just the coffee that was hot today.

"I really do," I admitted, biting my lip as I stared down at the cup. He'd gotten me one of the reusable ones after our conversation about the environmental implications of single-use containers. It was purple, and it made me smile.

"Then you keep getting them." His voice sounded far away, and I glanced up to see him contemplating the place where my teeth pressed into my bottom lip.

He was so cute. And sexy. It had been three weeks since that night he'd pressed me up against the wall in my hallway and almost made me come with a few flicks of his fingers. We'd fooled around since then, mostly making out on my couch or in his car after a date, but always stopped before anything could get too intense below the belt.

Waiting to have sex had seemed like a great idea a couple of weeks ago, but recently it was harder to see the merit. Our Friday date nights had expanded, and it was rare we didn't see each other after work these days. For drinks, or dinner, or to try a trivia night. Being around him almost constantly, wanting him so badly, and not being able to have him...it was torture.

His cheekbones heated when he realized I'd caught him ogling. Oh, to hell with it. My office door was closed. He was just too handsome, and I was just a little too horny.

"Thank you," I whispered, hooking my fingers into the collar of his shirt to bring him down for a kiss. A light, chaste peck. No more than a smooch.

Except the moment his lips touched mine, lightning darted straight through my core. My light, chaste peck turned into something a little feral. My fingers tightened on his shirt at the same moment his hands wrapped around my waist. He dragged me closer, mouth opening to flick his tongue against mine.

I couldn't help my soft moan. He was too hot, too good at this, and I had missed this too much. My head turned as his tilted. I gasped while he groaned. Tongues brushed against each other. It felt decadent. Electricity popped in my veins, making my brain feel fuzzy and hot, zipping between my legs. His arms felt strong around me, clasping me tight like he couldn't get enough.

We fought to get closer, to fuse together. I pressed against him, and he shifted. For an instant, with limbs tangled and head dizzy, it felt like we'd accomplished it. I couldn't feel where I ended and he began.

He backed me to the edge of my desk, rocking his hips so I could feel him hardening against my belly. I sucked his lip into my mouth while I shivered. I pulled on his clothes, despising the fabric between us.

"Tess," he groaned, tipping to rest his forehead against mine. The heat in his eyes incinerated the last shred of self-control I had left. I rose onto my toes, aiming to recapture his mouth, but he leaned back, breathing like he'd just sprinted around the building.

An involuntary whimper left my lips.

"I know, trust me." His face looked pained, filled with regret. He pressed into me once more, rolling his hips to underscore his words. "*I know.* But I figured you'd want to stop before we get into sex at work territory."

His words cracked the door back open on my sanity. I blinked, letting go of his neck. Somehow, I still held the latte in my other hand. I hadn't numbly dumped the whole thing on the floor in my scramble to climb him.

So much for a little smooch. "Right. Thank you." I smoothed my hands down my pants, like I could physically brush the lust away. "That's a good call."

He grimaced as I pulled away, rounding my desk to put some space between us. He adjusted his pants. "Was it?"

I laughed, breathless, finally placing the coffee next to my computer. I needed something colder. Like a bucket of ice water over my head.

"Probably. I've never had sex at work before. It seems like a point of no return kind of thing."

I made the mistake of looking at him again before I sat down. His dark eyes turned molten.

"That's not entirely true." His hands braced against the top of the desk. I could feel his breath against my face. "I fucked you on the desk when I got that corner office at Worther."

His words, the dark caress of his voice, and the memory of that night...I really, really needed that bucket right about now.

"Right," I managed in a strangled voice. I cleared my throat, but that did nothing to ease the tightness building up in my core. "Maybe I should have said, I've never fucked anyone in *my* office before."

"Well, now, that *is* a whole different story. Some list material, right there."

"You think?"

I knew he was teasing. No matter how much we wanted to, we couldn't get up to any frisky business at work. It was unprofessional, and he was going to be my boss soon.

The thought should have cooled the lust swimming around us, but it only amped it up. He seemed off-limits, even though he wasn't. Why was that so hot?

"Oh, I know so." He sized me up, no doubt cataloguing my flushed skin. My hair was probably a mess. When I reached up to smooth it down, his eyes skimmed to where my shirt lifted an inch, exposing a flash of skin. Was he getting impatient with our self-imposed celibacy, too?

His throat worked. He had to be. But he hadn't said anything, hadn't hinted that he might want to take things further. Almost as if he was waiting for me to...My eyes fell to the coffee cup.

Of course. I flushed for an entirely different reason. I'd been so *stupid*! Of course he was waiting on me. He was probably worried about pushing me too hard, going too fast, and messing up the incredible connection we'd rekindled. But it had been weeks, and as much as I loved getting to know this new Chicago Dylan, I also already knew a lot about him. Like what a great man he was, and how good he could make me feel.

I knew I wanted him.

"Dylan?"

His throat cleared, and he shook his head like he was snapping himself out of a stupor. "Yeah?"

Heat bloomed up my neck. How did one proposition one's long-term boyfriend who kind of was but wasn't still one's boyfriend? And in a corporate setting, to boot? "You know how we said we wanted to wait for...um..."

His eyes narrowed, heating. "Yes."

"What if we...uh...were done with that?"

The smirk on his face was absolutely wicked, tinged with a hint of the filthy thoughts he was probably having about me and this desk right now. "You tired of waiting, Angel?"

"Yeah."

"Good. Me too." He leaned closer, stealing the air between us. "You want it right now? It would be such a good addition to the list."

I gulped, eyes darting to the desk, my unlocked door, his face...his grinning face. "You're joking."

"Never about having sex with you, but maybe we want to wait for a more appropriate setting. Like, maybe on a well-timed business trip? With a hotel room? No interruptions?"

The sharp knock on my door was like a lightbulb turning on in a dark room. Sudden, unpleasant, and entirely unwelcome.

I sprang back from Dylan, sending my desk chair reeling. "Come in!" I yelled, fumbling for my seat with shaking hands. Across from me, Dylan looked amused as he eased into an armchair—all the time in the world, no fluster.

Must be nice. His eyes promised we'd finish talking about this later, and the thought sent a shiver of anticipation down my spine.

"Are you meeting to finalize the Botto presentation?" If the knock had been unwelcome, Victoria's voice was like nails on a chalkboard. I stopped myself from cringing. "I should be in on this."

"Really, it's okay," I started, but she was already marching into the room, laptop in hand.

"I had Noel send me the last round of updates directly, and I reviewed them last night. I still wouldn't have gone with the serif font." She glared at me like I'd kicked a puppy, instead of just asking the team to experiment with different font styles. Ironic, since she was the one derailing our usual review process by asking Noel to send the files to her first, instead of me.

Still, I wanted to shrink under her stare. Ever since that meeting a few weeks ago when I'd regained some control of this presentation and its strategic direction, she'd doubled-down on her negativity. I'd had to let some things slide in the interest of getting the work done. Like her whole rivets-and-metal concept that had somehow crept its way to the beginning of the slides. I'd told myself I needed to pick my battles.

Now, though, with the Botto presentation just a few days away, I didn't have time to coddle her. No matter how much my stomach hollowed at the thought, I had to put my foot down. I could feel Dylan's attention on me, and I took a breath, remembering his words. *I don't like the way she talks to you.* Well, I didn't like it either.

"Dylan and I are the ones flying out to New York tomorrow to present. We can go over the changes ourselves. It'll give us an opportunity to practice the presentation again." I took a deep breath, hoping she didn't hear the shaking in my voice. *Weak.*

"Well, you'll need me for the overview. I just finalized the last few slides this morning, and the most recent version is saved on my computer—"

"I'll need you to send me those files so I can review them myself." What I really wanted to say was, *"Why the hell are you making changes on your personal computer and not in the shared drive? Why are you making changes before I see them in the first place?"*

I tried to avoid moments like this. It was a harsh reminder of why I often felt like I wasn't cut out for the tedious politics of corporate leadership. All I wanted to do was design. Make something impactful. Recently, I'd thought it would be cool to lead a team to help *them* design. But instead, I had to tip-toe around this woman and her increasingly obvious hatred of me.

She gave me a sickly sweet smile, with an edge to it. "Obviously, I'll send you the files. As soon as my updates are finished. The last two concepts are, frankly, still all over the place..."

I let my eyes drift closed for a few seconds while she droned on, critiquing every aspect of the ideas the team had come up with—that *I* had come up with. I opened them in time to see her shove some folders on my desk aside to make room for her laptop.

Dylan's eyebrow arched. To the untrained eye, he was relaxed, leaning back in his chair, sipping from the neon peacock mug. I knew better, though. He glanced at me, an obvious question on his face.

Do you want me to handle this?

Truthfully, I didn't want to do *anything* about it. Victoria was annoying, and there was no love lost between us, but I'd have preferred to just duck my head and wait out the storm.

Except that hadn't been working for me lately, had it? Not for the last few months with this job. Not for the last few years, with my *life*.

Memories of the last month flashed before my eyes. Firing my mug, laughing with Meery, Dylan's face so content lying next to me on the pillow. I felt alive for the first time in a long time.

Old Tess would have thanked Victoria for her diligence, accepted her changes, and presented them to the client. But I was trying my hardest to evacuate Old Tess from the building.

"Victoria." I was still shaky, my hands sweating, but the sharpness of my voice at least halted her sneering monologue. "*I* am the one who directed the concepts on those slides. I will be the one to review and finalize them. In the future, do not tell the team to cut me out of the reviewing process."

Her eyes widened in exaggerated disbelief. "I was just trying to make your life easier. Save you some steps."

"I appreciate the gesture, but this is my job. I'll take it from here." I nearly asked her to send me the files from Noel, but thought better of it. The look she was giving me made me think she'd either flat-out refuse, or just send me the wrong documents on purpose. Instead, I stood. "Please get back to work. We have the social media meeting later today, and the new ad campaign for the healthcare app. I need you focused on that. Dylan and I will handle Botto."

I swung my door open, feeling her cold, venomous stare on my back the whole seven steps it took me. "Noel," I called, catching her attention at her cubicle. "Please send me the latest Botto files you sent Victoria last night. From now on, I'll be focusing on this account. We need Victoria's attention on other projects."

A hush fell over the bullpen. Carl and Chassie exchanged a glance as Victoria shoved past me, stomping down the hall.

"Of course! Sorry...Sorry, I should have sent those to you, too..." Noel had an apology written all over her face, eyes darting between me and Victoria, who continued clomping until she turned a corner. On her way to call Eric and complain? Maybe. Probably.

Oh, God. My stomach flipped.

I gave Noel a tight smile. "All good. I just want to make sure I'm as close to this one as possible. Cool?"

"Yes," Noel breathed. The others looked sideways at each other as I shut the door. The second it was closed, I nearly crumpled against it, the overheated skin of my forehead resting against the cool, smooth wood.

"I'm reconsidering my no sex at work policy. That was fucking hot."

Even my laugh sounded strained. My body was tense, trapped in the fight-or-flight response of confronting someone. I shuddered. There was a reason I never did this. It sucked. I felt horrible and scared and off-kilter.

"Well, you know." My shoulder shrugged, jerky. "Just trying to impress my new boss." When I peeked behind me, Dylan was still relaxed in his chair, a small smile playing across his lips even as his eyes dissected every aspect of my face. He must have known my anxiety was going through the roof right now.

"Oh, don't worry. I think you've made a very lasting impression." He grinned, playing along with my nonchalance. Bless him. My computer chimed, and I used the walk across my office to take a few breaths. *In for four...* When I sat, I gulped my coffee.

Spending your formative years with a lot of instability and a decent amount of shady characters hanging around, you learned early not to rock the boat. I had been around enough fights, drunken arguments, and uncertain times to understand the repercussions of speaking out of turn. It was easier to stay quiet. Survive.

But this wasn't a life-or-death situation. I wasn't a six-year-old girl hiding beneath the grungy tables at my dad's bar, or hunkering under the covers trying to block out the yelling and smashing outside my bedroom door. I was a grown woman, in a leadership role, in a controlled corporate environment.

My body hadn't gotten that message. Anxiety spiked again as I skimmed over Noel's email. Way more "sorry" and exclamation marks than I was used to. I winced. I'd have to check in with her later and reiterate that I wasn't mad she'd sent the files without including me...but that she shouldn't do it again.

"You don't think I was too harsh?" I whispered, opening the files and dragging them up on the big screen in my office to review.

"Not at all. I would have gone a bit harder on her, actually."

"You think?" Oh, those font colors were looking much better. I breathed through my nose as I clicked through them. Big in, big out. My heart rate was slowing. Dylan's hand rested on my wrist.

"Victoria's a bully, Tess. I don't have room on my teams for people like her."

I squirmed under his gaze and his touch. "She's been with the company almost since the beginning. She was the third hire."

"Third hire, yeah I know," Dylan spoke at the same time I did, shaking his head. "I've heard that once or twice. Doesn't change the fact that she's toxic. Sooner or later, people like that can tear an organization apart. You want me to handle it next time?"

Yes. Six-year-old Tess was still cowering in a corner of my brain, nodding frantically at the thought of having a savior. Dylan was good for that, I knew. It would bring an enormous sense of relief if I asked him to take care of it. Everyone thought he was just a consultant from our parent company, but Victoria knew he was a big deal. She'd listen to him.

But even as I considered it, I knew I couldn't take him up on his offer. Since he wasn't CEO yet, I wasn't sure about the power dynamics. What if he overstepped, and it made Eric think twice about him leading Jinx? Aside from that, how would I feel, knowing that I'd failed yet another test at this new job?

I was *supposed* to stretch myself. The whole reason I'd taken this role was to get out of my comfort zone. Without Dylan.

"No," I said with a sigh. He was still scrutinizing me, analyzing everything from the way I sat to the tone in my voice. I straightened in my chair. "I appreciate the offer, but this is my job. I need to be the one to handle this."

"You sure? I don't ask because I don't think you can do it." Dylan leaned forward, pressing his hands onto my desk. "You're so strong, Tess, but conflict isn't your favorite thing in the world."

That was being generous. I'd do just about anything to avoid a fight, or even the possibility of making someone uncomfortable. Anything, like work for months with a woman who humiliated me at every opportunity, and not speak up once.

Anything, like end a twelve-year relationship, only leaving a note in my wake as an explanation.

The thought made me wince again. It had felt like the right move at the time. I had been so mad, so sad. So done. It had felt like putting a period on a sentence that was already finished.

Now, though...how had I thought we were done? I could still feel the sizzling kiss we'd shared just a few minutes ago. We weren't done. We were so far from done, it felt like the beginning.

"I know. But that was old Tess. I'm...trying to be braver. Better."

"Better?"

I nodded, blowing out a breath. Starting pottery, putting myself out there with my friends, giving my relationship with Dylan another shot...all individual lessons that built into one big one I was discovering more and more every day.

"Just because something is hard doesn't mean it's not worth doing."

Dylan hummed, staring at me for a long time. There was a question hanging between us, that history we couldn't quite overcome.

Yes, you beautiful boy, I'm talking about you.

A soft smile flitted across his mouth. After another moment, he seemed to come to some conclusion, nodding. "Alright then, New Tess. Let's see what we're working with."

As we moved through the slides, discussing the concepts or making small notes and final tweaks, my pulse returned to a normal pace. My hands stopped shaking. My palm didn't leave a sweaty puddle on my mouse.

I knew eventually everything with Victoria would come to a head. In a few months, Dylan's trial run at Jinx would be up, and we'd have to decide what we were doing here, and if we wanted to keep going. In a few days, we'd be in front of Botto, pitching the biggest deal of my life. Then after...probably doing something else in that hotel room Dylan had mentioned.

If I thought about any of that too long, all my calm would evaporate into thin air. I wasn't sure what I was going to do about Victoria. I had no clue whether my warm, fuzzy (increasingly hot) feelings for Dylan would stick around, or if we'd both slide back into that cold, distant place we'd lived in together for so long.

All I knew was that right now, I had my coffee, my Dylan, and a solid presentation that would hopefully knock the socks off an international robotics enterprise and secure my job at the best company I'd ever worked for.

Old Tess could have never.

Eight months ago

Dylan

Sometimes it felt like my world had diminished to the neat piles in front of me. Dark stacks on the crisp, white bedspread.

"Hmm?" I asked, only half-paying attention. I did this often enough that it was down to a science, but I double-checked everything just in case.

"The tickets, Dylan."

Tess sounded worked up enough to finally snag my attention. She'd been talking about tickets? My brain raced as I looked at her, perched on the chair next to the fireplace in our master suite. *Airplane tickets*?

Her brows flattened. "For Fiona Winston!"

Oh. *Those tickets.* "I know."

"Do you?"

I slid the piles of clothes into the packing cubes for my beat-up suitcase. "Yes. Doors open at six-thirty, so we have to eat fast." This, at least, I remembered, because making a reservation at the nicest French restaurant in the city for five p.m. had made me feel geriatric.

Tess didn't say anything, but I could feel her eyes on me. I'd bet money when I looked back at her, she'd have that carefully blank expression, where none of her facial features moved, except her eyes snapped like she was mentally sharpening daggers behind them.

I looked up.

Yep. There it was.

"Tess, I know. We've talked about it so many times." Too many times. Her face didn't so much as twitch. I sighed, reminding myself that it was for her birthday, so it didn't matter if she asked me to retrieve the damn moon. I would make it happen.

I dropped a stack of shirts, skirting around the bed. "My flight gets in that morning. I'll nap, we'll hit an early dinner, and be rubbing elbows with Ms. Winston by six-thirty-one."

She nearly resisted as I pulled her from her chair and into my arms. She felt stiff when I wrapped around her.

"I'm serious, Dylan. This is important to me."

Irritation pricked. "Well, so is this multi-million dollar Japanese deal that will keep a roof over our heads for the next ten years." I tugged on her ponytail to soften the bite of my words. Her flat expression held firm. Apparently, that had been the wrong thing to say.

I wasn't in the mood to fight. Instead, I tried for a quick, close-mouthed kiss. Because that's what we did these days. I held in a sigh.

"Angel, I know it's important. I'll be there." Something flickered in her expression. Hope? Relief? It was enough of an opening that I leaned down again. I still had some time before the car picked me up for the airport. My tongue teased her bottom lip. Maybe we could...

She drew away. "You promise?"

"Yes," I bit, pulling away. So much for that. It was probably for the best, anyway. I wanted to take one more look at that contract before

I lost Wi-Fi during takeoff. My mind wandered down my miles-long mental to-do list. A few more packing cubes went into the suitcase.

"I wish this trip wasn't right on my birthday." I wasn't sure how an accusation could be delivered so softly, but Tess pulled it off.

"I can't set my work schedules around my girlfriend's birthday."

"I know."

My head shook. I really did not want to fight today. Or not fight. Whatever happened when we said things that pissed the other person off and then hardly looked at each other for a few days. I didn't want to get on a plane to the other side of the world knowing she was mad at me, but we were already heading in that direction. Might as well lean in.

"I don't think you do know." I knew for a fact she didn't, actually. Not about the pressure I was under or how much it took to make this house, *this room,* a reality. My feet shifted on the white carpet. "Our branch didn't hit our sales goals for this year, and the London office relies on our international contracts to stay billable. People's jobs are riding on my closing this deal. My bonus...our trip to Aruba? Doesn't exist if I can't make this happen."

Another cube stuffed into the case. Another. Sometimes her silence was so loud, it filled up every inch of our four-story condo.

"I'd rather have you here for my birthday than have a trip to Aruba."

I balled my hands into fists. I. Didn't. Want. To. Fight. Today. My jaw clenched. "It's a good thing I'll be here for your birthday, then. And I'll close the deal. And you can have both." The great thing about a smile was that you could still grit your teeth while you flashed it.

Another beat of silence stretched between us before she sighed and walked over to the dresser. I tensed as she got closer, lunging when I saw what she was reaching for.

"What are you doing?" I had to hold back a grimace. My sharp tone made her freeze. Tess was a deer in headlights if she thought someone was mad at her. I should have been cooler, but I'd panicked.

"I know you like to pack the socks last..." Her eyes darted between me and my sock drawer. "I thought since I was closer..."

"Don't worry about it." My fingers landed on the top of the dresser, palm hanging down to cover the sock drawer. If she wanted to open it, she'd have to go through me. *Come on, Angel. Take the hint. Walk away.*

Her brows furrowed. An expression. A miracle. "Right." Her eyes searched my face like she was trying to decipher a piece of art she'd never seen before. "Well, then...have a good trip. I guess."

"Don't have too much fun without me." Another peck and she was gone. I waited until I heard her in the kitchen, checking over my shoulder before opening the drawer to reach into the back. My hand wrapped around the thick winter socks shoved there, fingers pulling the tiny velvet box from the folded bundle. I flipped it open. The diamond glinted back at me.

I wasn't usually so reckless as to keep something this important in a sock drawer. What a cliché. But I needed it close if I was going to propose on her birthday. And I was going to propose.

This time, for sure.

Chapter 14

Dylan

"I swear, this is the first presentation this week that didn't make me yawn all the way through it." Botto's head of U.S. markets, Angela, pumped Tess's hand so hard her shoulders shook. I had to stop myself from reaching over to stabilize her.

Then again, I hadn't had to interfere much during the presentation earlier. Why start now?

Tess had been charming, bright, and smart. She'd led the Botto team through the presentation thoughtfully, her quiet voice forcing the people in the room to sit up and pay attention. The concepts were distinct, well-thought-out, and dramatically different from what any of Botto's competitors were doing. She even managed to spin Victoria's metal design into something mildly interesting.

I had to stop underestimating her.

"Obviously, we'll need to accommodate for our other markets, but as we discussed, we should easily be able to add in the other business verticals. Right?"

Tess's soft smile hid a wince only I could see. No presentation was perfect, though I knew Tess had been hoping this one would be. The chef character was a hit, but Botto also wanted to continue promoting their other manufacturing products.

"Of course," Tess agreed, still gripping the other woman's hand. I was getting seriously concerned about a traumatic brain injury. Angela needed to tone it down. "I already have a few ideas."

Angela beamed. "Brilliant. We have one more presentation to sit through on Monday morning, but then we'll make our decision about who we want to present in the next round. Probably Monday afternoon. We'll give you a call."

"We'll keep our phones on," I assured her, offering my hand, sacrificing myself to spare Tess from any more shaking. And they say chivalry is dead.

"Other products," Tess groaned the second the elevator doors shut behind us. "I should have added a few sketches and covered those bases."

"Were we in the same meeting? Where they were glowing about your ideas?"

Our eyes met in the elevator's reflection, and Tess's cheeks turned pink. *Adorable.*

"It was the team's ideas. Group effort. And you handled all the business-y stuff."

"Mmhmm. Sure. And was it the *team* who just had Angela practically salivating at the idea of putting this creative out in the market?" A slow grin made its way across Tess's face. "That's what I thought. Nailed it, Livingston. Fucking nailed it. Botto is in the bag."

"You think so?" Her whisper was so high it sounded like a squeak. I bit my lip to keep from smiling as we walked through the big marble-and-glass lobby to stand on the busy New York sidewalk.

"Trust me, Angel. We should start getting the next round presentation ready." My head tilted towards the building. Tess followed, her eyes tracing up the glass like she'd be able to sneak a peek at the conference room where she'd very likely just doubled Jinx's annual revenue in a single proposal.

"Yeah." She had a happy, far-away look in her eyes. "We're a good team. We should have done this more together at Worther. That was fun."

"Very fun," I agreed, just as our car pulled up to the curb. I opened the door and let her slide inside. "And still more to come."

She stilled as she pulled her seatbelt over her body. The heat of her gaze seared across the seats. "Oh, yeah?" Her lips tugged into another smile. Not quiet, or happy, like before. *Hot.* The smile of someone who knows they're about to get something they want.

"Oh, yeah."

***

"Adjoining rooms? You could have just canceled mine altogether." Tess thought she knew what was going on, but she had no idea.

The Botto meeting had been late in the day. Too late to hop on a plane and come back afterward. Or at least, that's what we told ourselves, fiery eyes roaming each other as we booked our flights and rooms. I'd just happened to call ahead this morning and make sure those rooms were as close as possible.

"Seemed presumptuous." My eyes snagged where Tess was pressing her teeth into her bottom lip. I was so busy staring at her—bright eyes, flushed cheeks, and the long, loose stride of a woman thinking about sex—I almost flew right by our rooms.

"Presume as much as you want. All over me, even."

God. She was so funny. And sexy. How did she deliver such ridiculous innuendo and still manage to turn me inside out? Her eyes traveled from my bobbing throat down the row of buttons on my shirt. Lower. Her finger stroked the same path.

"So...your room, or mine?" she practically whispered, tilting her head back to look at me with enough heat to start a blaze. I nearly groaned.

"Your room," I started, pointing to the door on the left. Tess opened her mouth. "And, my room. I'll be in touch."

I swiped my keycard, leaving Tess, a cloud of lust, and her baffled expression in the hall behind me. My suitcase landed on the bed before I even looked around.

Didn't matter. Hotels were pretty much all the same. Next door, I heard Tess's latch click closed. The muted sounds of her moving around her room filtered through the wall as I yanked two garment bags out of my suitcase.

For this to work, I needed surprise on my side. A little awe didn't hurt, either.

Only a minute or two had passed by the time I rapped my knuckles on the adjoining door. But when she opened it, her gaze widened, running up and down my body and the suit I'd donned with lightning speed.

Ah, there was that awe. Excellent.

"Um, hello?"

"Told you I'd be in touch," I answered, grinning at the way she kept looking at me. Like I was an unexpected room service order, but she was going to devour me, anyway.

"Ri-i-ight," she drawled, glancing behind me, like that would hold the answers to why I was in her doorway looking like I was about to walk a red carpet. "I guess I didn't realize I'd be so underdressed when you came knocking."

"Easily remedied." I handed over a garment bag, praying like hell the dresses in her closet hadn't lied and she could fit into this thing. She stared at the bag before delicately looping the hanger over her fingers. I checked my watch.

"It's almost five-thirty. You have two options. Get ready fast, and come have a drink at the bar with me. Or..." I trailed off, allowing my attention to wander all over her. I had so many plans tonight, it was hard to keep my thoughts straight.

"Or?" Tess took a step forward, her eyes darkening a shade. The lavender of her hair caught the light streaming from the window. She was perfect. And I was getting distracted.

"Or, get ready slowly. And let me watch."

"Ready for what?" She sounded breathless. A glance at the mirror behind her showed me I was baring my teeth, wolfish. I wanted to eat her whole.

Instead, I reared back. "Tess, it's the sixteenth."

Her brow furrowed. I could practically see the wheels turning in her head. The moment she came up empty. "So?"

"You think I'd forget your half-plus-a-month birthday?" I paused, but her face still looked blank. "I'm not missing such an important occasion just because we're in a different city."

Understanding dawned. She looked down at the garment bag dangling from her finger. "We have reservations or something?"

"Or something."

"It's a work trip. I just assumed we'd eat at a Chili's and then go at it like bunnies." She slid the bag's zipper down while I laughed.

"For your seven-twelfths birthday? Give me some credit. Though, maybe the second half of that is still doable..." I was still laughing when her breath caught in her throat. She stroked the material of the dress. Simple, elegant. It shifted when the light hit just right. Blue like her eyes, then a faint sheen of lavender caught a stray sunbeam.

"Dylan."

"If you hate it, I have a backup." I wasn't laughing anymore. Not when she looked at me like I was the one shining warmth and light down on her, not the sun. I would have given every one of my stock options to freeze this moment and live in it forever. My palms grew sweaty.

"I don't hate it," she whispered, stepping even closer. The backs of her fingers brushed the fabric of my jacket.

"Good."

"This is a little crazy."

"Maybe. But I owe you." I grabbed her fingers, bringing them up to my lips. Feeling her was a compulsion. A vital function of my body. She melted against me, the dress crushed between us. My lips grazed her forehead. "Now, Angel. What'll it be? Fast? Or slow."

She only had to think for a second before she rose on her toes to plant a kiss on my lips. "Fast." I caught a flash of her smile before the door between us slammed in my face. I tipped my head back and cackled.

***

"Butter," Tess murmured, her head propped on my shoulder, one hand resting on her stomach. She'd moaned that she couldn't eat another bite, but the whole time our car sped around the city, she'd been talking about every single thing she'd consumed. "The French just know how to use it better than we do."

"Magic. That pâté..." I trailed off, running my fingertips along the slope of her neck, where it dipped to meet her shoulder. Every inch of her could be a work of art. The shadow of her clavicle, the soft skin around her throat.

She groaned, and the sound went straight to my cock. "So good. It reminded me of that French place in Nashville. You remember that place?"

Your favorite restaurant with that chardonnay you always ordered? That time we dared each other to try the escargot, and you liked it so much we went back three times that month? "Yeah."

"That was a good place. I think I liked this one better, though." When she smiled up at me, she looked soft, dreamy. She'd had three glasses of champagne, and the bubbly went to her head faster than regular wine. "Even the band was phenomenal. Am I into jazz now?"

"We could be jazz people."

"You think?" Her nose wrinkled when she was thinking hard about something.

"Oh, yeah. We'll be very hip. Listen to everything on vinyl."

"We'll need to buy more turtlenecks. Jazz people always wear turtlenecks."

God, she was cute. "I don't know. I like this neck. It'd be a shame to cover it up." When I placed lingering kisses against her skin, she shivered. The fabric of her rainbow dress caught on the passing streetlights.

"You did good tonight, Morris."

"Mmm," I agreed, licking the freckle by her lips I'd always been fond of. "It's not over yet," I reminded her, nuzzling the soft skin underneath her ear, where she smelled like lavender and rain.

"You're right," she murmured, leaning closer, planting her own kisses across my jaw. I glanced at the driver in the front seat. He was looking ahead, paying us no attention. Thank God. Surely he had some idea what was going on back here.

Tess curled around me, gripping my jaw.

And all thoughts of our driver vanished from my mind.

Her lips opened underneath mine. The brush of her tongue across my mouth hijacked every single one of my senses. Taste, touch, smell.

All of it was Tess.

There had been a lot of hard parts about her leaving. I missed her the way someone misses air when they've been pushed underwater. Her absence hurt, but it was the torture I inflicted on myself that cut the deepest.

Remembering the feel of her body against mine. The sound of her breath in the morning, soft and even. How her face lit up every time she saw me, even towards the end.

I wrapped my arms around her, hauling her closer and growling when she got tangled up in the seat belt.

This wasn't a memory, it was real. She tasted like champagne. She felt like a better life than the one I'd been living.

I licked into her mouth. Teeth nipped enough to sting. To make me crave it even more. I cupped her cheek, lifting her, tilting her chin, and taking control. Tess was so careful, so thoughtful and composed, with everyone except me. I wanted it all.

"Dylan," she gasped when our mouths clashed again. I inhaled the sound, wanting it tattooed into my skin. Her fingernails scraped against my neck, fluttering as she tugged on the top button of my shirt.

I captured her wrist. I was gone for her, but not enough to strip in the back of a cab. But we could still...I chased the thought, sucking her lip into my mouth while my other hand smoothed down her dress. My fingers radiated lavender sparkles wherever they touched.

The hem fluttered a few inches above her knee. Just short enough that I could see the definition of her thighs. I wanted to lick them up and down. Then up again. My thumb slid up an inch, exposing more.

"Sir? Ma'am?"

Tess stilled, reality barging in like a battering ram. Our driver rattled off the address I'd entered when I called the car, unimpressed that we were practically dry humping in his back seat.

A breath rushed out of Tess's mouth. I felt it against my skin before she scrambled backwards. "Thank you," she gasped, fumbling with her seatbelt.

I cleared my throat, adjusting my pants. "Yes. Thank you." I pulled out my phone, already leaving the driver a hefty tip, when I heard a little squeak.

My hands shot out just in time, catching a slightly tipsy Theresa Lynn Livingston before she hit the asphalt. "Thank you!" She giggled again as the car slid away from the curb.

While I was slinging her around, I decided I should pull her up against my chest. She washed up like a wave to shore.

"I think that guy caught us making out," she whispered, leaning her weight on me.

"I think so, too," I whispered back, ducking my head down. She was easy to see in the flooded lights of New York, but I wanted to be closer. I wanted to be back in that cab. Or, better yet, back in our hotel room.

Her fingers twined around my hair, playing. "Good thing we... This isn't our hotel."

I shook my head, brushing a smudge of lipstick from the corner of her mouth. I wiped mine as well. No telling what they looked like. More than likely marked with light pink gloss and bite marks. I didn't mind it. If I had my way, the whole world would know she was mine, and that we liked kissing in cabs.

But for this...we should probably both be presentable. Tess would die if she walked in there with lipstick all over her face.

I stepped back, scanning her body. A quick tug on her dress shifted it back from where it had twisted up in the car.

"Why are we in a strange neighborhood in a strange city after dark?"

I nearly snorted. *After dark*. She sounded pretty scandalized for someone who had been about to take my shirt off in a cab.

"You got me," I admitted, grabbing her hand to stride toward the big brick building. "It's been a long con. Twelve years of manipulation, and now I'm finally ready to murder you."

"Dylan," she scolded while I pressed the button.

"Tess," I replied, swinging the door open when the lock buzzed. I towed her across the hall.

"I'm serious. What is this? And why aren't we back at the hotel?" She caught up to me, her last words whispered and urgent in my ear as she stroked my arm. It was tempting, so very tempting, to turn around, march back to the street and hail the first cab I saw.

But I'd already screwed this up once. I wouldn't do it again.

"For this." I nodded behind Tess to where a large black door covered in bronze dragonflies swung open. A woman stood on the other side. Tall, draped in printed silk scarves, she looked like the Barefoot Contessa, but with graying hair that fell past her waist.

"Tess?" The woman looked at Tess expectantly. She received a blank stare in return. "Dylan has told me so much about you in our email exchanges. I've been looking forward to this all week."

Tess's mouth opened and stayed there, like the words had only loaded halfway and were getting stuck on the way out. I eased forward to offer my hand.

"I'm the Dylan who's told you so much about her. Thank you for inviting us here tonight."

Her handshake was delicate. I had to be careful not to grip too hard.

"Fiona Winston?" Tess croaked, finally coming out of her stupor. Fiona smiled, offering her hand to Tess, who took it automatically. When she realized who she was touching, Tess wrapped her other hand around Fiona's, like she was scared the woman would vanish.

"One and the same. Your man here told me you missed my show when it came through Nashville last year. What do you say to a private tour?"

Fiona cracked the door, revealing a long hallway filled with watercolor paintings, from massive, six-foot creations to tiny, postage-stamp-sized portraits. They were pinned to the wall like butterflies, fluttering with the air conditioning unit. Beyond the hall, we could see a large room filled with light. More paintings.

"A private...?" Tess's eyes were wide, ready to capture every color she saw. "Do you have an exhibit going on right now?"

Fiona's eyes crinkled. "Nothing like that, dear. This is my studio. Want to come have a look around?"

It shouldn't have been possible, but Tess's eyes grew even bigger. She looked at me, stunned, like she was asking for permission to go inside. Or, maybe, asking if I was seeing this, too?

"Go on, birthday girl," I murmured, tucking a strand of hair behind her ear. "We've got all night."

Tears pooled in her eyes. "Dylan, I..." She looked back at Fiona. At me. Fiona, again. "I'm so sorry. I'm really overwhelmed. I am so inspired by your work. It's been my dream to see your pieces in person."

Fiona wrapped her arm around Tess's shoulders. "Dylan tells me you're a painter, as well? Maybe we can have some fun once you're done looking around. I'm working on a new technique I could use a second opinion on."

As they walked into the studio, Tess looked up like she was entering the Sistine Chapel. She glanced back again, her amazed, disbelieving face framed by hundreds of watercolors as Fiona led her down the hall.

I watched her take it in. The wonder. The joy. The disbelief.

What a waste these past seven months had been. These past few years. Did I really think anything was more important than *this?*

Tess's smile lit the hallway. I stepped inside, following her through the room filled with bright colors and muted shapes. And vowed then and there I'd never take her for granted again.

Chapter 15

Tess

"The work she's doing with the geometric patterns is incredible," I gushed. Dylan's hand on the back of my neck led me through the door to his room.

"The sharpness of the lines," he muttered. I grinned.

"Exactly! That contrast of the bold edges with the softness of the watercolor. You can't recreate it twice. The way she dilutes the pigment is so..."

"Organic," Dylan supplied, tugging on my shoulder to stop me before I ran into the dresser. I glanced up from the little postcard-sized painting I'd been staring at ever since leaving Fiona's workshop.

She was everything I'd wanted her to be and more. She was so smart, carelessly throwing out various techniques and theories that made me want to grab a pen and take notes.

"Organic. Exactly!" I beamed at Dylan, then back at the paper in my hand.

In her workshop, she'd let us experiment with her inks. I'd sketched out a little dragonfly on a lily pad, and drenched it in color. It was nothing like Fiona's work, but I'd shadowed it enough that the dragonfly popped, nearly 3-D from far away.

"Mmm, excellent dimensionality. We could play with the light a little next time," Fiona had commented when she saw my paper. "Do you mind if I borrow the concept? Mess around with it a little?"

I had nearly died. If Dylan hadn't been there, holding me up, I would still be passed out on Fiona Winston's studio floor. He'd managed an interesting-looking squiggle, washed with blues and greens and purples. Fiona had called it a "beautiful expression." Expression of what, I wasn't sure, and I'd been too overwhelmed to ask her to clarify.

"I know I should stop babbling about Fiona Winston, but I just *met Fiona Winston,* and she *liked my painting,* and I think this is the greatest night of my life."

"I'm glad."

When I looked up again, Dylan was sitting on the bed, folded hands hanging between his spread legs. A lamp in the corner illuminated the room in a soft orange glow.

Earlier tonight, opening the door to him had done ridiculous things to my hormones. He'd looked like a model in his crisp, well-fitted suit.

Now, though, he was less than picture perfect. He'd shed his jacket, sleeves rolled up. His hair curled around his collar in the humid night air. A soft smile played across his mouth.

And he was gazing at me with such aching fondness, my heart squeezed. This man, *my* man, had done this for me.

I might have floated on a cloud all the way here, but now I landed back on Earth. In a hotel room. Alone. With Dylan.

I licked my lips. "I really should stop talking about Fiona Winston." My voice came out as a whisper. The smile deepened at the corners of his mouth.

"Or don't. I love how happy you are right now." He looked like he loved it. Like he loved me.

My heart thudded in my chest, landing like a stone against my ribs and then picking up speed like it was trying to take flight.

I gently placed the painting on the dresser beside Dylan's. "No, I...really think I need to stop talking now." I didn't want to fan-girl over a painter. I wanted to get my body as close to his as possible and see what happened next. I'd been looking forward to this trip for days, weeks even, thinking longingly of *New York* and the *hotel* every night he left me at my door with the taste of him on my tongue.

Sadness flashed through the affectionate look on his face. "I haven't done a very good job of making you happy in the past. I've learned not to take it for granted."

My racing heart fissured straight down the middle. "Dylan." I stepped closer. Touching him was imperative.

"We both know it's true. Tonight makes me remember how being with you can feel like magic." Tonight *had* been magic. The dinner, how we'd hung on each other's every word. Laughing with Fiona as Dylan accidentally splattered paint everywhere. Perfection, all of it.

Yet...I took another step closer, swallowing, my mouth suddenly dry.

If I'd been looking forward to New York for a long time, I'd been scared for longer. Long-nurtured fears and regrets bubbled to the surface, threatening to crack our perfect evening into pieces.

"What's that face? You don't agree?" Even though he was sitting, he didn't have to crane his neck to see me. He was so tall, larger than life. And I was so small.

So small I sometimes became nearly invisible.

"Tess?"

In the end, it was the careful caution in his voice that made me speak up. I couldn't keep this bottled up if it would hurt him, too.

"Tonight *was* magic. But it's not always like this," I said, my throat dry as I voiced the concern that had been prickling my brain for weeks. "What happens when things get back to normal? When it's just boring life stuff again?"

"Boring life stuff?"

"I mean, we can always make new lists, but sometimes it's just...life." My hands lifted, searching for the words. "Sometimes I get over-whelmed and it might take me time to come back out of my shell. What happens if you get this job at Jinx and you lose yourself in work again? Or when it's just a Tuesday and we have pasta and go to bed early?"

Will this still work? I wanted to beg him for an answer. For some guarantee that twelve years from now, we wouldn't revert to the cold, separate place we had been. *Will you still love me when I babble about art? Will you still look at me like that when one of us forgets to pick up the groceries?*

"I like Tuesdays."

It wasn't the answer I wanted. "Dylan—"

"I'm not done." He grabbed my hands, bringing them up to his chest and holding tight. I shuffled forward until his thighs bracketed my legs. "I like Tuesdays. With you. I like pasta. And holding you while we sleep. That sounds like a great fucking day to me."

I tried to pull back. He wasn't getting it. "That's...I'm not asking about pasta." He held tighter.

"I know, Angel. I know exactly what you're asking." He gripped my chin, drawing my gaze from the ceiling. "You're scared it'll go back to the way it was. That the 'boring life stuff' will get in the way of this." He squeezed my fingers. "I've done the boring life stuff with you before, Tess. And I'd rather have a lifetime of Tuesdays with you than Saturdays with anyone else."

His words reached into my throat and squeezed. My heart fluttered again.

"Boring doesn't scare me, Theresa Lynn. Doing it without you, though..." He shook his head, heart in his eyes, shatteringly sincere. His thumb reached out to catch a tear I hadn't felt fall. "I've done that before, and *that's* what scares me."

I swayed forward, powerless to fight the pull towards him. He *knew*. He got it.

My lips brushed his, butterfly soft. I wanted to savor this moment. Maybe it would carry me through all those Tuesdays. Because he was right. Life happened, and we weren't perfect. But we were better together than we were apart.

His mouth parted underneath mine. He whispered my name like a plea. A benediction. I let my hands slide across his shoulders. Cup his neck. Pull him closer.

All this time of quiet retreating and living separate lives. It was done. I was done.

"I love you." He'd told me a million times, but this felt like that first time. Like laying on his bed at the frat house, galaxies of possibility thrumming between us. "I've never stopped, Tess. Not for one minute."

We hadn't said those words to each other the whole time he'd been in Chicago. One time in our lives, we'd exchanged them like breathing. *I love you. I love you, too.* Constantly.

Maybe we'd said them so often, we'd forgotten what they meant altogether. But I remembered now.

"I love you, too," I whispered. He smiled into my mouth. "Even while I left, I never stopped. Not for one minute," I repeated his words, pressing my lips more firmly against him. Hot palms circled my legs, sliding up the back of my thighs to pull me closer. One of his arms clamped around my back while the other continued its exploration, easing over the curve of my hip, smoothing up my spine.

We were close enough that I felt rather than heard his groan. I nipped his lip with my teeth, grinning bigger when he hauled me into his body, forcing my knee to brace on the bed, straddling him. His fingers made circles down the back of my thigh, teasing the hem of my dress when he made the journey back up.

All the while, his breath was hot, tongue darting out in increasingly daring licks. "This dress," he moaned, balling the fabric up then releasing it. "You look like you're wearing rainbows."

"Sounds cute." I pressed light, close-mouthed kisses along his cheek.

"Oh, the dress is cute. The things I want to do to you in this dress?" He yanked, sending me sprawling against his chest. "Definitely more X-rated."

My pulse pounded in my ears when I looped my hands around his neck. We were molded together now, not an inch of space between us. The contact was debilitating.

"Does that mean I have to keep the dress on?" I'd meant for it to sound teasing, but the words exited my mouth on a gasp. I barely finished speaking before his mouth was on mine. His tongue licked at my lips, demanding entrance. I surrendered.

With another groan, he pushed inside, savoring like I was the sweetest thing he'd ever tasted. Pressed against his lap, I relished the undeniable feeling of his desire underneath me.

"If you really want to ruin that dress, Angel, I can rip it off you," he panted, groaning as his tongue swept down my neck. "But I haven't felt your skin against mine in weeks. I haven't been inside you in *months*." The word shuddered out, like he was confessing the ultimate sin. He drew back, eyes almost black.

"That little rainbow dress will not survive what I have planned."

A full-body shiver wracked me. That soft, floating feeling burned away as mad, scorching lust flooded my system. His hands were everywhere, sliding and grabbing, like he was greedy for every inch of my skin.

"Please tell me your plan is fast," I begged, my fingernails scratching against his neck. I fumbled with his buttons, already mentally working him out of his pants. It wasn't enough to have his body pressed against mine. I wanted skin. I wanted him all over me. *Inside me.*

He groaned, fingers gripping my ass tight enough to leave marks. My hips jerked against his, the thought taking everything to a whole new level. I wanted his mark on me. I wanted real, physical proof of how much he wanted me.

"We should go slow," he grunted. His words lost all meaning when he surged upwards, taking me with him. In an instant, I was on my back, the frilly hem of my dress shoved up to my waist. He loomed over me, eyes darting across my face, my body, until he dipped lower to plunder my mouth. I arched beneath him.

"Or not," I suggested, grabbing at his waistband. His shirt pulled free, granting me access to the corded muscles of his back. My hands slid and grasped, just as his smoothed over the bare skin of my thighs, playing with the lace edge of my underwear. We moved against each other like waves on the sand, gliding and grinding everything to dust. Starting over with every touch.

"You're trying to kill me," he panted, looking down at how I was splayed open for him, pressing his hips into mine like he couldn't control himself. Sparks flew across my vision. "I want it to be...special. This first time, again."

This first time, again. That was a good way to describe it. I remembered viscerally how he pulsed inside me. The sounds he made, and how he lost control at the end, snapping his hips and clenching his jaw.

The knowledge of what it was like to make love with him fueled my urgency. I knew how good it could be, and I wanted it. Now.

"It's been too long." I sounded whiny and needy, but that's how I felt. As my fingers scrambled to undress him, he did his best to melt my brain, pressing my legs open further, exposing me to him. Kissing me until I couldn't breathe, shoving his hips into mine again and again, sending exquisite pressure between my legs where I was growing wetter, hotter.

"Shit." He cursed when I finally slid my hand inside his pants. His cock was long and hard in my fingers. I reveled in the way he moaned, hips flexing as I moved up and down his length. His mouth tore away from mine, growling with every breath. "Too good."

"So good," I whispered, high on the feeling of him losing control against me. It was heady, powerful, making my head spin even more than it already was. I gripped him harder, needing to see what he looked like when he completely fell apart for me. It had been so long since it had felt like this. I wanted to capture all of it.

He cursed again, yanking my wrist to pin my arm over my head. The movement stretched me long underneath him, and his eyes drifted down my body, lingering where my heaving chest pressed against the fabric of my dress. It bunched around my navel, baring thin, lacy blue underwear to him. His eyes narrowed on the wet spot between my legs. I flushed, gasping, like his gaze was a physical thing pressing against the damp lace.

His fingers tightened on my wrist, driving my hand into the pillows. "Did that get you wet, Tess? You like teasing me?"

My hips churned underneath him. He didn't require an answer. We both knew exactly how turned on I was.

His teeth flashed, and for a moment, I wanted to know what they'd feel like against my skin. "We can see how you like it. How hot can I make you with just my fingers? You want me to tease you, Angel?"

Yes. No? I wriggled, pulling on my arm, but he pinned it mercilessly to the bed. Something about the restraint ratcheted my desire even .

My mind emptied as his hand found my core, stroking between my legs. With a single, deft move, Dylan pushed the fabric aside and slid his finger through my wetness, making me shudder and arch.

"That's it, Angel. Damn, do you feel how wet you are?" His thumb circled my clit while his fingers stroked, adding to the aching pressure building low in my stomach. The feeling shot through my body, zipping down my limbs. My feet scrabbled for purchase on the smooth comforter, bunching and twisting it. I was losing myself to the pleasure, every second stealing more of my thoughts, dissolving them into pure feeling.

"You like that?" His voice was a low, inaudible growl. It flooded my senses, a deep rumble in my chest. I whimpered, then cried out as he speared a finger inside me, his leg pinning my knee to the bed, holding me open.

Despite the heat burning across my skin, and his frantic breathing, his invasion was slow. Gentle, almost like he wasn't sure how rough he could be with me. He'd barely pressed inside before he moved back, pulsing softly in between my legs. The whole time, he kept constant pressure on my clit. Ecstasy and torture.

"Dylan." I definitely whined this time, reaching down to grip his wrist with my free hand, pulling, trying to persuade him deeper. Harder. "More, please."

I nearly cried out when his fingers left me, gathering my other wrist above my head, neatly securing both my arms in one hand. The other trailed back down my body. "I told you I wanted to go slow."

His head dipped, tongue swirling across the tops of my breasts. He left sucking kisses across my skin, not enough to mark me, but enough for me to feel the little pulling pulses between my legs. I tried to squeeze my thighs to ease the pressure there, but his hips rested on mine, holding me in place while he jerked the dress down, exposing my breast. His teeth scraped across the bottom curve, tongue licking in a lazy circle, avoiding my nipple.

Even when I strained, he held fast, keeping me stretched out under him. He'd never physically restrained me like this before, but the more I struggled, the more I realized *I liked it*. A lot.

I hooked my leg over his to press against his cock. He gave me a warning look, his free hand darting down to press my hip back into the bed.

"I'm trying to go slow," he growled. Even as he spoke, his chest heaved, hand gathering the fabric of my dress to jerk it even higher. Hungry eyes trailed my body. My core clenched while I writhed in his hold.

His throat worked as he watched me. "So fucking beautiful."

"I need more," I whispered, pleaded.

He and squeezed my wrists almost to the point of pain. Eyes raised and clashed with mine, a storm of lust and raw, masculine need. "You don't think I know what you need, Angel?" His voice was deceptively soft, and didn't prepare me in any way for how he thrust two fingers inside me, suddenly filling me exactly the way I wanted.

I yelped, straining my hips against his fingers. That slow, gentle exploration was gone. He shoved against me, thumb firm on my clit, maintaining a pressure that built in my throat. I could hardly drag air into my lungs.

"I know exactly what you need. And I know exactly how much you can take." He demonstrated, hooking his fingers inside, practically melting me into the mattress. My eyes closed, trying to hold the intense pleasure pinging through my veins. I was close. So, so close.

"You know why, Tess?"

A low moan rattled out of my throat when he worked faster, circling harder. He was making a point, proving his mastery of my body with incomparable skill. "I..." I'd lost my words, my breath.

"Tell me," Dylan demanded, shoving his fingers inside, rocking me closer to the inevitable orgasm that was sparking at the edge of my vision. "How do I know? Why can I make you go crazy like this?"

"Because," I gasped when his fingers twisted. Close, close, close.

"Tell. Me." His words lashed, stripping any protections I had left, laying me bare.

"Because I'm yours!" It was a truth I knew down to my bones, the words I knew he wanted. My eyes fluttered open again, just in time to see the triumph flash across his face.

"Mine."

I barely heard his declaration, especially when he swooped down to pull my nipple into his mouth, laving it with his tongue, teeth teasing the tip with just enough pressure to set me off like a rocket. I gasped and cried as the crest of pleasure washed over me.

Heat shimmered through my blood, flooding every corner of my body. Above me, Dylan grunted, his words a litany of my name and "mine" and "yes, Angel, yes." I lost myself in it, floating in ecstasy for another moment or two.

His hand tore away with a curse. I blinked my eyes open to see him tearing at his pants, pushing them down his thighs with one hand. His other was still braced above my head, holding me in place.

"Too good, Angel. Fuck, I have to feel you." His weight settled on me, and I felt him finally, *finally*, pushing at my entrance, his cock hot and hard.

Chapter 16

Dylan

I slid against her, her slick entrance coating me in her desire. I'd done that; I'd made her go crazy underneath me, writhing and screaming.

She was mine, no question about it. We might have lost our way, but I had always known her body better than my own.

"I wanted to go slow." I didn't recognize my voice. Low and harsh, I sounded like I was accusing her of something. Maybe I was. Of making me crazy. Of making me throw every single plan I'd had out the window as soon as I'd seen her eyes darken when I held her wrists.

Thank fuck she liked it, because I liked having her here. There was a possessive satisfaction in the sight of her spread out underneath me, her tits red from my attention, underwear pushed to the side, pussy bare and shining.

She must have gotten a wax sometime this week. I'd nearly come at the first feel of her. She was like silk and honey, her sweet little body pulsing around my hand. I slid forward again, this time catching my tip on her entrance before gliding up her clit.

One more look at her had me nearly breaking into madness. She was panting, wild, completely succumbing to the mind-bending heat between us. Damn. I really *had* wanted to go slow. Re-learn every inch of skin I'd missed since she left.

But I was just a man, and she was a goddess, spread beneath me, panting and pleading. Her lilac hair flowed across the pillow, silky and sweat-drenched, while her creamy skin turned pink with desire.

How could I deny her?

I reached between us, teasing her folds again. "I brought condoms."

This, at least, I could pause for. An offering, an olive branch. Maybe a memory to patch the rough edges of that night a few weeks ago, when all my carefully laid plans and expectations had crumbled around us. It had seemed important to her, then. Maybe it still was.

"No." Relief rushed through me. I couldn't remember the last time we'd used a condom—not since early college—and I didn't want anything between us now.

I surged forward, mouth capturing hers once more as I slid inside her warmth. Her neck arched, head thrown back while I pressed in.

Yes.

She panted my name as I drew back, pressed again even further. With one more gasping kiss, I moved, losing myself completely. The world fell away, and every ounce of my existence constricted down to the places our skin met, sliding and sticking.

I sank into her like I was dying for it. I didn't recognize the sounds coming out of my mouth. Words rushed and slurred, blending with groans I couldn't suppress, as the heat seared through my brain.

So long. Too long. How had I ever taken this for granted? The perfect beauty and captivating completeness of pushing into her, surrounded by lush skin and her mewling breaths. I ducked my head, swirling my tongue around her nipple once more, craving the taste of her in my mouth.

The action set her off again, her inner muscles clamping and spasming around me as she cried my name. It sent a fury of heat into my cock, tightening my balls.

I wanted to empty inside her, to answer her call.

Not yet, though.

She protested when I pulled out. I nearly shoved back in, dying to feel her pulsing and twitching against me. In a quick move, I flipped her onto her stomach, sliding a pillow under her hips while I held onto her wrists. "One more, Angel. Like this."

My palm smoothed down her ass, shoving her underwear to the side again. My thumb dipped into her core, feeling her aftershocks. Slickness smeared across the inside of her thighs. It was achingly perfect.

"Can you stay still like this?" My voice was like gravel, rough and rasping in her ear. I licked up the shell, unable to help myself. She shuddered, pressing her hips against mine. Without thinking, I cracked my hand across the globe of her ass. Light, but enough for her to feel it.

She froze, eyes going wide as I stroked her skin, easing any sting. "Still, Angel. Can you do it?" *Is this okay? I just spanked you and you haven't had control of your hands for ten minutes. Are you with me?*

I had been her first. We'd gotten up to some fun stuff in the last twelve years, but nothing close to this. Light spanking and bondage was so far outside our realm of experience, it was laughable. But the caveman in my chest was howling for it.

"Never let her leave again." The instinct I had to claim her, right here, right now, was primal.

"Yes," she whimpered, turning her head to look at me. Lightning struck. Her swollen lips pulled between her teeth, eyes glittering in the soft glow of the lamp. Her soft, open expression told me everything I needed to know.

"Tess," I murmured, leaning down to kiss her, to smooth my tongue across the grooves her teeth had left in her plump skin. I tasted her, whispering about love and perfection while my hand roamed the sloping expanse of her back. I tucked her fingers between the mattress and the padded headboard.

"Leave them right there, Angel. Don't move. So good." I groaned when she nodded, curling her fingers, bunching the fitted sheet in her hands.

I sat back on my heels, eyes taking in the feast of smooth skin before me. The little almost-heart-shaped birthmark on her left shoulder blade. The smooth, regular protrusions of her spine. The wrinkled, ruined fabric of her dress, hiked and forgotten around her waist.

That. Ass.

I lined myself up against her again, thinking about how I could spill all over that perfect skin. I knew from experience she looked utterly gorgeous splattered with my come.

I groaned, shoving myself back inside her slick, hot core at the thought. Yes, she'd look brilliant with me spilling across her spine, running down her sides, soaking into her rainbow sparkles.

I shouted as the thought, the feel of her like this, nearly shot me over the edge. God, I wanted to ruin her. Later, I promised myself. This first time, I wanted to be inside her for every instant I could.

I glanced down, growling when my shirt hung in the way, obscuring my view. I yanked it up, tightening my fist around the fabric at the sight of my cock shuttling in and out of her.

Her face burrowed into the pillows as she keened and cried out, fingers dutifully tucked against the headboard. She gripped so tightly the sheet snapped off the corner of the bed.

My arm looped around her hips, pulling her up as I pushed another pillow there. The new angle shattered me. The room melted around us, pleasure and hot need whipping into a maelstrom that threatened to take me down. I gripped her waist, frantic, pulling her back against me again and again and again.

She was panting my name. Screaming, scrambling to hold on to the bed as I rocked her up and down over and over. Finally, her heat and gasping cries became too much. The familiar pressure gathered at the base of my spine.

I hadn't even come yet and I was completely lost. I needed her mouth on mine when I spilled inside her. An anchor, a breath in my lungs. I was gasping, dying and coming alive against her.

I pulled her back, and she came willingly, twining her arms around my neck as she craned her head around for a kiss. I gripped her hair, ravenous while I claimed her lips, fucking up into her, a guttural cry leaving my mouth when I finally came.

I barely registered her scream, my hands too busy gripping her hair, locked around her hips while I drove inside. I felt her moving against me while I came down, and distantly realized she'd come again, too.

Finally, after another minute of pulsing inside her, my hips moving like I could make it last, I stilled, settling back on my heels and taking her with me. Slowly, in increments, I came back to myself. I released the fingers I'd clenched hard in her hair. Her lips didn't leave mine.

I stroked the backs of my fingers down her neck, afraid I'd hurt her. I pressed apologetic kisses to her mouth before looking at the wreckage around us.

Pillows had fallen haphazardly to the floor. The sheet had pulled away from the mattress. The comforter was toast, crumbled somewhere behind us. She'd slipped out of her heels somewhere along the way, but I...

"I still have my shoes on," I panted in disbelief. We had obliterated the room. Each other. And I was still mostly dressed.

Tess's lips were puffy and red; streaks crossed her chest from my five o'clock stubble. One of the straps of her dress fluttered, torn and useless. Her hair was a tangled halo around her face. From her wide, surprised eyes, I assumed I didn't look much better. Wrinkled shirt under my armpits and my pants pushed down just far enough for me to ravage her.

I still had my *shoes on*.

In the quiet aftermath, a giggle bubbled out of her lips. She brought her hand up to her mouth, glancing back to me, then to the ruined bedding around us. "We really made a mess," she laughed, eyes dancing.

I snorted into her shoulder, dragging kisses there as I eased out of her. We both groaned, and she collapsed, twisting onto her back. She had the biggest smile on her face. My heart ballooned inside my chest.

Perfect.

I eased onto my side, pulling her against me and finally toeing my damn shoes off. "I really did plan to go slow," I said, kissing her hair as she snuggled in.

"Next time," she whispered, fitting her forehead against my neck.

I sighed and pulled her closer.

Later, I would carefully peel what remained of her dress over her head and gently tuck the comforter around her. I'd shuck out of my own clothes, turn off the lamp, and we'd watch the lights outside sparkle through the sheer curtain.

Later, I *would* go slow, running hands and tongue and teeth over every inch of her, careful of the sore places where I'd been too rough.

For now, though, I held her close, pressed together in the wreckage of what we'd done. Absolutely certain that if I could go back and do it all over again, I wouldn't change a thing.

Chapter 17

Tess

I didn't have the heart to tell Dylan I was getting a little tired of lavender lattes. Especially not since he'd ordered three different artisanal syrups, which arrived at my doorstep the same day as the fancy electric milk steamer.

He started sending a lot of things to my apartment, actually. Mostly because neither of us wanted to leave unless it was absolutely necessary. Since returning from New York, we'd been holed up here, fueled by incessant sex and the news that we'd made it to the final round of the Botto bidding process. Our only competition in the next presentation was a local firm in the city, and Angela assured me that while the other agency had strong ideas, they were nothing like Jinx's offerings.

"—and the formula we're using makes her fart like a trucker—Oh. Hello, Satan." Vanna sneered when Dylan appeared behind me on the phone screen.

"Morning, Vanna!" he chimed, smacking a kiss on my cheek and edging me out of the way to finish the eggs I was cooking. Her face scrunched.

"So that's still a thing?" She asked me the same question every time we talked, like she thought Dylan would magically disappear. I smiled at him.

"Still a thing."

She pretended to gag. "Alright, I'm leaving before you force more of this lovey-dovey bullshit on me. I have to go get farts outta this baby."

"Tell Adrianna I said hi!"

"Yeah, yeah. You look happy or whatever. You'd better stay that way. You hear me, Satan? Make it stick this time!"

"Yes, Boss!" Dylan shouted back. Vanna rolled her eyes, but I caught a hint of a smile on her lips just before she hung up.

"Okay, we're both thinking it, so I'll say it," Dylan declared, tipping the eggs onto plates. He looked like devastation wrapped in corporate clothing. Hair still damp from the shower we'd shared, freshly shaved and smelling like my flowery body wash.

"What's that?" I took another sip of coffee and eyed the eggs.

"We gotta wash the sheets." He sighed. "I know, I know, it will involve actually leaving the apartment for something other than work. But after last night, we've veered into safety hazard territory."

I laughed, glancing at the rumpled bedding across the room. We'd swapped out the sheets mid-week for my extra set, but last night *had* gotten a little out of control.

That shower this morning was necessary.

"Remind me again why we can't use the perfectly nice-looking washer and dryer in the corner?" His lips pressed against my neck, setting the baby hairs there on end. I tilted to give him more access.

"Don't let it fool you. It *looks* nice, but it's a demon. Turn it on and watch water spray in all directions, soaking the floor and everything you hold dear."

I added a sad piece of toast to each of our plates. There wasn't even jelly in the fridge, and the butter had run out yesterday. We needed to go to the store, or at least get some necessities delivered. He grinned like we hadn't just concocted the world's most pitiful breakfast.

"Thank you. Why hasn't your super fixed it? Or replaced it?" He glared at the stacked units while I settled at the coffee table that doubled as the dining room. Yeesh, this place really was tiny. "How long has it been out of commission?"

"Mmm, since I moved in. I've never even done a full load in there," I muttered around a mouthful of dry toast. I watched as he stared the machines down, hands on his hips.

"I'll call someone. Your landlord *should* do something, but if he won't, I can take care of it."

"I can email them again," I offered, guiltily remembering I'd only emailed them about it once or twice, and had promptly given up after getting brushed off. Maybe the third time was the charm? I didn't want Dylan to go out of his way and hire someone to fix a rental washing machine when another email from me might suffice. What did washing machine maintenance cost these days, anyway?

"Don't worry about it." He winced as he sat on the low couch. His knees poked up at an awkward angle. When I'd bought it, I hadn't had six-foot-something men in mind. I opened my mouth to argue, but he handily derailed my train of thought with a kiss. "You deserve to have clean sheets without making the trek down to the creepy basement."

That, at least, I couldn't argue with. "Well, you can call someone, but we'll need to wash sheets tonight, anyway. Do you think you're going to want to get drinks with Danny, or something? I'm sure you have a lot to catch up on."

Danny Ricci, Worther's Chief Operating Officer, was technically Dylan's immediate boss, but back in Nashville, the two of them had acted like one sales automaton with two heads.

Henry called them the Dream Team, and it was easy to see why. Danny had just joined Worther last year, and he was only a few years older than us, with the same magnetically charming personality as Dylan. I'd seen them bring down big deals over the course of a corporate dinner like lions tackled prey. Danny was...fine, even though he suffered from the same issues that had swamped Dylan when he was at Worther, too: workaholic, unshakeable drive to succeed. Business first.

"Nah. I'll leave work with you like normal. We've kept in touch," Dylan commented, spooning eggs onto his toast. I blinked at him, both because of his breakfast ingenuity and my surprise.

"You've 'kept in touch' with Danny?" When did he have the time? Even before we'd started shacking up in my apartment, he spent his working hours practically glued to my hip, or in meetings with Eric.

My eyes narrowed. "What did you get up to at that hotel after work hours, anyway?" It wasn't the first time I'd wondered about his life in Chicago. Aside from his book club and new pickup soccer league, most of his energy was spent wooing me with coffee and snacks. What was the routine he'd left behind when he brought his suitcase through my front door last week?

Dylan smiled. "Oh, this and that. Staring out the window, pining for my lost love a few blocks away. I wrote some truly excellent poetry. 'Roses are red, I love you to bits—'"

I smashed my hand over his mouth. "If this ends up being an ode to my breasts, I will kick you out," I warned, actively trying not to laugh.

He licked my fingers before I could pull back, making me yelp.

"What, are you five?" I wiped my hand on my pants. "What will Danny think? A month away from Nashville and you've regressed by about two decades."

Dylan's crooked, unrepentant smile sent butterflies pinging through my stomach. "He probably won't recognize me. It feels like it's been years, not a month." The edges of his mouth softened, and he leaned forward to brush a kiss across my cheek. "I'm practically a whole new man."

My hand around his neck stopped him from pulling away. I enjoyed the smooth skin of his face under my lips, knowing that in a few hours, it would feel rough again. "Chicago looks good on you, Morris."

"*You* look good on me," he countered, sweeping me into his lap, our dry toast forgotten on the table.

***

"I swear, it felt like Christmas when this guy told me y'all were back together." Danny sank into an office chair, grinning ear-to-ear as he glanced between me and Dylan. It was surprisingly good to see him.

"Same, trust me." Dylan's eyes sparkled, light and happy, as they met mine. "But we're trying to keep it on the down low around here.

We don't want to give people the wrong impression while I'm still ramping up."

"Oh, sure!" Danny threw an over-exaggerated wink at us that was so ridiculous, it made me smile. "I'll keep my mouth closed. I'm just glad to see you two together. He was moping around the office for months."

"I wasn't much better, I promise," I assured him, perching on a chair. The spare office Meery had assigned to him for his visit was small, but the three of us could sit and chat for a while without the rest of the office listening in.

Danny grinned at me. "Better together." He seemed so...pleased. Another surprise.

Even though he worked closely with Dylan, Danny and I had never interacted outside of work events. It had been easy to relegate him to "one of the evil people corrupting my boyfriend," and dismiss him out of hand, especially towards the end, when he'd spent more time with Dylan than I had.

Now, though, seeing his genuine happiness for us, I regretted not making an effort to connect with him more. Part of me always thought his over the top charm and endless energy was faked, just a side-effect of wheeling and dealing all the time. But now he had me wondering if he was the real deal.

The shrill ringing of a cell phone made the two men pat at their pockets. Dylan pulled his out, flashing the screen in our direction. "It's Grant. Let me get this."

I watched him duck outside, the door closing softly behind him.

"We had a pool going in the office, you know. How long it would take you to come back? We never thought he'd be the one to come here, but you know what? Good for him." Danny shook his head, sliding his laptop out of its sleeve and setting up on a corner of the desk. "I don't know how he's doing it—working two jobs and fixing things with you. He looks more rested than I would have thought."

"Two jobs?" Did he mean, like, shadowing me *and* Eric? Sure, Dylan's days were pretty busy, but I wouldn't call it "two jobs."

Danny snorted. "I mean, Henry let him decrease his workload to come try this out, but not *that* much."

A queasy feeling settled in my stomach. Maybe I was misunderstanding? I glanced at the frosted glass, watching Dylan's shadow pace in front of the door. "Henry...but Dylan works here. At Jinx. He's...on track to replace Eric as CEO."

Danny shrugged, like this was a normal conversation, not confusing at all. "He's not CEO yet. And you know Henry. He'd rather cut off his own hand than lose his golden boy. He hasn't made it easy on him. Old man is holding on tight, hoping Dylan will see the light and come running back to Nashville." Danny winked at me. "Something tells me Dylan's planning to stick around though, if he can."

If he can. My pulse fluttered. It was becoming increasingly clear that I was missing something. Maybe lots of somethings. *Big* somethings.

"So, Dylan is still doing his old job, too? Besides all the stuff he's taken on here?" My brain was spinning. That math didn't add up. He worked with me. Here. All day. He had meetings and made coffee runs. And when he came home at night, his phone got chucked on the table until it was time to leave in the morning.

Danny paused his desk setup to look in my direction. Something flashed across his expression—uncertainty or wariness. It cranked up the unsettled feeling in my stomach. "Dylan hasn't talked to you about this?"

"Oh, I mean, of course...I guess I just didn't realize how much he was still...handling."

Was that right? It was hard to bullshit my way through a conversation I didn't truly understand, but it was crucial I get this information from Danny right now.

His expression smoothed, turning empathetic. "It's a lot, yeah. In the last week or so, there have definitely been a few balls dropped. Usually, I get flurries of emails from him at night, but the last few days? Nothing. That's why I'm here. The only way I can get his attention to prep for the pitch in California on Friday is to get in his face. It's going to be a beast and we need him focused."

My stomach pitched, and everything in my abdomen felt like it was sliding down to my feet. Dylan was working two jobs? Dylan was doing a pitch with Danny? In California?

For so long, his career had felt like the imposing third partner in our relationship. I thought he was changing. I thought he *had* changed, and that coming here with a fresh slate.

It was like finding a secret stash of love letters from your partner's ex dated from last week. I'd thought he was done with all that.

Guess not.

"California pitch. When are you leaving for that one again?" My voice sounded faint, but I had to keep going, even if it hurt me. Every detail I uncovered from now on would just sink the knife deeper, but I had to know.

"Flight Wednesday, pitch on Friday. Want to get there a day early to schmooze a little bit. And the time change is a bitch, pardon my language." Danny offered me a crooked smile, but must have seen the stricken look on my face. "Tess, you okay?"

My lips tried to smile back, but they trembled. Something dangerously close to betrayal flooded my veins. "I'm good, I just—"

"Sorry about that. He's freaking out over a calculus test." Dylan sauntered in with a bright smile. "What are we talking about?"

He looked so happy, carefree. And he was lying to me. By omission, perhaps, but...

I'd thought he'd changed.

"Sorry, I have another meeting. Good to see you, Danny." I flung the goodbye over my shoulder as I hightailed it out of his office. Dylan said my name as I passed him, but I squeezed my eyes shut, blocking him out.

I couldn't do this right now.

I fled down the hall.

Chapter 18
Dylan

"—if we go back to slide six..."

"Danny," I groaned. My patience had worn thin an hour ago. "Change slide six on your own. You can do this without me. I know I was at Worther longer than you, but it's time to spread your wings and fly, man."

We'd been stuck in this office for most of the afternoon, and I could practically *feel* the emails flooding my inbox. Now that I was spending my evenings with Tess instead of alone in my hotel room, juggling my roles—and workloads—at two different companies had become considerably harder.

But it was worth it. Tess's face this morning, her giggling shriek as I swept her into my lap...it made the escalating tension easier to bear.

Old habits died hard, and part of me knew I'd never fully leave my workaholic ways in the past. I'd been conditioned this way, nearly from birth, by my father, then by Henry. Strive. Succeed. Push.

But losing Tess had made me realize I could do all those things and still have a life outside of work. I had to, or I'd go insane. I had to, or I'd lose her all over again.

Speaking of...

"I'm serious. Ask your questions now, because as soon as the clock hits five, I'm out of here." In fact, I'd be speed-walking to the elevators. I hadn't seen Tess much all day, and I didn't like the way she'd run out earlier.

Danny scoffed, shaking his head even as he grinned. "You really have changed, man. Thriving. Meanwhile, Henry's still stomping around the office, mad as a bear that his next-in-line flew the coop."

A pang of guilt sliced through my chest. "I know. But Tess loves it here and"—I looked around the room at the bright orange and signature purples—"it's a special place."

Danny glanced around too, with a more critical eye at the riot of color. "Whatever you say, man. But...you should know, the old man is still talking about shutting it down." He lowered his voice as he delivered the mother lode of bad news.

Surely not...

"He said if we got the Botto account, he'd give me another year to triple revenue." Jinx was small but mighty—emphasis on small. Eric had been happy to pick and choose his clients and grow the agency at a moderate pace, but Henry didn't do moderate anything.

On paper, the mandate from Worther's CEO had been simple: Triple profits and you can have Jinx. Show me you can still make money all the way up in Chicago, and I'll hand over the C-suite title you've been working for your whole life. Oh, and your girl, too.

In reality, it was more complicated than that. Bagging the Botto account would help, but it wouldn't get us all the way there. Sure, there was room to stretch the Jinx team's workload, but I'd vowed to myself

I wouldn't push as hard. I'd learned my lesson—I couldn't burn myself out at work, and I couldn't expect others to do the same, either.

I needed a creative solution to meet Henry's expectations, and I still hadn't quite figured out the plan. But it shouldn't have mattered. I had time. Or at least, I was supposed to.

"He wants the prodigal son back. You haven't lost any accounts from your Worther roster, but they haven't grown, either. Our close rate is down across the board. He's used to seeing numbers go up, not stay flat. He's freaking."

"Worther can weather a few months of flatline as the new team gets in place." The team I'd hand-picked to replace me and who I delegated practically everything to these days. It had taken hiring four people to manage my workload.

No wonder Tess had left me. I'd been drowning and hadn't even known it.

"True, but he's not happy with how this acquisition has gone, either." Danny gestured around, and my heart nearly stopped.

"Jinx is profitable, too. Where is this coming from?"

"Sure, it's profitable, but it's all getting put back into Jinx. Henry wants to see returns sooner, rather than later. Especially if he feels like the Worther bottom line needs a boost. He's started running the numbers on closing up shop. Might get a better return if he can absorb Jinx's clients into other Worther offices and funnel the revenue directly back to us."

My gut clenched. He wouldn't. He *couldn't*. Of course, my mentor hadn't been happy at my change, but he'd promised me.

"What happens to the people here? The staff that makes this place profitable to begin with?" *What happens to Tess?*

Danny grimaced and, to his credit, looked uncomfortable when he replied. "Maybe they take jobs in some of our other boutique brands, or at Worther? Maybe they just..."

The words he didn't say ballooned, stretching and contorting into a tangible thing.

Tess might be out of a job. Or, maybe, she'd get shoehorned back into a position at the mega-corp she'd left in the first place. I wasn't sure which was the best and which was the worst-case scenario. Tess had done good work at Worther, but it had taken her soul away, one day at a time.

"I won't let that happen," I vowed.

"That'll come down to you and Henry. You know you coming up here ruined all of his plans. Listen, you didn't hear all this from me, alright?" He sighed and closed his laptop. "Just know, you might want to get a little more aggressive about closing some deals around here. I figured you deserved a heads-up."

"Thanks, man," I mumbled through numb lips. *We'd had a deal. He wouldn't just close this place down. We'd shook on it.*

"Least I could do. I know why you're really out here, and it has nothing to do with a profit margin."

I grunted in agreement, and Danny smiled.

"Maybe this time you put a ring on that finger? Lock it down?"

"Yeah..." I sighed, trying to come to terms with the new roadblocks that had just been lobbed into my path. "Maybe."

***

I didn't knock on Tess's open office door when I slipped inside. Her nose was scrunched, eyes locked in on the newest iteration of the Botto concepts. I got the feeling a marching band could parade through the cubicles and she'd barely glance up.

It reminded me of when I'd peek into her studio back in Nashville to find her hunched over an easel, so absorbed in her work it took me physically touching her for her to realize I was standing there.

It was the look she got when she disappeared into something she loved.

I couldn't let Henry close this place down. She belonged here.

At her elbow, Tess's afternoon coffee sat, full and untouched. I'd asked Meery to deliver it, since I'd been stuck with Danny for the last few hours.

"Oh, so you only drink the latte when it's hand-delivered by *me*. Noted."

She blinked, brow furrowing as she came back to reality, glancing at her cup and then at me. "Oh. Right."

"It's probably cold by now. Might I suggest swapping it for a glass of wine? We could grab a bottle on the way home." That was the ticket. Danny was great, but diving back into Worther-world with him had made me itchy, old habits and the nearly inescapable compulsion to check my email tackling me from behind. Some wine on the couch with Tess, though, was compelling enough to keep the feeling at bay.

"I need to catch up on some work here. Just leave without me."

A trickle of unease slid down my vertebrae, and I closed the door behind me.

"I'd prefer not to. What's wrong, Angel?"

Her shoulder jerked as she spun back to her computer screens. "Nothing. Just need to focus."

The trickle turned into a flood. She was shutting me out. Again. I crossed the room in an instant, spinning her to face me. "Hey, don't do that. Tell me what's wrong."

She let the silence stew before she gave in with a sigh. "When were you going to tell me you're still working with Worther? Or that you're going to California this week?"

Her accusations were fast, sharp. My brain scrambled to catch up, mostly because she was only half right. "Where did you hear about that?"

"It doesn't matter where. I thought we were past this, Dylan. We were doing so well, and now I hear you're leaving for *days* and didn't care to fill me in? It's like Nashville all over again." Disappointment dripped from her words. Something went spiky and blood-red in my brain.

"I'm not going to California, Tess." I sounded calm, wholeheartedly trying to suppress my rising blood pressure.

"Danny said—" *Ah. Of course.*

"*Danny* is going to California. I'm attending the presentation virtually, from the Jinx office." I shook my head, but I wasn't sure if it was to assure her, or out of disbelief. "Danny's taking over more of the meetings because I'm actively reducing my workload at Worther. Yes,

I still have my job there, but I'm offloading as much as I can to focus here."

Hopefully. I really needed to get Henry on the phone. But not until I sorted this out. In her orange swivel chair, Tess looked suspicious, which just took my irritation up a notch.

"You're offloading your Worther work?"

"I'll transition fully in a few months, but I have to tie up loose ends before I can solely focus on Jinx."

Tess's eyes narrowed into slits. "You're not going to California?"

"I never planned to go to California. In fact, I insisted on setting the time of the meeting so it would be done by five, Chicago time. So I could leave with you, like I have been every day for the last month. You'd have known that if you'd just asked." The last part sounded more accusatory than I'd meant, but the more I thought about her reaction, the more frustrated I became.

I paced a few steps, restless, before stopping to look at her again. "Were you planning on pouting about it by yourself until you realized I hadn't gotten on a plane?"

Tess's arms crossed, her face twisting in a scowl. Now we were both getting worked up. Lovely. "Don't say that like it's out of line for me to need some space. Do you not remember how many times this has happened? That I'd just get a text from you out of the blue that you'd be gone for three days on some work thing? Or, better yet, figuring it out for myself after you forgot to tell me you'd jumped on a plane? Because that happened too. Forgive me for being triggered by the long-standing pattern of shitty behavior."

My stomach sank. She was right, of course she was right. But still...My fingers ran through my hair, and I ordered myself to calm down. "I'm sorry you were triggered. I understand, I do. But I told you I'm not that guy anymore. I've been here, with you, every day for weeks, and you still jumped to conclusions."

Was anything I did ever going to be enough? The question reverberated uncomfortably in my head. My chest.

"I'm sorry. I guess...I guess I'm still more hurt than I realized about...everything that happened before."

"I thought we were moving past some of this together. Fresh start." My shoulders sagged. I really had thought we were in a better place. How long would it take to win her trust back? Could I ever? She was still hurt, and as a twisting heat curled around my intestines, I realized I was, too.

Had any of this mattered? The cold, shocked feeling of the night she left floated uncomfortably close in my memory. Had we made any progress here at all? Maybe we had new hobbies and a new appreciation for each other, but was she still going to pull away from me at the first sign of difficulty?

"We were." She picked at her cuticles. I hadn't seen her do that in weeks. "We *are*. It just caught me off guard."

I swallowed the tightness in my throat, trying to see it from her perspective, feel what she would be feeling. I had a long history of neglecting her for my career. I could understand that.

Maybe I was asking the wrong question. Maybe it wasn't "*will she pull away again?*" and more "*am I going to let her pull away again?*"

I was on my knees in front of her before I could fully process that thought, already committed. I rubbed soothing circles around her ankles.

"I need you to talk to me, Angel. When something bothers you, or you're worried." I squeezed her knees. "I'm sorry you felt like it was old times again. I should have told you I'm still working on some stuff with Worther. I honestly didn't think it mattered. But I can be more transparent about that if you need, as long as you *talk to me, too*."

Her body relaxed as I spoke, face transforming from doubt to relief to something like an apology. "I'm sorry. You're right." Her forehead pressed against mine, fingers stroking my cheeks. "I should have handled it differently."

"It's okay if you need time to think about something, or need to be alone. But you have to tell me what's up. Then come back, eventually." *Please. Don't leave me again.*

I felt her nod, my eyes falling closed as she wrapped her arms around me. "I will. I'm sorry."

"I'm sorry, too."

Her lips were warm against mine. We were good. Now that I knew she had this trigger, I could avoid it in the future.

Lying in bed that night, Tess's even breaths blowing across my chest, I stared at the ceiling. It was lit up every few minutes by silent texts from Danny, who was still churning through that presentation.

Even though I left my phone where it was on the side table, I had the uneasy realization that I had triggers, too.

Three Years Ago

Tess

"I'm almost done." Dylan spoke before I'd made it fully into the doorway of his office. This was such a frequent exchange for us, I apparently didn't even need to speak anymore.

Still. "It's almost midnight."

"I know."

"And it's not even a school day tomorrow," I cajoled, wrapping my arms around his chest from behind. Friday night usually meant ordering a pizza and throwing on HBO, but that little ritual had been getting skipped a lot recently.

"Every day is a school day now," Dylan murmured, eyes on his laptop. I tried to ignore the tightness in my stomach. Ever since his promotion a few months ago, it felt like I lost a little more of him every week.

I should say something, I thought. I hated how he was so consumed with work. He needed a break, and I...needed him. I missed him.

Dylan's fingers tapped decisively on the keyboard and an email jettisoned off into the Internet ether.

He spun around, sliding his hands from my hips to my ribcage as he pulled me into his lap. "Hi."

"Hi." I smiled. This was more like it. Maybe he'd just had a busy couple of weeks. This new role was hard—more demanding than he was used to. I wasn't losing him; it was just the ebb and flow of working at a higher level. Now that he was working with more international clients, it was normal to have wonky hours, right? This wouldn't be forever.

My skin tingled where his hands roamed—my arms, bare legs, arching neck.

"Shouldn't you be in bed?" he teased, leaning forward to run his nose up the length of my throat, inhaling.

"*You* should be in bed," I shot back, tilting my head to give him better access. "You know I don't sleep well without you."

"Poor thing." His lips pressed hot against my skin. "We can't have that now, can we?"

He rose, carrying me across the room and down the hall. I snuggled into his chest, my legs wrapping around his hips. I loved this. Feeling so small and safe. His fingers squeezing into the soft flesh of my butt. It was everything I'd been missing for the last few weeks.

I used my teeth to scrape the skin of his throat. *Remember me? Us?*

Later, naked and panting, he gathered me close, squeezing me into his chest like I was precious.

"We should go for a walk in the morning. It's supposed to be nice." I broached the topic I'd been hesitant to bring up all week. But he was here now, with me. Not just sitting with me, but actually thinking about a spreadsheet.

He grunted. I could feel him already slipping into sleep, arms growing heavy around my stomach.

"We can walk over to that new coffee shop that just opened up," I whispered. "They have something called a lavender latte."

"Sounds gross," he muttered, breath shifting a few strands of my hair.

I pinched his arm, and he grunted again, pulling me closer to bite my shoulder.

"I wanna try it so bad."

"Then we'll go."

When I woke later that night to the sound of Dylan's phone, I shifted, watching him rise and answer the call.

"Is everything okay?" I asked when he came back into the room.

He bent, placing a kiss on my forehead. "Issue with one of the UK clients." The next morning when I woke, he was already gone.

***

Two weeks later
Dylan

"It feels great out there," I told Tess, coming in from grabbing the mail that had been piling up our mailbox. Bills. Coupons. More bills.

I dumped all of it on the counter.

Tess mumbled something affirmative, curled up in her favorite squishy armchair by the window, soaking up the puddle of sunlight with a book in her lap.

Winter was just beginning to melt into spring. The air was warm without being hot. The kind of day that brought people into their yards for the first time in months to mow and have a beer with their neighbors.

And I, somehow, had a pause in the incessant deluge of work, calls, and emails that consumed my life. I wanted to take advantage of it.

I studied Tess for a few more moments, bare feet crossed, legs hanging over the arm of the chair. She looked warm. Comfortable. Like home.

I rubbed my chest, suddenly guilty about all the hours I'd been putting in at the office. She hadn't complained, but she'd started asking more and more for me to come home at a reasonable hour, or grab dinner together. I'd probably said no too many times over the last few weeks.

A vague, sleepy memory surfaced. *Lavender latte.*

"Hey, didn't you want to go to that coffee shop a few streets over? We can go for a walk. See if that farmers' market has anything good for dinner?"

Was it my imagination, or did her shoulders hitch up a millimeter? Her brow furrowed. "I'm not really in the mood."

"You can finish your chapter, then we'll go," I tried again. I hadn't had a day to myself in...too long to think about. I wanted to hang out with Tess. Feel the warm air on my skin. Hold her hand. Hear about what she'd been up to for the last few weeks.

I saw her every day, but she felt distant right now, like we were orbiting around each other and never quite connecting.

"No, thank you."

When I peered back at her, she looked the same. Sitting in the same spot, same position, same thoughtful frown on her face. But everything felt weird.

"Are you okay?"

"I'm fine. Reading." She raised her book and her eyebrows at the same time, the universal 'you're bothering me' face. I held my hands up in surrender.

"Must be good. I want to hear about it later."

I tried not to take it personally when she didn't respond. She didn't look up when I passed through to the kitchen. I stood there, glass of water in hand, looking around my house like it was a strange new planet.

What did I usually do with my free time?

Hell, when was the last time I'd had any?

Fabric rustled as Tess shifted in the other room. I thought about the emails I'd left untouched last night, knowing they could wait until Monday.

I grabbed my briefcase from the chair in the kitchen and made my way to the office. I could work with the window open.

Chapter 19

Tess

"I'm wondering if we could push those timelines up even more."

My eyes narrowed at Dylan's question that wasn't really a question.

"Um." Noel glanced at me.

"I took another look at that opportunity to pitch the pharmaceutical campaign. That weight loss drug? I think it's worth a shot. If we can shift some things around, we could free up bandwidth for the pitch. It's a hot market right now."

Every red flag, alarm, and shred of intuition in my body began waving, blaring, and pointing straight at Dylan. *Something is wrong.*

I forced myself to take a breath. It had been a few days since our misunderstanding about California. His pitch had gone well, and all our Jinx projects were on track. Our team usually liked to spend some time on Monday morning celebrating recent wins and debriefing on priorities for the week ahead, but Dylan had hijacked our usually peppy, laid-back touch-base.

I didn't like it one bit. Just like I hadn't liked him walking around the office last week, asking people about progress on various projects. Just like I didn't like how he still slept in my bed, held me close, and brought me coffee, while his mind was clearly somewhere else.

Every cell in my body was alive with warning, along with a healthy dose of déjà vu.

Noel's face looked panicked. I used my newfound corporate confidence to interject. "We're at capacity right now. Besides, we all decided that project wasn't for us. We'd rather work with smaller organizations."

"That aren't evil," Carl muttered, bumping his fist with Chassie. I bit back a grin.

"That aren't evil. Exactly." I glanced back at Dylan, who looked deep in thought.

"Weight loss drugs aren't evil."

I scoffed. Were we really doing this? "Of course not. Medicines aren't intrinsically bad. But when the organizations that sell them jack up the prices of things like insulin for no other reason than to turn a profit, one might reasonably say the corporation isn't squeaky clean."

"I'm with Dylan on this one."

I just barely stopped my eyes rolling. Of course, Victoria just had to wade into this. She'd been oddly quiet since I'd taken her off the Botto account. I knew it couldn't last forever.

"The vision for Jinx before most of you joined was to get bigger and better accounts. I'm in favor of pushing ourselves harder."

"Botto *is* a bigger account, and we've almost closed that deal. I don't want us to take on more than we can chew and get burned out."

"But if we don't take on bigger clients, we can't expand. Hire more people," Victoria argued. She leaned into the table, looking past me to Dylan. "I'd be happy to take the lead on the pharma pitch. I'm not afraid of a little overtime if it benefits the company." She speared me with a glance and a raised eyebrow.

She probably wanted this shiny new account all to herself. Something else to lord over me.

Maybe it was the weird there-but-not-there tension simmering between me and Dylan, or my newfound courage, or the fact I was just *over it* with Victoria, but I snapped. "Victoria. I am the creative director. I think I know how to run this team, and the direction the organization wants to go in."

Awkward stillness fell. I wasn't sure what I expected after my clipped words, but her triumphant grin wasn't it. And I certainly wasn't prepared for what she said next.

"I don't think you do. We all know this role was a huge jump for you. I think you're only here because you happened to be fucking the right person at the right time."

I froze as the knife-edge silence in the room sharpened.

"What did you just say?" Dylan's voice was hoarse and low. If you heard it on the street after sunset, you'd throw your wallet in his direction and run away.

Victoria's face transformed into something pinched and ugly. "You heard me. Danny is so interesting, isn't he? And such a talker. Yapping away on his phone in the parking garage about how happy he was that you two were back together." She cast her eyes around the stunned faces of the Jinx staff. "She and Dylan dated since college. He got her a job at Worther in the first place. But Tess gets an offer from Jinx and suddenly she up and leaves him. Super convenient timing to rekindle that flame right as Worther puts pressure on us to close more deals.

Worked once, right? Maybe putting out again will help you keep your job this time around."

I gasped, unsure if I could dignify that with a response. Dylan didn't have the same issue.

"Everyone. Out." His words snapped like a whip, emptying the conference room of everyone but the three of us.

Dylan stood, glaring down at her. "Pack your things. You're done at Jinx."

Shock registered on her face. "You have no right to do that. You might be a big deal up at Worther, but here, you're just a consultant. All I did was expose this for what it is. Fraud. Favoritism. *I* should have gotten the creative director job. We never hire externally for leadership roles. Our culture is too important. But then *she* shows up?" Victoria sneered at me. "It didn't make sense. But now it does. You just happened to be sucking the right cock."

Adrenaline and disbelief surged from my hair follicles all the way to the tips of my toes. Everything inside me wanted to curl up into a little ball and crawl under the table. What was happening?

"That's enough." Dylan's voice echoed through the empty room. "I have months' worth of documented harassment not just of Tess, but of your other Jinx colleagues who have had enough of your bullshit. As to your claim that I don't have the authority to fire you, Eric was planning to announce next week the plans for me to take over as CEO. I guess we're announcing a little earlier than planned. Now, pack your shit and go."

In the back of my head, some disconnected train of thought floated by, noticing that Victoria looked like a puffer fish, gaping, cheeks round and flushed. "You...CEO? You can't."

"Can. Did. Eric gave me the green light to fire you weeks ago. Obviously, this isn't how we wanted to announce my transition, and I was hoping this issue could be resolved without my intervention, but you've forced my hand." Dylan punched numbers into the conference room line. "You have ten minutes to collect your personal items. I'll call security while you pack."

Within minutes, two security guards appeared, hovering as Victoria threw pencil cups and picture frames into a box.

"You will never last as CEO here, you hear me? This place used to mean something. Everything changed since it's gone corporate," Victoria ranted. "You know what? I don't even want to work here anymore."

"Works out for the best, then," Dylan drawled, scrolling on his phone while everyone else watched the drama unfold. Meery looked like she wanted to grab a box of popcorn.

Victoria rattled off more sputtering, angry vitriol as the security men walked her to the elevators. The office was quiet as the doors closed.

"Too soon to blast 'Ding Dong the Witch is Dead' through the speakers?" Chassie asked.

"On it!" Meery cheered, rushing back to her desk. Dylan cracked a grin, pocketing his phone.

"I hate to let people go, but I think we can all agree this one was overdue." Murmurs of agreement met his words. He projected his voice across the space for everyone to hear. "I know this isn't how we wanted to announce I'll be taking over for Eric. A lot more drama than I'd envisioned." A few people chuckled. "You might have noticed Eric is pulling back from the company. He has his own reasons for leaving, and I'll let him tell you. He's on his way in and we'll hold a meeting in about an hour to talk it out. I guarantee he'll be sticking around for a while here, making sure we're in a good groove before he officially leaves. I have a feeling we won't be able to get rid of him completely, anyway." More laughter. I wasn't sure how he made this seem important and lighthearted at the same time. He sounded so...in control.

"In the meantime, if anyone has any questions about Victoria's departure, or concerns, my door is always open. On that note, it hasn't been a secret, but I'll go ahead and officially inform you all that Tess and I are dating. We've been together almost since college, so this is not new, and our relationship has nothing to do with her getting a job at Jinx."

He paused to smile back at me, teasing. "Though she might have had some impact on my moving here."

Noel audibly sighed in her cubicle.

"Again, let me know if you need anything. I know this is a lot, but we're all going to be better off. We'll talk more when Eric gets in."

Mutters of agreement, even thanks, followed me as I trudged down the hall to my office. I couldn't feel my feet. What had just *happened*? The click of the door sounded behind me, and I realized I'd been standing in the room, staring blankly out the window.

"Are you alright?" Dylan's voice was quiet behind me. "What she said, how that all went down. It was unacceptable."

I turned to face him, lips numb. "I agree."

"Angel, I'm sorry she said those things." Dylan stepped closer, but I shuffled away.

"Not her. You." Dylan's head reared back, but I kept going, my words keeping pace with my racing heart. "I told you I wanted to handle Victoria myself."

His demeanor shifted on a dime, frustration reading in every line of his body. "Are you serious right now? Did you not hear how she spoke to you?"

"I would have handled it, but you didn't let me. You can't just come in here and take over everything."

"It's actually my job to come in here and take over everything." He stalked around the room for a few paces, furiously combing his fingers through his hair. "But even if it wasn't, she's been targeting you for months, Tess. If you really had it handled, she'd have been gone a long time ago."

I winced. His words cut so deep into my insecurities, it felt like a physical blow. *We all know this role was a huge jump for you.*

"That's not how I meant it." He reached towards me, but I stepped back, running into my desk and rattling the pens. His fists balled. "I meant it is my job to lead the people of this office. Her attitude has been horrible for months. But even if I weren't about to be CEO, I can't tolerate someone speaking to you like that. You might be okay with her using you as a punching bag, but I'm not."

"Whatever. It's done."

"Obviously, it's not. You're still upset. Talk to me about this. Is it really Victoria you're mad about?"

It wasn't Victoria. It was the fact I'd been worried for months that I wasn't cut out for this job, to *lead* people, instead of just following. And he'd just proved me right. I should have cut Victoria weeks ago. Months, even, but I'd been too scared or…worried that she was right. Maybe something *would* fall apart without her here? As if she was the only thing holding the team together.

I realized now I'd given her that power, though. She'd walked all over me and made herself out to be the queen of the office, when I should have had the guts to step up and lead, instead of letting her manipulate me into whatever direction she wanted.

Maybe I wasn't cut out for this. Maybe everyone back home was right, and I would never amount to anything. Dylan would always be above me, and I'd never have the courage to step out of my comfort zone, no matter how many lists I made.

But I couldn't say all that now, not in the middle of the office, with all these realizations crashing into me.

"It's fine. Look, I'm going to finish up some work at home. I'm sure you have things to focus on here. Meeting's in an hour." They didn't need me for that. It was the Dylan and Eric show from here on out.

He blocked the door, bracing as if I was going to rush him to escape to freedom. Maybe I would. My hands were sweating, mind racing. Between this and Victoria, it was too much. I'd never been good with conflict, and now I was drowning in it.

"I won't let you do this. I won't let you pull away from me when something is obviously wrong. You did that for years, Tess, and it nearly killed us."

Heat rolled down the back of my neck, hair prickling. "Me? It was you who killed us. Your obsession with work and money and *stuff*. I'm sorry if it was too painful for me to talk to you when you clearly didn't care about me at all."

"Didn't care? Tess, everything I have done has been for you. Your car, the house, your painting studio. I was trying to give you the life you didn't have growing up. Stability. Things you enjoyed. Ironic, now, because I realize you never enjoyed it to begin with. I found that house by myself. It was on me when the credit card bill came in. I bent over backwards to build that life for us, and you threw it away, anyway."

I leaned back onto the desk, bracing myself. Dylan and I'd had a lot of fights, but I'd never seen him look like this. Pinched and red. There was a vein bulging in his neck. I had a fleeting thought that he'd been keeping this bottled up for a long time. He had to have been. There was too much resentment spewing out of him for this to be fresh.

I could feel my defenses rising higher, brick by brick. Years of hurt and neglect welled to the surface, threatening to pop.

"I didn't want all that stuff! I wanted *you*. And you were married to your job. Maybe that's why you never married me."

The instant those words left my mouth, I should have felt regret, but I didn't. I didn't want to tip-toe around this forbidden topic anymore. I wanted to hurl everything in my arsenal at him. To hurt him like he'd hurt me. It was twisted and horrible, but I didn't care.

My chest heaved, breaths filling the silence between us as his face lost a bit of color. His arms fell to his sides.

"I did it all for you, Tess. But the more I gave you, the more you pulled away. It was like nothing I ever did was good enough. I didn't want to start a life like that."

A small shred of decency plucked at a nerve in my chest. *Listen to him. He's telling you something important.* I shoved it down.

"If you were so unhappy, why didn't you just leave, then?" I could feel my upper lip pulling into a sneer. Maybe this was why I'd left in the night months ago. I knew if all this anger and pain ever got loose, it would turn me into someone I didn't recognize.

"I was willing to fight, but you never were. You're the one who left."

I might have dealt a blow, but he could throw one right back.

Every moment of guilt and second-guessing that had chipped away at me since walking out crashed into me at once. Heavy and sticky.

You left. You gave up. I could see it in his face.

I was the bad guy.

Reality trickled into the rage boiling through my veins. I opened my mouth.

I'm sorry.

I still love you.

Fuck you.

I shouldn't have given up on us.

I didn't mean it.

You're worth fighting for.

Am I?

"I think you should go."

As I spoke, his phone buzzed in his pocket. A muscle in his jaw clenched.

"Yeah, I think I should, too." He looked at me, the vibrations the only sound in the room. "I'll sleep at the hotel tonight."

He turned and left without waiting for my response, already answering his phone. Back to work.

Chapter 20

Tess

Jasmine took one look at my face when I walked into R³ and handed baby Xander to Connor, who didn't miss a beat strapping him into a carrier across his chest.

My protests were weak, and she was strong, leading me by my elbow into Molido, the coffee shop that shared a parking lot with R³. She sat me at a table before I could catch my bearings. My brain spun, heart splintering. Snippets and accusations from today swarmed around me like a cloud of bees, stinging every time they settled.

If you really had it handled, she'd have been gone a long time ago.

I bent over backwards to build that life for us, and you threw it away, anyway.

You're the one who left.

It must have shown on my face. Molido's owner, Santiago, stopped by the table, tapping the shining wood to get my attention. "Caffeine or booze?"

"It's not even three in the afternoon," I responded, woodenly, hunching forward in my chair until my shoulders touched the table.

Tiago and Jas exchanged a look.

"That's chocolate. Maybe a beer," Jordan, Santiago's partner, grunted, kneeling to place a huge, meaty hand on my shoulder. His touch was light. Warm. "You good, Tess?"

He, Jas, and Santiago peered at me. Their attention made tears well up in my eyes. The café bustled around us, but the two owners had stopped everything to check in on me. I must have looked as miserable and confused as I felt.

"I'm okay." I did not sound okay. Jas reached her hand across the table.

"Is it Superman? The guy?"

"Yeah," I croaked. "We fought, and it was bad. I think we said a lot of things we had been holding back for a really long time, and now I'm not sure where that leaves us. And this woman who hates me...we had to fire her today. Well, Dylan did, but I should have done it and I'm probably not cut out for my job." As I spoke, my voice dragged, lurching and tightening until it was a mere squeak.

They exchanged looks.

"All of it?" Santiago asked.

"Three alarm heartbreak," Jordan agreed.

"We'll need backup."

"I already texted Lainey. She's off today, so she's on her way." Jas scooted her chair closer as the men retreated behind the counter in a flurry of cups and plates.

"I really only came for a workout," I whispered. "You don't have to bug Lainey."

Failing at my job *and* everything with Dylan *and* imposing on these people who I hoped to call friends but worried I wasn't close enough to was too much. A tear dripped down my cheek as Jas rubbed slow circles across my back.

"You're not bugging her. We're your friends. We're here for you."

"Connor's working, and I made you stick him with the baby," I sniffled.

"He is that baby's father. If he has a problem with holding his son, I have bigger issues than you do."

"And Lainey is so busy, and she has Sam, and she doesn't have time to come down here just because I'm sad."

"...Okay, and?"

Jas's reply caught me off guard. I blinked down at the wood grain in front of my nose. "And...Tiago and Jordan have other customers they need to focus on."

"Uh huh. What else?"

"I...I don't know you all that well," I whispered, the tightness in my throat squeezing to the point of pain.

"Well enough for what, hun?" Jas's hand kept up those slow, soothing circles across my shoulder blades. She was probably a really excellent mom.

"Enough for...this. To drop everything just because I'm...having a bad day."

She was silent beside me for a moment, still stroking. "When did you learn you had to do everything on your own, Tess?"

My eyes met hers, and tears began streaming down my face. Because I'd learned I was on my own from the first minute I could comprehend it. Sometimes, it felt like I'd always been on my own.

And that thought, more than anything else that had happened today, or over the last month, or years, cut me so deep that everything I'd been holding onto, all the strands of anxiety winding me so tight, frayed loose.

Because I'd been alone before, but with Dylan, I'd thought maybe I didn't have to be. I'd been wrong. He'd abandoned me for work, just like my dad abandoned me and Mom. Just like Mom abandoned me for the men and drugs and booze that ultimately killed her.

I was so tired of being alone.

"Okay." Jas pulled me into her arms, hugging me close. A sob escaped my mouth. "We can work on that later, maybe."

"Okay," I whimpered, laying my head against her chest. She felt solid, but soft. Like I could fall apart on her and it would be okay. So I did.

***

"And all this has gone down over the course of, like, a month? Where the frack have I been?"

"Starting a new job, living it up with your hot new boyfriend," I supplied. Eventually my tears had dried. Santiago had delivered a tray full of iced, caffeinated, carbonated, and alcoholic beverage options, and Jordan had presented a mammoth cheese board, complete with a heaping plate of his signature brownie bites. My favorite.

I loved Jordan.

I loved all these people. I wanted to shrink myself down and live in their pockets.

"Oh, that." Lainey waved her hand casually, like those big life events didn't matter, but her lips quirked up in a smirk. "It sounds like things were going well, though. With you and Dylan. And work? I'm just wondering if this is a fight or a *fight*." She arched her eyebrows on the last word.

I sighed, picking at the brownie in front of me. "The second one, I think. Everything was going so well, but...I don't know. I guess we were still holding on to a lot from our past."

"I have a question. And feel free to tell me to fuck off, but why *didn't* he ever propose?" Santiago was taking a rare break, propping his feet up on a chair next to me and plowing through a salad and espresso.

"Tiago," Jas warned.

"No, it's a valid question. I mean, I know some people don't want to get married. There are amazing couples who can live their whole lives together without involving a church or legal documentation. I'd understand if that was Dylan's position, but...we always talked about it." My stomach seized up when I remembered how I'd flung it in his face today. "We talked about it, but it never happened. It was always after this promotion, or after we settled into the house, or whatever. I thought he was putting it off because he wasn't sure about us, but now I'm realizing it's because I..."

My tear-soaked brain churned through these new realizations. It really had felt good to lay it all out there: Dylan's workaholic behaviors, how they'd driven me to withdraw, how I hadn't recognized myself for a long time, until recently.

Jas was right. I shouldn't have tried to muscle through life on my own.

And I didn't have to. Everyone at the table remained silent, allowing me to process my thoughts.

"I understand now why he was so focused on success. It just wasn't what *I* considered success. He thought he was providing, and I thought it was abandonment. I just pulled away." Seeing both sides of our story was a real punch in the gut. "I wouldn't want to marry someone like that, either."

I appreciated that my confession wasn't met with empty platitudes about me being enough, or how Dylan was in the wrong. The table absorbed the comment and thought on it.

"I hate to play the doctor card," Lainey started.

"You love to play the doctor card," Jas countered, making us all laugh. Lainey shrugged.

"Ok, well, *forgive me* for playing the doctor card, then. And I'm no psychologist, but the way you're talking about withdrawing and losing yourself makes me wonder if your avoidance is something deeper. Have you talked to someone about all this? A professional?"

"Not since after my mom died. That was...not a good time, and my relationship with my mom was complicated. It all hit me at once, and it felt like a crisis I actually needed help to get through. But this has just been..."

How to describe what it felt like to look up from your life one day and realize you'd been slowly freezing? Every time Dylan walked away, every time I made the choice to sink further into myself, was a quiet, incremental slide into frigid water.

Then, all at once, I'd found myself neck deep in ice, unable to move or feel or break free. It wasn't like the shock of losing my last remaining blood relative.

"The death of a relationship is its own type of grief, isn't it?" Jas said. "It doesn't have to be dramatic. The ending of something so big, however slowly it happens, is its own sort of implosion."

I'd thought it would be impossible for me to become more limp, but taut muscles turned to jelly, and I slumped further in my chair. "That's...exactly right." My tears had run out, but my throat could still signal the emotion choking me up. "I'm not the person I used to be."

"What changed?" Tiago took a swig from his espresso, nearly black eyes swallowing me up.

"Well, I...I've always been alone." I glanced at Jas, who nodded like I'd just confirmed something she'd known all along. "Then I found Dylan right at this moment when I was ready to strike out on my own. He made it easy for me to be bold."

I trailed off, voice scratchy. I gulped the glass of iced tea Lainey slid in my direction. "Then, after a few years, when I started losing Dylan...Maybe I felt like it would be easier just to give up. To lose myself, too. I mean, it *hurt*. He was supposed to be my other half, and I kept reaching for him, but he wasn't there."

Nods around the table as they considered.

"You said he started withdrawing into work more?" Lainey asked, biting her lip and staring off into the distance. "When I was going through a tough time, I threw myself into becoming a doctor. I got transferred to the best cardiac hospital and decided I'd be the best resident I could be. Then the best fellow. Then the best doctor. My ex and my friend...they hurt me. I couldn't control that, but I could control how I did in the OR. I realize now I was self-isolating for *years*, trying to avoid being vulnerable again."

More nods. Jordan stopped by to drop a kiss on Tiago's cheek and give him another espresso. He nudged the plate of brownies in my direction before he walked back to the counter.

"I don't know Dylan, so I can't speak for him," Lainey continued, laying her hand flat on the table, "but maybe he was reaching, too, and you just didn't see it? And when he got hurt, he pulled back into what he could control?"

Jas hummed. "When Connor or I hit a rough spot, usually one of us gets really distant."

"You and Connor have rough patches?" My voice was small and stunned. "You two are solid."

They were one of the most stable couples I'd ever encountered. They joked and laughed and seemed to genuinely like being around each other. Maybe it was my upbringing talking, but it had never occurred to me that two people like that, so in sync, could have issues.

"Oh, Lord, yes! We've been together since we were seventeen. We've both lived like six different lives since we met. Two of them in the last year. We work really well together, but not because we never have issues. Because we're willing to talk about what's going on. Get on the same page. Sometimes it's a struggle, but it's worth the fight."

I was willing to fight. But you never were.

My eyes prickled again.

The more I gave you, the more you pulled away. Maybe Lainey was right. I'd always assumed Dylan had retreated into his work because he was more interested in that than spending time with me. Something about the money and the clients and the wins were more compelling than coming home on that random Tuesday to watch TV on the couch. Maybe I'd been wrong, though. Maybe he'd only pulled away because I had.

The thought burned a hole straight through my chest.

"Dylan said earlier he was willing to fight, and I never was. Is that...am I the reason everything is messed up, then?"

"No!" they all spoke at once, but Tiago was the loudest. "You both drifted apart, sure, but he lost himself, too. Besides, it sounds like he wasn't really fighting all that hard, was he? If he were, wouldn't he have said something to you when you started getting distant? Forced the conversation?"

"Yeah..." Tiago had a point, but I didn't know what to do with it. I felt like I was sitting alone in the crater of my relationship's implosion, and I wasn't sure who'd pressed the red button.

"I don't think it's something that can be blamed on one person," Lainey offered gently.

"Takes two to tango." Jas nodded.

I felt heavy. "So, where does that leave me?"

"Do you still love him?" Lainey asked.

Jas held her hand up. "Rephrase, do you still *want* him? You can love someone and still need space."

I paused, even though I didn't have to think about it. "Of course." It was that simple, and that complicated.

"Of course?" I wasn't sure who asked, still too caught up as the gears of my mind sluggishly turned.

"He's the best person I've ever known. Smart and confident. He's so kind. He believes in people; that's what makes him so good at his job. He's..." *mine*. Even after all this, he was still mine.

"That is a great place to start. You still want him. Now what?" Jas asked.

"Now, go back to his place, bang it out, and tell him you're both going to stop being idiots."

I snorted at Tiago's suggestion while Jas frowned. "As hard as this might be for you to comprehend, not every relationship issue can be fixed with orgasms."

"But have you *tried?*"

Despite everything, the day, and the emotional exhaustion, I grinned.

I really, *really* liked these people.

"Okay, well, let's say that's Plan B." Jas glared, throwing a napkin in his direction, where it fluttered to the floor.

"You're picking that up." Tiago pointed at her. I bent to retrieve it.

"So, if that's Plan B, what's Plan A?" At Lainey's question, all eyes turned to me.

Well, if that wasn't the question of the hour. The question of the last few months, even.

Dylan had come here on the slimmest hope. He had put everything aside—his life, his career—to make this work, even though there was no guarantee I'd give him another chance. If he hadn't showed up, where would I be?

Probably still miserable. Alone in a new city with hardly any friends or hobbies. Still quietly collapsing into myself, like a black hole that would eventually cease to exist.

I thought back to the first night Dylan and I met. The hopes I had, the incredible, massive crush. How he'd made everything seem possible. He'd turned my list into our list. He'd been on my side since day one, fighting to give me everything I wanted.

Maybe he lost sight of what, specifically, that looked like, but he really hadn't ever stopped.

My heart squeezed.

"I need to see what he's thinking. We need to talk about this. And not just skip over it and forget this ever happened and start fresh. I mean...I need to know if he still wants this, too."

"And if he does?" Jas was smiling as she asked, like she already knew the answer, and just wanted me to say it out loud.

I gulped, glancing around. That crater wasn't so lonely anymore. It was their faces that gave me the last push, that last hit of confidence I needed.

"Then I fight. Like hell."

Chapter 21

Tess

I had only ever been to Dylan's hotel once. It was one of those long-term stay places, almost like an apartment.

His suite had a little kitchenette, sitting area, and a big king-sized bed. It was all white and cream, washed out and bland. When we'd stopped by to get him some more clothes last week, I'd pouted and told him he never had to come back to this sad little not-an-apartment ever again.

But the door opened, and here he was. Sad and beige in this sad and beige room. The surprise on his face clenched my heart into a fist. He hadn't expected me.

Well, I couldn't blame him for that. I was good at running away. Not so good at running towards. But that was going to change.

"Hi."

"Hi." I had rehearsed what I wanted to say on the drive over here, but I hadn't thought about how I'd get invited in. Shit. Hadn't his last words in my office been about staying here tonight, away from me? I should have called him before rushing over. "Um, can...do you mind if I come in? It's okay if you don't want me here...I mean, if you still need some time..."

He was already swinging the door open. Thank God.

"You seem relieved." His voice was like sandpaper. I wandered into the little sitting room, perching on the edge of a taupe, pleather loveseat.

"I didn't know if you'd want me here."

"I always want you."

I felt the urge to sigh, like those words had the potential to flip a release valve on all the pressure bubbling around in my chest.

"You sure? Even after...everything?" I finished lamely. He sank into a chair opposite me with a blank look on his face.

"Of course."

Of course. That simple, that complicated.

"I'm sorry I didn't call on the way over, but I was on the phone with my landlord. Yelling." My eyes flicked up to Dylan, gauging his reaction.

His eyebrows bounced upward. "Really?"

"Yeah, he's getting someone to fix the washing machine tomorrow."

"That's...great." His lips tipped up as he tried to smile, but didn't quite make it. He wasn't sure, yet, what this had to do with him.

"And I should have fired Victoria months ago. She was toxic and pulling the team down."

A divot appeared between his brows, then smoothed. "Alright," he intoned, woodenly.

"And I never should have left you."

That, at least, got his attention. His eyes lost some of that glazed detachment, focusing, darting around my face.

"It was probably one of the biggest mistakes of my life," I went on, clammy palms scrubbing down my pants. "Not the biggest, though.

I stopped being there for you. You're so right, I withdrew from you a long time ago and I'll never be able to make that up to you." It hurt to think about all the time we'd lost, all the pain we were feeling now that could have been avoided if I'd just...tried. If he'd just worked a little harder on *us*.

Dylan's elbows rested on his knees as he scrubbed his hands through his hair. "Tess, I was too harsh earlier. I didn't mean what I said. All this is my fault. You wouldn't have left if I hadn't taken you for granted."

"But it's not just your fault, is it? You wouldn't have sunk yourself so deeply into work if I had made sure you felt important to me."

I watched as his jaw ticked at my admission.

"You are, by the way. Important. No matter what your salary is or where we live."

His eyes went glassy and wet.

Mine felt prickly, too. "I'm sorry I didn't make you feel that way before."

"I'm sorry, too. I should have tried harder to be there for you instead of..."

I reached for him. I felt like I'd been in this relationship by myself for too long. I wanted to hold on to him, feel his skin, know he was right here with me.

His fingers tangled in mine.

"We both pulled away. It's not just your fault. I know..." Darn. I thought I'd gotten all my tears out back at Molido. Dylan stroked one away as it rolled down my cheek. I continued, choked. "I know how painful it is to want to connect to someone and feel like there's nothing on the other side. We weren't connected for a long time there, and I think both of us share the blame."

A deep sigh left his body; he wilted in his chair, as if I'd taken all the air out of his lungs. "I think so, too. When I came to Chicago, I was so set on just focusing on you, on what I did wrong. But you're right. I had a lot more resentment than I let myself feel."

"Me too. Maybe it was easier to see the ways you slipped away instead of owning the ways I did, too."

"Thank you." His forehead bowed to rest on our entwined hands, shoulders easing down even more. "Thank you."

I bit my lip, for the first time really comprehending what Dylan must have felt all this time. How much he buried inside himself to come to Chicago and win me back, even though we were both to blame for the way everything fell apart.

His skin was warm under my hands. I ran my fingers up and down his forearm, feeling the twists of veins, the beat of his pulse. It felt like mine.

"Now what?" Dylan raised his head, a question in his eyes. I wasn't used to seeing that. Some time ago, that uncertainty would have caught me off guard, made me falter. Dylan always had a plan. He always knew what to do.

But now, I smiled. I didn't just have a plan. I had a Plan B, too.

"I don't want to be Sad Tess anymore," I confessed, pulling my hands away. He held on, chasing me until he realized I was heading into his lap. I straddled his hips, breath catching when his arms closed tight around my waist. "I want to want things and be curious and try stuff, even if it means it might hurt or be embarrassing."

"You are never embarrassing." His voice sounded stern as his forehead tipped to meet mine. I was close enough to hear his throat working in a swallow. Close enough to hear his next words, even though they were hardly a whisper. "I don't want to be terrified you're going to leave again. You left me in pieces over the course of years, and I had no clue how to stop it. I lost myself because I lost you. I don't want to lose either of us again."

"Then we won't." Again, that simple, and that complicated. Of course it would be hard, and all of this was easier said than done, but I wasn't satisfied just retreating and watching the world happen around me. I would fight for him over and over if I needed to. I brushed my lips across his. "You are enough, Dylan. You don't have to work at it. You just are."

"You're enough, too. Even if we just watch TV and eat pasta every weeknight."

"Only Tuesdays," I choked, because those damn tears were back, but this time, they felt like hope. He laughed, but it was lost when my mouth closed over his, sealing in these words, this new energy that was us.

It wasn't starting over, and it wasn't what we were before. It was completely new. Not just sweeping something under the rug, but an actual next step forward. Together.

"I love you," I whispered.

Dylan's hand tightened in my hair, gripping like he wanted to hold on for dear life. "I love you so much, Angel."

"I want to fight for you."

"Well, that's good." His nose brushed against mine. "Because I will never stop fighting for you."

I smiled as I kissed him again, my tongue dipping between his lips to taste more. He pulled me closer, using the locks twined through his fingers to turn me this way and that, taking my mouth deeper, then teasing, nipping, only to dive back in again.

We kissed for a long time, seconds turning to minutes, and the sheer joy of being together again flooded me. These last few weeks, we'd been together physically, but it had felt like we were making up for lost time. Like nothing had changed in our relationship except we missed each other and were trying to make that be enough.

It wasn't.

It was nothing like *this*. His hands, running over me not to grasp, but to cherish. The teasing smile that brushed the edges of his lips like he, too, couldn't believe we were here. The feeling like we were on the other side of something, and we'd made it out alive.

When he sighed my name, arms clasping me tighter, I felt the growing bulge beneath me, and the contented, comfortable feelings started sparking at the edges. His palms ran down my back, then up underneath my shirt. The rasp of his hands on my skin struck a match.

"I need you."

The raw confession, paired with the desperate flex of his hips beneath me, roared into an inferno. I caught fire as a mix of love and adrenaline and relief and Dylan washed over me.

"Yes," I gasped. The word was hardly out of my mouth before he surged upwards again, this time bringing me with him. My feet landed on the gray-striped, utilitarian carpet so quickly my head spun.

"Take this off. All of it." He sounded feverish, pulling and grappling with my workout tank. "Not like New York, Tess. I need all of you. All of this off."

My shirt was barely over my head before his mouth slammed down on mine. I moaned as his tongue delved inside, spearing between my teeth to taste me again and again as I worked his buttons open.

We pushed and pulled, flew and fumbled and somehow made our way across the room. I sensed the moment Dylan stumbled, tripping on the mattress behind his knees, and I followed him down. We landed hard, groaning when bare skin met bare skin. I shivered at the silken slide of him against me. The way he gripped me tighter made me lightheaded.

I loved it. I sank over him to capture his mouth, and he opened for me with a groan, hips bucking. The hard jut of his cock against my belly flooded desire between my legs. He shifted again, pressing once more on my low back, grinding me against him.

"Tess." My name, strangled in his mouth, finally broke through the haze of lust. He was working to move me, raise me up so he had better access to my pants. I huffed out a laugh even as I scrambled off of him. He rose to his elbows, like he meant to follow me.

"Tsk," I clicked my tongue, peeling my leggings down and onto the floor. "You too."

He shoved at his waistband so hard, the button popped. I snorted again, watching as our clothes and shoes made a pile at the foot of the bed before Dylan sat up and dragged me close.

The hiss of our sigh was palpable, like the air being let out of a compression chamber. No matter how much sex we'd had over the past few weeks, this, right here, was real. Liberating.

I grasped him tighter, rising up on my knees to take him inside. He said my name again, called me Angel, called out to God, but I was swept away, overcome by the feeling of him.

It never got old. We could do this for another dozen years, another twenty, fifty, and I'd still lose track of my senses the moment he was inside of me. I was swamped, fingers fluttering, core stretching to accommodate him.

His smell was all over me, his taste on my tongue, his skin sliding against mine like velvet. It was overload. It was too much. It was perfect.

I rocked over him again and again, panting and clawing at his back. His thumb brushed the tip of my nipple, making me gasp and tighten around him.

"Fuck, that's it. Ride me, Tess. Take me."

His words sharpened everything to a point. My mouth opened, truths spilling out before my brain could catch them. "I want to take you. I want to make you mine."

Dylan bucked, groaning. His hand cupped the back of my neck, pulling me closer, millimeters from his face. "I'm yours, Angel. I've always been yours. I will always be yours."

"Always."

"Always." He growled the promise into my swollen lips, and the sound of it rushed down my spine, setting off a chain reaction I was helpless to stop. I cried out as the peak rushed over me, whimpered when he tweaked my nipples, rubbing my clit to prolong my pleasure.

Before I'd taken a full breath, I was flying again, flipped onto my back, Dylan bearing down on top of me. I sucked in a gasp at the look on his face, so harsh and pained I almost asked what was wrong.

He buried his face in my neck before I got the chance, keeping up a pounding rhythm that had my still fluttering nerves on edge again. "Perfect," he groaned, scrambling for purchase to pound into me harder, deeper. I arched, nearly screaming as the pleasure rose again.

"Dylan," I gasped, the only word I could form before I crashed under the waves of ecstasy once more. He moaned above me, shouting while his hips snapped a jerky rhythm. I rode it out with him, holding him tighter when I started to come back to myself, stroking his back as he panted into my neck.

"I almost..." he whispered, the softest flutter of lips against my pulse. "...there was a part of me..." His words were stilted, strained. "I thought maybe I'd lost you earlier."

I closed my eyes, letting his breath and words wash through me.

"I thought since I walked away..."

My heart broke. I wrapped my fingers in his hair and pulled him up to look at me. He'd thought since he'd walked away, I wouldn't come to him. That I wouldn't fight.

I stroked his face, tracing his jaw. "Walk wherever you want. I'll just follow."

His lips tipped up into the gentlest, most heart-stopping smile I'd ever seen. "Yeah?"

"Yeah." I kissed him because I couldn't stop myself. Because he was mine, and it was a travesty that he'd ever doubted it. "I'm sorry, Dylan. For everything."

"I'm sorry, too, Angel." He kissed me back before scooting up the bed to wrap the covers around us. "For everything."

We laid there, curled around each other, pressing kisses and I love you's into each other's skin until my limbs grew heavy in the warm circle of his arms.

"Tess, what you said earlier today...about not marrying you..." Dylan started. I waited for the familiar sensation of alarm to slither its way into my brain, but I just felt content. Quiet. I drifted a little deeper, hovering on the edge of unconsciousness.

"It's okay," I whispered, stroking his shoulder. "We can talk about it later." I was already fading, half-asleep.

"Tess." Even with my eyes closed, I heard his smile. "We should talk about it. I want everything out in the open."

"We have time," I whispered. My jaw cracked in a yawn. "I'm not going anywhere, Dylan."

His fingers traced my temple, brushing a few hairs away from my cheek. "Promise?"

"Promise." A few beats passed while I battled my weighted eyelids open, looking at him across the pillow. "Now you promise, too."

His face softened as he pulled me closer.

"I'm not going anywhere either, Angel." He murmured into my hairline, pressing kisses there. "I promise."

Chapter 22

Tess

I woke up and, for a clouded, dizzy moment, thought I was back in Nashville.

But that wasn't right.

I was in Chicago, on crisp hotel sheets that crinkled when Dylan rolled away, drawn like a moth to flame toward that familiar, abhorrent ringtone.

Everything in the room was dark, but the screen illuminated his face. He winced, the lights probably burning his retinas.

"Hello?"

I blinked. Another moment, another flashback. I was living in two worlds. Nashville, tense, hating every moment that Dylan wasn't next to me where he should be. Chicago, confused, but happy. Waiting for him to return to me, like we'd promised.

Only he didn't.

"What?" he hissed, and the leftover cobwebs of sleep cleared from my brain. "You're sure?"

My heart pumped once, thudded. Something wasn't right. Dylan shoved to his feet.

"They...right, yes. Yes, right." He yanked the charger out of his phone, beelining to the closet. I sat up, clutching the sheets to my naked chest.

"Are you okay?" I whispered when Dylan threw his suitcase on the bed, shoving it open. I thought he glanced at me in the dark, but I couldn't be sure.

"You'll have to shut down the client updates...yeah. Shit, we have to talk about China."

My face screwed up, trying to follow all the work words spilling out of his mouth. China? When was the last time he'd said anything about the foreign markets?

When he'd worked at Worther. I bit my lip, reminding myself that he still worked at Worther.

Some of the initial panic subsided. At least it wasn't an emergency with his family. Right? He wouldn't be talking about client updates if it was his family...

"Is it the twins? Your dad?" I hissed in the dark, just to make sure. Dylan's head shook sharply once before he returned to his conversation, throwing clothes and electronics into the suitcase.

"...on a flight in about an hour. Yeah, text me the confirmation number."

I stilled at his words before leaping out of bed. What the fuck was happening? What time was it? I scrambled to the couch where I'd dropped my phone last night, tapping the screen to life.

Four a.m.

I blinked at the sound of the zipper winding its way closed. Dylan was still talking about markets and emails and board members. I sank onto the bed, waiting. He didn't even glance in my direction, rushing around the room and peeking into his briefcase, shoving his legs into a pair of jeans without his phone leaving his ear.

"Hold on," he murmured to whoever he was talking to.

Finally. I leaned forward as he muted the phone, glancing at me. He'd turned the bathroom light on, and I could see his face. He looked...numb. Distracted.

"I have to go. To Nashville. I'm not going to make the Botto meeting tomorrow."

My blood froze. "What?"

"I'm sorry, Tess, but I know you'll knock it out of the park."

I sucked in a breath. Why was he talking about the Botto presentation like it mattered? Didn't he realize there were so many other things to talk about right at this moment? Namely, why he was walking out the door in a frenzy at four a.m.?

"Is everything okay?" What more could I ask? That seemed like the first thing to get out of the way before I grabbed onto his leg and held on so he couldn't leave.

"It's...I..." His eyes darted over my face, then back to his phone. I curled into myself, acutely aware of the fact that I was completely naked.

He rubbed at his brow. "I can't get into it right now." He paused, conflicted. "Trust me when I tell you, Tess, I wouldn't be leaving if I didn't absolutely have to. Do you believe me?"

Would I believe the Dylan from eight months ago? Absolutely not.

Now, though? I thought about our lists. His obsession with crafting me the perfect latte. His promise last night.

I'm not going anywhere.

"I believe you." The words rasped out of me, and I could only hope I actually meant them.

Dylan sagged, as if his knees had literally weakened for a moment. "Thank you," he whispered, leaning forward to press a kiss into my forehead. "Stay in the room for as long as you want. There's a key on the entry table. I'll...I'll call you. If I can. Just...Tess, please...trust me."

His plea traveled all the way across the room. He was already opening the door, rolling his suitcase through.

"Okay," I whispered to no one as the door swung shut with a soft snick.

I crossed my arms over my chest in the cold room, glancing around and wondering what the hell had just happened.

And why did it feel like two hundred steps backwards?

Chapter 23

Tess

The walk of shame didn't sting as much before the sun came up, but making my way home, still feeling cold despite cranking up the heat in my car, did.

At my apartment, I texted Dylan, asking him to call me when he got the chance. By nine a.m., I'd showered and made my way to the office, and I still hadn't heard from him.

My stomach was a ball of snakes, lurching and curling and making me so nauseous I would have thrown up all over the elevator floor if I'd had anything to eat today.

I blew out a breath, staring at my strained expression in the mirrored doors. I had promised Dylan I would trust him. And I would. This was surely some sort of post-traumatic reaction to him flying out the door without an explanation, like I'd seen him do so many times before. Not some gut-twisting premonition that just as we'd been about to settle into our future together, I'd lost him to the siren song of his mistress, Worther.

This wasn't that at all.

At all.

I was so focused on reassuring myself, I nearly plowed headfirst into Danny as he hurried out of the break room, holding two paper cups full of coffee.

"Ah!"

"Crap!" I squeaked, watching the hot liquid slosh onto his hands. I lunged towards him as if I could do anything to help. "I'm sorry!"

"It's okay. Probably my fault. Had a rough night." The dark smudges under his eyes stood out against his skin. He looked a little gray.

"Yeah..." I trailed off. If something was going on at Worther, Danny would know too, right? "Dylan got a crazy call a few hours ago."

Danny snorted. "I bet. They had my ass on a plane in the middle of the night. I'm just laying over here to talk some stuff over with Eric before I head to Nashville." He nodded for me to follow him as he walked down the hall to Eric's office. I just about keeled over when I saw the CEO, himself, walk out of the door.

I assumed he was here yesterday for the emergency "Dylan's going to be CEO" meeting, but I hadn't seen Eric in weeks. He'd taken the off-boarding thing pretty seriously.

"Tess." He nodded in my direction, taking the coffee from Danny. "How are you this morning?"

His voice lacked its usual pep.

"I..." I wasn't sure how much to say. "I was just talking to Danny about his early flight. Dylan had to get up early, too."

"Right. That's right." Eric's usual personality broke through for a moment as he winked at me. "I always suspected there was something going on with you two."

"He didn't say anything to you, did he? About Worther?" Danny interjected. Eric glanced between us.

"He just said he had to go, and he was talking to someone on the phone about a lot of work stuff I didn't catch." I swallowed around the lump in my throat that had been there for hours. "He asked me to trust him."

I wasn't sure why that last bit popped out, but it seemed relevant somehow. Like the men in front of me needed to know I was out on a limb here, too. Deep down, I hoped they'd give me some information to ease the roiling in my gut.

Eric looked pointedly down at his coffee. "Maybe for the best," he muttered, just as Danny nodded.

"Give us another day, Tess. It'll all come out in the open soon. Just...not right now."

Dylan being cagey was one thing, but all three of them? It was like I'd stumbled onto some kind of international conspiracy, which was ridiculous. We were an advertising agency, for Pete's sake. What could be so secretive?

"Tess!"

Before I could demand answers, Noel burst from the other side of the office, Carl hot on her heels. She looked panicked, and for a wild second I wondered if she knew what was going on here, and was coming to tell me.

"The Botto files are gone."

I blinked, staring as she practically sprinted closer.

"What?"

She skidded to a stop in front of me. "All the Botto files. Gone."

"The presentation for tomorrow, the source files, all our previous iterations. Even the original RFP is corrupted!" Carl was practically panting, worry emanating from him in waves.

"What do you mean, gone?" Corrupted? What? My poor, sleep-deprived brain was being whipped around. From a lonely hotel room to a corporate conspiracy, and now whatever this was?

"It was Victoria. We can see the timestamps. She logged into everything yesterday after she left the office and somehow erased it all or corrupted the files. We can't get to anything." Noel bit her lip, fingers twisting together.

My stomach swooped, brain finally clicking in. "Nothing? Not even previously saved versions?"

Their heads shook in unison and I glanced at Danny and Eric, as if they'd have any brilliant insights for me. Eric was rubbing his forehead, looking pained. Danny winced.

"That would have been Dylan's job to cut off all the access. Maybe he forgot?"

My intestines squeezed tighter. I was sure he had forgotten. And I knew why. Because of the crazy fight we'd had in my office immediately after Victoria had left the building.

My breath hitched, like I was being constricted from the inside out. "Alright. Alright." What to do? First things first.

"We need to make sure all her access is revoked. Passwords canceled, accounts closed, everything. See if there's anything else she's messed with, so there won't be any more surprises down the line."

"That, I can do," Eric jumped in, eager.

"Let's salvage everything we can. Anything that's been saved on personal computers, sent over emails…Is there some sort of backup somewhere? IT?" I looked again at Eric, who nodded and pivoted to stride into his office.

"I'm not sure what they can do if she's messed with the file histories, but I can ask."

Noel sprinted back to her cubicle, Carl close behind.

"We can…see what we can recover and, if we need to, piece together the presentation again. Most of the work was already done. It won't be perfect, but we can get it close." I babbled to myself, wringing my fingers.

"When's the presentation?" Danny asked.

"Tomorrow morning."

His entire face fell, and I just knew, on top of every other shitty thing that had happened today, he was about to pile more on. "Damn. I really thought you were going to do it." He shook his head, eyes pitying.

I groped for the half-wall of the cubicle behind me. I had a feeling I'd need some support for this. "Do what?"

Danny huffed, glancing around. We were alone. "I guess it doesn't matter if you know now. Nothing we can do about it. Worther is going to close Jinx down."

Every ounce of oxygen got sucked from my body. "*What?*" I was getting really freaking tired of asking that question today, but it seemed I'd woken up in Wonderland and everything was determined to go belly-up.

"That's why Dylan was here. Henry wanted to see bigger margins from this branch, otherwise..." Danny trailed off, shaking his head. I got the picture.

"That's why Dylan has been so focused on the accounts and new pitches? Margins?"

"Henry wants tripled profits within the year. Botto will make a dent, but you'll need more. Henry wants—er..." Danny trailed off in a strangled cough. "Well, I'm not sure what will happen now."

"We...Dylan and I fought about it. I thought he was just being a workaholic."

If Danny looked any more pitying, I was going to die. "He was dead-set on saving this place, Tess. Took a pay cut, even. You know, Henry wanted to announce Dylan as his successor a few months ago."

"As CEO?" Did I sound shrieky? Because I felt shrieky. I'd known Henry wanted Dylan as CEO eventually, but he'd been offered the job *now*? And Dylan had just...given it up?

"Yeah. Then Eric started talking about retiring, and Henry starts thinking about shutting this place down. Honestly, I think it was the push Dylan needed to finally put his foot down and tell Henry he was leaving no matter what. Talked Henry into letting him give it a shot here." Danny's voice got soft. "He told me you'd sacrificed a lot so he could have the career he wanted. You deserved a shot at your dream job, too."

Blood rushed to my head. Why didn't he tell me? I knew he'd come here for me, but he had *come here for me*.

And now he was gone.

The Botto presentation was gone.

Jinx was, maybe, going to be gone soon, too.

As I glanced around, I noted people's faces. Chassie, and their love of all things pop culture. Meery, and her burgeoning social media career. Tobias, who had two kids at home and another on the way. Noel, and that house she wanted to buy.

A crushing weight pinned me to the ground.

It was a twisted sort of irony for me to get a glimpse of what Dylan dealt with daily. I wondered how often he felt like this? This panicked, out-of-control feeling where everything was on my shoulders and all I wanted to do was grab every ball in sight to make sure it didn't drop.

If he'd felt like this, I wished he'd have told me. Maybe I'd ask him when I saw him again.

But I had things to do first.

"Jinx is not closing."

"Huh?" Danny's face screwed up in confusion, so I repeated myself, louder this time.

"Jinx. It's not closing. Not now, at least."

Something sparked in Danny's eyes. Curiosity. Respect, maybe. "What are you going to do?"

"Salvage this Botto presentation, to start. Then bag a few more clients. And then..." I glanced at him. Or maybe glared, given the way he flinched backwards. "Then you're going to tell me exactly where Dylan is and what is going on, so I can fix that, too."

Chapter 24

Dylan

Tess's airy voice trickled through the speaker of my office phone, followed by a beep. Voicemail again.

After a few texts and a brief round of phone tag yesterday morning, she'd gone radio silent, just like when I was in Japan and she'd left. Only this time, I was keenly aware of every minute that passed without her.

I'd tried to call her a few hours ago on the way back from the hospital, but my phone had died. Thank God I knew her number by heart. Not that it was doing me any good.

I left a stumbling, slightly incoherent message telling her I hoped the Botto presentation had gone well. I almost asked her to call me back, but I could already see Ron, the head of the board, striding down Worther's hallway. My free time was up. I was about to get sucked back into the nightmare I'd been living in since yesterday morning.

"Anyway, I'm sorry I have to go...I love you...Please just..." Please just what? Trust that I wasn't choosing work over her again, even though I clearly was? "Just let me explain after all is said and done. It's almost over, okay?"

I waited for a beat, as if she would respond, then remembered I was just talking to her message system and fumbled to hang up the phone. I chugged the dregs of the cold hospital coffee I'd been nursing for the last hour, rubbing gritty eyes as I ducked out of my old office and headed back down the hall to Henry's.

My gut clenched.

Henry.

My larger-than-life mentor, the billionaire media mogul, had looked so small in that hospital bed. Beth, his wife, had looked even smaller, like a shell. I'd blinked down at him, unconscious and hooked to a million and one machines, and let the words "blockage" and "cardiac arrest" and "heart attack" wash over me.

I kept walking down the hall, even though the memory of that private hospital room made me want to turn on my heel and call Tess again. Get on a plane and fly as fast as I could to Chicago. Grip her shoulders and shake her and tell her I never wanted this. I didn't want to be that man, working my body to the breaking point just for...for what? Work?

Fuck. I wanted Tess. Hopefully, I could remedy that soon. As long as everything wrapped up in the next few minutes, I could be on a flight back to Chicago tonight.

"If we push the UK director into the global ops position, we can keep Tindell where he is in California."

Ron was talking at me before I'd fully stepped into the room. Gina, another board member, Danny, and Ramón, Worther's Chief People Officer, all sprawled around Henry's office. We'd been camped out here on and off since I'd landed the day before. Had it been yesterday? Day and night lost meaning when we were frantically trying to put out fires before they started.

I blinked, trying to re-orient myself to the conversation we'd been having before I'd left earlier. To see Henry. Who might never stand in this room again.

"I thought we already decided Lochlan was the best choice for CEO." At least, that had been the plan before I'd left for the hospital, and I was banking on it *staying* the plan.

"And we already told you, Lochlan announced his retirement for next year. We can't announce a temporary CEO after all this instability. It'll make us look even worse," Ron blustered, lowering his bulk into a chair around Henry's conference table.

"It's not corporate instability, it's a cardiac event," I argued back, sick to death of Ron and pretty much everyone else except Danny. How had I ever thought I could spend hours and hours a day navigating these people and all the politics and the endless decisions and responsibilities they'd thrown in my lap over the last thirty-six hours?

Life had been a whirlwind from the second my plane touched down, fielding calls from clients who hadn't heard from Henry, dropping into meetings I was only half tuned into, endless calls and video conferences with the board and the Worther network's CEOs as we all scrambled.

"I call it instability when he didn't have the decency to name who he wanted as the next CEO," Gina muttered, scowling at Henry's desk like the man himself would magically appear there so she could give him a piece of her mind.

"Well, technically he did." Ron stared at me from across the table. I sighed. I was exhausted and sad and had spent the whole day barely comprehending all the meetings I'd been shoved into. *Nothing to see here. Just Henry's right-hand man sitting in on this meeting instead of the CEO. Don't think too hard about the fact you haven't seen him around here in months...Everything's fine.*

Ron scowled when I rubbed again at my eyes. "Forgive me if you think this is tedious, Morris. Some of us are trying to clean up the shitstorm you caused."

I scrubbed my hands down my face. Leave it to Henry, stubborn ass that he was, to refuse to do any succession planning while I was in Chicago. He'd been so sure I'd come back. "I told you all when I got here, I'm not Worther's CEO."

"Henry seemed to think you were. I don't see what the issue is. Everyone expects it. Just take the fucking job and let's move on," Ron jabbed a stubby finger in my direction.

Bile rose in my throat, panic at being forced into the position I'd given my blood, sweat, and tears for. I didn't want it now. "It's not that simple."

"It is, actually," Ramón chimed in, steepling his hands in front of his face. "We have another day, maybe, before word of Henry's condition gets public. We have to make an announcement before that happens, look like we are in control. If we announce Dylan as CEO, the way he planned, it shows consistency within the organization, and it's an expected choice. A *stable* choice. Our stocks will tank if it looks like we weren't prepared for this."

"No one is ever prepared for a massive heart attack, Ramón. I think they'd forgive us."

"We're a global corporation with no one at the helm," Gina chimed in this time, tearing her eyes away from Henry's desk. "Everyone knows you're supposed to be the next in line. What happens when we announce we haven't just lost one leader, but two all at once?"

Every eye in the room focused on me. I could feel the weight of it crushing my chest. This is what happened when you became the fix-it guy. People expected you to fix stuff.

Seconds passed, then more. Danny sighed when I didn't respond. "Surely the shareholders will understand if we take more than twenty-four hours to restructure our entire organization after an emergency medical event."

Ron sputtered. "That's just it!" His hand slammed onto the table, the sound ringing in my ears. "We are a multi-billion dollar enterprise. How is it going to look if the death of a single man topples the whole organization? No. We announce the news on our own terms, with a clear plan in place. Keep everyone calm. Let them know we have it handled."

"We do have it handled," Danny argued. "Normal operations don't stop just because the CEO is incapacitated."

I kept my mouth shut. Sitting down had been a bad idea. My head was swimming. Too much stress, not enough sleep. Had Tess slept last night? Where? At my hotel?

I would have given my right hand to transport myself to Chicago and burrow into her questionably rickety mattress and not come out for days.

"So, we just tell everyone, 'Hey, Henry's about to kick it. We don't know what's going to happen next, but we're sure everything will be fine?'" Ramón was already shaking his head. "Then the questions start. Who's signing off on paychecks? What if an emergency happens again? How do I know this won't affect the company long-term? How long do you think we can keep that up before we start losing clients?"

The door swung open. I blinked.

Tess stood on the threshold, cheeks pink. I blinked again. I was hallucinating. The lack of sleep and the shock of Henry's hospitalization had done something to my brain.

"Hey." She walked into the office, nodding at the others in the room. They gaped. Her hand on my face didn't feel like a hallucination. "Dylan? Are you okay?"

I stared up at her, feeling like every muscle in my body was made of stone. "Henry's in the hospital."

Tess knelt next to my chair, rubbing soothing circles on my arm. "I know. Are you alright? Have you slept?"

"Excuse me, ma'am, this is a closed-door meeting. Highly confidential," Ron snapped. Neither of us looked in his direction.

"Not really," I mumbled. Her fingers felt good on my skin.

"Eaten?"

My head felt like it was full of sand when I shook it.

A frown marred her brow. "Alright. I think you should go home."

I sighed, leaning closer. Home sounded divine. I didn't even know where home was anymore, but I knew she'd take me there.

"He's not going anywhere until we know exactly who we're going to announce as CEO and the impact that will have on the rest of the organization and the price of our stocks."

Tess turned to stare at Gina for a long moment. The other woman eventually shut her mouth and sat back in her chair. It was a wild, uncharacteristic display of dominance, and I wanted to pinch myself. I wanted to see it again.

Tess rose to her feet, taking in the state of the office. "All this can wait."

Everyone in the room but Danny started talking at once, jumping at the chance to tell her exactly why this couldn't wait. Tess held up a hand and waited for them to stop.

Who was this woman?

"We are not the government. We're not the U.N. People's livelihoods depend on us, yes, but not their lives. Stocks might go down." Tess shrugged. Ron gripped his chest like he was feeling his own palpitations. "It's just money. We can make more. Henry is in the hospital, and the first thing you think about is stocks. Don't you want to go home and hug Diane? Because Henry might never get the chance to hold his wife again."

Tess narrowed her eyes at Ron, who seemed to finally realize who Tess was and that she was well-acquainted with him and his wife. Tess had been on my arm for every company function for the last decade.

His mouth snapped shut.

"But what will we tell the shareholders? What's the statement for the press release?" Ramon fidgeted when Tess turned to look at him.

"I think Tess said it perfectly." Danny sat forward in his chair, resting his elbows on the table. "Henry is ill. Our thoughts and prayers are with him and his family. We're using this time to appreciate the work he put into building this incredible organization, and remembering how precious life is, and we hope others will do the same. If we need to put a name forward in the interim, just to calm people down, use mine."

Ramón pursed his lips. "We'll need someone from PR to workshop it, but it's not *bad*. We'll still need..."

I didn't hear the rest. Tess was pulling me to my feet. I looked back once, but Danny waved us out. I could still hear their bickering voices all the way down the hall.

"How..." I trailed off, noticing Tess pulling my luggage behind her, the bag I had packed in a frenzy and only cracked open this morning for a new shirt after a few fitful hours of sleep on my old office couch. "What are you doing here?"

She hummed as we entered the elevator. "Call it a rescue."

"I'll call it whatever you want." I felt loose. When the elevator dropped to one of the garage floors, I nearly tilted forward. Tess wrapped her hand around my bicep as we walked, finally easing me into the front seat of a silver rental car.

"I'm so sorry," I babbled as soon as she was behind the wheel. "They want to keep everything quiet until we have a plan in place, or until they knew more about Henry's condition. I couldn't tell you."

"I know. I convinced Danny to spill the beans before he flew down here." Tess smiled, lacing her fingers through mine as she maneuvered the parking garage like a pro. She had worked here for as long as I had, but it had been years since we'd driven to work together. What a tragic waste.

"You're incredible." She snorted at my praise, but I continued. "I've been trying to get out of that room for hours, and you managed it in under ten minutes. How do you keep getting more amazing? I hated it in there, every minute. And everyone's looking at me to solve all these problems, and I hardly even work there anymore."

I could sense myself talking, but something in my mind disconnected. I sounded slurred. Finally, I fell silent, only rousing when familiar streets rolled by.

"Where're we goin'?" I asked, head lolling on the seat to look at her. She was beautiful.

"Home."

I frowned. "Where home? I sold the condo."

The car jerked, and I rolled to the side before she righted the wheel. "You sold the condo?" she demanded.

"Of course I did. Months ago. Your half is in an investment account whenever you want it."

"Why?"

I snorted. "You weren't there. And it was so cold. Why didn't I realize how cold it was?" I raised my hands in front of me like I was trying to craft my thoughts into a tangible pattern, then gave up and let them fall into my lap. "You need life. Color. Plants. We should get a dog."

She put the blinker on and stared at me in the glow of a red light. "I'm allergic."

"Cat, then."

"Poop you have to scoop by hand? No, thank you."

I laughed. She was funny. I loved her. "Fine. A baby, maybe. I'll put a baby in you. I'd love your baby so much, Tess. I want to clone you."

My eyes drifted closed. Today had been too much. I didn't even know what I was saying anymore.

"Dylan. Where were you staying? Before Chicago? After you sold the condo?"

"M' dad's..." I murmured.

Her soft, sighed curse was the last thing I heard before I drifted off, her fingers still clutched in mine.

Chapter 25
Dylan

I woke up groggy, mouth tasting foul. It took a few blinks to orient myself. Dad's house. Guest room. Tess was nowhere to be seen, though the indent on the pillow told me she'd spent the night here, too.

What time was it? Had anything changed with Henry? Damn, I should call Ron and the board. I rolled to a seat on a groan, glancing at the bedside table for my phone and finding only an empty expanse of wood, save for a glass of water. I didn't remember coming in last night. I hardly even remembered leaving the office.

Had I left my phone at Worther? *Shit.* I needed to be reachable, especially with Henry in the OR. Even if the board went with Danny's suggestion not to announce a new CEO immediately, there were still clients to handle. Meetings and calls and emails I needed to be on to make it seem like everything was under control.

My heart sank as I trudged to the attached bathroom. I'd have to go back. No matter what unexpected, badass magic Tess had worked to bring me here, my phone was probably already blowing up with more emergencies. More needs. More things to do.

I wanted to crawl back into bed and pull the covers up over my head.

There was a time when I would have jumped at the chance to be CEO. Now, looking at my haggard face in the mirror, gray and drained after just two days back here, it was clear that version of me was long gone.

Working at Jinx, focusing on Tess and the things that made me happy, that's what mattered. Leading people, connecting them, fostering their passions, and helping them bring businesses to life. Books. Soccer. Pasta on Tuesdays.

That's what I wanted. Unfortunately, in the harsh light of the morning sun, I felt like I was just back to where I'd started: In Nashville, crashing at my dad's house, with the weight of a multinational organization on my shoulders.

Until I saw the note.

Good morning. Brush your teeth and come find me. Don't forget to drink some water! <3

Right back where I'd started, except for one massive difference. Tess was here.

***

My dad's recently renovated Brentwood bungalow was nice, but it wasn't huge. It was easy to follow the sounds of scraping and rustling in the kitchen.

I looked at the stale art on the walls while I padded down the white carpet. It reminded me of our old condo. A memory flashed.

You need life. Color. Plants.

I stopped dead in my tracks on the threshold of the kitchen. Had I told Tess we should have a baby? For the life of me, I couldn't remember anything other than snippets of our conversation in the car last night. Had she been mad? Disappointed?

She was here, right? Wasn't that a good sign?

"Dylan?"

I glanced up to find my dad sitting at the kitchen table with his computer, surrounded by piles of papers and folders.

"Hi."

"Hi." He looked at me, taking in the rumpled clothes I'd been wearing for over twenty-four hours. "Rough night?"

I laughed humorlessly, looking around. Tess wasn't here. "Yeah."

"Tess told me about Henry. I was sorry to hear it." Dad's lips tilted down before he shoved away from the table to pour a cup of coffee. "She told me a lot of things, actually." The look he speared in my direction froze me. I'd been about to excuse myself to find her, but something about his face locked my knees.

"Oh?"

"Oh. Your girl's feisty. Never realized." He handed the mug over without meeting my eyes. "I should probably apologize for that. In fact, maybe I should apologize for a lot of things."

In the morning's fuzziness and with everything that had happened clouding my brain, my last encounter with my father had faded to the back of my mind. Now it came roaring back. The accusations. The bristling fight.

I sighed, staring down into my coffee. "Dad, I don't think now's really the time—"

"No, I think it is." He motioned for me to sit on one of the upholstered chairs at the kitchen table. "Tess came knocking late last night, and before I could get a single word out, informs me that my son has been through a trauma and that I was going to open the door and let you both sleep here."

Even with the tension filling the air, I smiled. Tinker Bell really had relocated that spine of steel. "Yeah, that's my girl."

Dad grunted. "Since she woke up this morning, she's been on a tear. Commandeered my office." He gestured at his laptop and the papers on the table. "She's been in there on calls and video meetings all morning, and she has your phone."

"My phone?" A wave of relief crashed over me. I hadn't left it behind.

"It started buzzing three different times when she was in here grabbing coffee. She checked the screen, silenced the call, then flipped it back over."

Everything inside me was liquifying. She'd told me...yesterday? Two days ago? It didn't matter when. She'd told me she'd fight for me.

I hadn't expected a warrior.

I should have.

"I've been, er, thinkin' a lot about what you said to me the last time I saw you," Dad began, fidgeting with a pen. "I know I might have...overstepped some. I assumed a lot of things about your relationship that I shouldn't have."

"Dad," I started again. I didn't want to have a come to Jesus moment right now. I wanted to find Tess.

"And Tess didn't mind telling me this morning that I've made a lot of assumptions about other areas of your life, too." Dad winced, finally looking up at me. "I always just wanted you to be happy, son. And I realize now I might have pushed you too hard to do that on my terms. I haven't given you the chance to find your own happiness. And I'm sorry."

I let the words sink in, taking a deep breath. "Thank you for saying that."

Dad grunted. "Well, I mean it. I might have...well, I *know* I've been hard on the twins, too. Maybe...takin' some things out on my kids that I need to work on myself."

"What did she say to you?" Magic words, maybe? Only something supernatural could have caused my bitter, single-minded father to apologize, let alone admit to his failures.

He surprised me again by chuckling. "Plenty of things. She told me about everything goin' down at Worther, and I said that was great." He winced. "She practically ripped me a new one, talkin' about how I should be ashamed for pushing you so hard into a job that might have run Henry Worther into an early grave. And how you're happy, really happy, for the first time in a long time, and maybe you wouldn't have stayed so long in that place if I hadn't put so much pressure on you to...be something you didn't want to be."

My throat tightened. Dad took a sip of coffee before he continued. "I'll give her credit, though. She didn't totally throw me under the bus. She said we'd both failed you in our own ways, making you feel like you weren't good enough when you were just trying to do right by the people you loved."

I glanced away before my father could see the moisture gathering in my eyes, but I couldn't escape him entirely. His calloused hand closed over mine.

"She and I agreed on that. She said you've been doin' a lot of work to figure out who you are outside your job. I'd like to hear about that someday, if you'd like to share."

"Yeah?" My voice was rough with the grip of emotion I was trying to ride out. This was the most vulnerable conversation I'd ever had with my dad, and it was hitting me when my defenses were down.

"Yeah." He sounded a little choked up, too. "I might want to take some notes."

I bit the inside of my cheek, finally looking up at him as I flipped my hand over. "Sounds like a deal."

"Deal."

We shook once, a fragile thread of lightness winding through me. My dad wouldn't change overnight and, hell, maybe he wouldn't change at all. But this was a step. His words, his recognition of how he'd affected my life trajectory, closed a cut I hadn't realized was open. For now, at least, I could appreciate his outstretched hand for what it was.

An apology, a deal, for something new.

"Well, you weren't too far off base, pushing me so high at Worther," I told him, smiling when I thought about Jinx, how excited I'd been to start over there, how much fun I'd been having in a smaller, more laid-back environment.

"Oh, yeah?"

"Yeah. I'm…really good at my job."

"Course you are. You're my son, aren't you?"

"Maybe I just need to try it in a different place."

Dad clicked his tongue, smirking. "Nashville not good enough for you anymore, hot shot?"

I grinned. "Something like that. Now," I sat my empty mug down. "You know where I can find my girl?"

***

My dad's office was an add-on in the back, decked out with oak paneling and floor-to-ceiling windows. Tess had, in fact, taken over. Her bright pink laptop case and rainbow notebooks spread across the heavy wood desk in the center of the room.

I took my time, taking advantage of the rare opportunity to watch her work without other people around. The little crease at the top of her nose. The way her eyes flicked back and forth across the screen.

I sighed, hoping my ramblings about impregnating her hadn't completely bombed.

She smiled when she caught sight of me. "Hey, you."

Thank God. Maybe I hadn't said something *totally* out of line during my sleep-deprived monologue. "Hey...you look good in here."

She spread her hands on the table in front of her, taking up more space. "It just screams 'Beer Angel,' doesn't it?"

The laugh that left my mouth went straight to my head. "Tess, I'm sorry I had to leave like that. I was right there with you, so happy, then suddenly Ron's yelling in my ear and Henry's in the hospital, but no one can know yet...I didn't know what to do."

"I think you did what you needed to do. Even though I sat alone in that hotel room for like an hour trying to figure out what had just happened."

I winced, crossing the room to reach for her. She stood and met me halfway. When I swept her into my arms, she smelled bright and fresh. Felt like home. "I'm so sorry," I apologized again, because I didn't know what else to say. Her fingers stroked up and down my spine.

"I know it was a lot." She pulled back to clasp my face. "I trust you. I still love you even if you have to do work after-hours every once in a while."

I brought my hands up to trap hers. I'd never get enough of her skin on mine. "Thank you." I could have fallen to my knees and repeated it over and over if she'd let me, but a vibrating sound stopped me.

Tess leaned over to glance at my phone screen, read the name scrolling across the top, then promptly dismissed the call. She nestled her head back into my chest, and I stared at the phone, watching it go to voicemail.

Ron's name taunted me.

"Do I want to know how many times he's called?"

She grumbled something that got lost between my pecs before she pulled back. "No, you don't. Between him, Ramón, and all the others, it's been nonstop. I'm considering dropping it down the garbage disposal. I've always hated that thing. This would give me the perfect excuse."

"I can always replace it, if that's what you need. It could be a nice fresh start. Ritual cleansing, or something like that."

"We'll need to get some sage."

I pressed a kiss to the top of her head. "Maybe just a new ringtone."

"That might work." Her head tilted back to look up at me, and the urge to kiss her was so strong it seared into the very marrow of my bones. She spoke before I could bend down, though. "The only call I've answered today was from Beth."

My heart leaped into my throat. "Is Henry…"

"Stirred this morning, but still unconscious. I told her about Lainey."

I closed my eyes, enjoying the feeling of her fingers threading through my hair, comforting. "Lainey, your heart surgeon friend?" She'd mentioned Lainey and Jasmine a few times. The faint memory of a woman with a mop of brown curls in the gym parking lot resurfaced; from a time when I'd been holding onto the fragile hope of Tess ever speaking to me again.

"Cardiothoracic surgeon," Tess corrected, pulling away to lean against the desk. I nearly collapsed into a chair, tired and sore despite passing out for hours last night. "I texted Lainey, and they're going to connect. See if Beth can get a referral so Lainey can take a look at his tests. She might see something the doctors here can't. Or maybe have different equipment up at Mercy."

She looked so calm. Collected and in control. "That's amazing. I'm sure Beth appreciates that." I paused, picking my words carefully. "I appreciate that, too."

She nodded. "He's like a second father to you, Dylan. He might have contributed to you running yourself ragged, but he's family. I'd never have wished for this."

"I know you wouldn't." The clock on the wall said it was after ten a.m. As wonderful as it had been to sleep in, recuperate, there was still work to be done. "You keeping track of what's happening at Worther?"

A smile ghosted across her lips as she tapped her laptop to life and turned it in my direction. "They announced Henry's condition this morning. Sent an email to the shareholders. It says it's from Ron, but it's got Danny all over it."

I snorted as I read, already finding the bright optimism of Danny's voice imprinted on the email as it discussed how Henry was irreplaceable, and the Worther team was praying for his swift recovery. The letter said nothing about a new CEO or a succession plan, but it didn't need to. It sounded strong, but...human.

"You think Danny's gonna make a run for CEO?" I asked Tess after I'd read it through twice.

"He'd be a great choice."

"Better him than me," I murmured, returning her computer. She tilted her head.

"You sure about that?"

"Tess—"

She held her hand up to stop me. "After all the craziness that went down with Botto yesterday, and everything with Henry, I had to do a lot of thinking about your job."

"Wait, what happened with Botto?"

"I'll tell you in a second. Focus." She speared two fingers in my direction. "I know you're important to Worther. Henry wanted you at the helm, and I think in some ways, you wanted to see yourself there, too. If that is what you want, we can find a way for both of us to get back to Nashville."

My smile was breaking across my face. "Tess," I tried again, just for her to cut me off. Again.

"I love Jinx, but I know its future is somewhat up in the air." I frowned at that, but kept quiet. *What had happened after I'd left Chicago?* "If your dream is Worther, and you think you can do this without falling into the black hole again, then we should talk about that."

Her hands clenched on the desk. I gazed lovingly at where her knuckles were turning white. "Really?"

"What sort of partner would I be if I didn't let you go after your dream when it came knocking?" She peeked through her eyelashes. "You always wanted this. I can't be the reason you don't get it."

"You're not the reason," I assured her, leaning forward to cup her hips in my palms, pressing my cheek against her belly. "Not the only reason, at least. Theresa Lynn, I've wanted a lot of things in my life. The CEO position, my car, that condo across town. But you are the only thing I've ever needed."

She cradled my jaw. "You can still have me and have this at the same time. If you really, really, really, *really* need to."

I rose, wrapping my arms around her. I pressed a lingering kiss to her cheekbone. "Thank you for saying that. I know it probably physically hurt you."

"You have no idea," she sputtered, pulling me closer. "I mean it, though."

"I woke up thinking how grateful I am that I don't have to be on the hook for the whole company. I spent all day yesterday nauseous because I thought Ron was going to force me into the job."

She blinked, adorably nonplussed. "You're not just saying that?"

"Absolutely not. I like leading. Managing people and thinking about the intricacies of an organization. But maybe Jinx is more my speed these days."

She bit her lip, hope shining through her eyes. "You're sure?"

"I'm sure, Angel." I kissed the tip of her nose just because I could. "Besides, if I went back to Worther, you'd be exhausted standing up for me all the time."

Her eyes narrowed. "How much of last night do you remember?"

"Enough to be completely awed by you." I couldn't stop myself anymore, brushing a kiss across her mouth. She tasted like lavender and sunshine. "Apparently, you gave my dad quite a dressing down, too."

A guilty look flashed across her face before she tilted her chin up, defiant. "Well, maybe that conversation was a little harsh, but it was overdue. And Ron and the rest of them were out of line. Someone needed to step in."

"Thank God I have my very own angel willing to take on the job."

I savored the soft skin of her lips once more.

"Only sometimes," she whispered as she pulled back for a breath. "I don't think I'm cut out for all this confrontation. I said I'd fight for you. I didn't really mean with other people."

When I laughed, it was like every last ounce of worry, uncertainty, and dread spilled out of me.

I'd have to answer the phone eventually, and more than likely, I'd have to head back to Worther while the board figured out who would take Henry's place. But with Tess in my arms, the prospect didn't make me want to run back to bed anymore.

The phone buzzed again, this time Danny's name scrolled across my screen. I groaned, resting my forehead against hers.

"I need to get that."

"Probably," she admitted without loosening her hold on me.

"And you need to tell me about Botto."

"Mmhmm..."

"Even though I won't be CEO, I'll probably need to stick around Nashville for a while longer. I have to call Eric...there's going to be a lot to do."

Tess hummed, tilting her head back for one more kiss. "Sounds like we should make a list."

Chapter 26

Tess

One week later

Botto was ours. It had taken days' worth of negotiations and another presentation to Botto's CEO, but we did it.

When we'd gotten the email approving the contract, the entire Jinx office had erupted in cheers, and Eric had shut everything down early to celebrate. I'd popped into Willy's for a few sips of a watered down cocktail, but had hightailed it out of there as soon as was socially acceptable. Only this time, it wasn't because I wanted to go home and wallow in my sad solitude.

I practically flew up my stairs, thinking how nice it was to come home to someone. I grinned, wondering if we should get that cat after all. I wasn't ready for a baby—yet. Besides, it looked like Dylan would split his time between Nashville and Chicago for the next few months while Danny got his feet under him and Eric officially retired from Jinx.

And then...We'd be here. In Chicago. Together.

I couldn't wait.

I'd only been in Nashville for a day before I'd had to head back. There were a lot of forts to hold down, and things to put in order, and

Dylan had been needed at Worther. I'd missed him so much it was like an ache.

My keys rattled in the lock, and then Dylan was there, shoving the door aside to sweep me into his arms. We kissed like it had been six months, not six days, since we'd last seen each other. It was a little ridiculous to feel such a strong surge of rightness and love and affection for this man. But I couldn't help it.

We'd turned a corner together. We'd gotten through everything and now that we were on the other side, I just wanted to hold him.

"I missed you," he growled into my mouth. I swallowed the sound down, yanking him closer and wrapping a leg around his hips. He boosted me up easily.

"You two gonna put on another show?" Mrs. Ramirez drawled from across the landing.

I went rigid in Dylan's arms. He pulled back, coughing, though he didn't put me down. I'd finally plucked up the courage last week to re-introduce myself to my neighbor, and now she was smirking at us.

"You saw that? Ma'am?" He gave her his best sheepish, southern-boy smile, enhanced by the touch of pink across his cheekbones.

"Just the first bit. You two sure were making a lot of noise." She winked, her little dog prancing around her ankles. "I shut the peephole before I could get too much of an eyeful. I'm a classy lady, you know." She patted her curlers and pulled her mumu closer around her.

"I can see that, yes, ma'am. We appreciate that. We'll...try to keep the...shows to a minimum."

"Or not." Her smirk turned wicked. "Nice to spice things up now and again." With those words of wisdom, she shooed her cockapoo down the stairs and left in a waft of Chanel N°5.

"I'm never going to be able to look Mrs. Ramirez in the eyes again," I warned as Dylan backed into the apartment. He almost knocked over his suitcase where it sat by the door. His laptop and a few files took up most of the kitchen counter. We were going to need a bigger place. Worther was still paying for his long-term hotel room, but in a few weeks his work with the mother ship would be done, and he'd need space to put everything he currently had in storage in Nashville.

"I don't know. She seemed cool. 'Spice things up' is pretty great advice, as we know."

"Yes, we do." I slid down his body, but kept my arms looped around his neck. "I missed you, too, by the way."

"Good...that's good..." He glanced at the coffee table, then back to me. "Tess—"

"How's Henry?" While we'd been apart, Lainey had reviewed Henry's files and assured us the situation was severe, but not dire. He'd woken up two days later, and the first thing he'd asked for had been his wife, Beth.

"Good. I saw him before I left. He's got a long road to recovery, but they're hopeful he'll be back on his feet soon. The doctor said Lainey is brilliant and competent and a pain in their asses."

I snorted. "Sounds about right. She's a force of nature."

Dylan stepped back, rubbing his neck. "Yeah. I'm glad she's in Henry's corner. Listen, Tess—"

"And your dad?" I toed my shoes off. I wanted to curl up on the couch and talk with him forever. I wanted to rip his clothes off. I wanted to snuggle up and sleep. It had been a long week.

"Fine, hey, we need to talk," he rushed out, running his fingers through his hair the wrong way, making it stick up everywhere. I stilled where I was pouring a glass of water.

"What's wrong?" For the first time, I realized he looked stressed. Harried, maybe. Or nervous? "Is it something at work?"

A laugh blasted out of him, taking me off guard. "No, Angel, this isn't about work. Come sit with me."

"You're freaking me out," I warned. So simple, those words. Last year, maybe I would have kept my mouth shut, stewed in my uncomfortable feelings alone. Now, though, I trusted him. The same way he trusted me.

"I know. Just…let me get through this, please." He reached into his carry-on backpack while I sat, pulling out a shoebox.

It was blue, with worn corners. I had vague memories of seeing it stuffed in a closet somewhere in our condo. "I got this from my lockbox back in Nashville. There's one thing we never fully put to rest between us."

I frowned, more jittery by the minute, especially when he pulled the lid off with a quiet reverence usually reserved for priests or the parents of a newborn baby.

What was in that box?

"Last week, you mentioned how I never married you because I was already married to my work." His throat worked as he produced a small black velvet box and popped it open. Every atom in my body seized as

I stared at the bright gold band, sparkling with a rainbow of tiny gems. It was beautiful. Colorful and unique. A sob unfurled in my chest as I stared at it.

"I bought this the day we graduated college."

I blinked at the ring, then him. Then the ring again. The sob turned into a rock lodged in my throat. "What?" He'd been holding onto this thing for eight years? "*What?*" I repeated, because it seemed so inconceivable.

He laughed, but it sounded like sandpaper. He rubbed a shaking palm over his jeans, carefully setting the ring on the table between us. "You brought so much color into my life, Tess. From the very first moment you tapped that keg, I knew you were the one. But then I got a little up in my head, I guess. We were really young, and I wasn't sure if you wanted something more traditional, you know?"

I shook my head. I didn't know. If there was a ring in the world more perfect than this one, I didn't know of its existence.

"So then, I saw this one." He produced another tiny velvet box. Inside was a gorgeous solitaire diamond in a platinum setting with tiny baguette diamonds on either side.

"What?" I gasped. That seemed to be the only word left in my vocabulary. Because really...*what?*

Dylan set it next to the first. "I had to save for a while to buy it, just out of college. Neither of us was making anything at all, but I thought it would look beautiful on your hand. But then you lost your mom, and I know that was a lot. The last thing I wanted was for you to feel like you couldn't grieve for her the way you needed. I didn't want to distract from that."

"Okay..." I could understand that. Kind of.

"And I saw this one on a trip to New York, right after I got that first big promotion at Worther." He placed another ring on the table. A brilliant sapphire set in gold. It was followed by another—a diamond in rose gold with a gorgeous halo surrounding the cushion cut. An art déco style emerald, the band studded with rubies. A hexagonal onyx stone with three diamonds trailing asymmetrically down the side of a glowing, brassy gold band.

I stared at them all, lined up in their multi-hued boxes on my scratched, second-hand coffee table. I wanted to snatch them up and find them somewhere better to sit. They were stunning. Every single one.

"I always thought I had the one. But then things kept changing. The only thing that ever stayed the same was how much I loved you, but I didn't...feel like I had the right thing to offer yet."

My lips wobbled, a tear sliding down my cheek. This was too much. I needed to call Lainey. A person's heart wasn't meant to squeeze and swoop like this. "Dylan." My voice came out as a whisper and I had to swallow, reaching out to squeeze his arm to give us both strength. "You could have given me a paperclip and I would have been the happiest person in the world."

More tears escaped. Dylan's face scrunched, too. "I know that now. But you don't deserve a paperclip, Tess. You deserve it all. All of me. My best and my worst. The good and the bad. Every moment, every phase. I want to be there for it, even if I fall short."

"You could never. You're so tall." My stupid joke was a squeak, because I was actively sobbing now, arms hugging my midsection as

Dylan kneeled before me. He laughed, even as he hastily wiped his eyes.

"Theresa Lynn, I have wanted to marry you since the first day I met you. It hasn't gone away. Not when we were together, and not when we were apart. Please, please tell me you'll marry me. I know we're still working through things together, and we don't have to have the wedding soo-OON!"

I tackled him to the ground, and he caught me before we could both tumble onto the rug. When I grabbed his face, it was sloppy, taking me a few tries to locate his mouth. A breathy sob caught in my throat as I kissed him. "Yes."

His head jerked off the floor, banging into my face. "Yes? Fuck, sorry. *Yes?*"

"Yes!" I laughed, pressing my lips into his again and again as he tried to sit up to examine my nose. "I will marry you tomorrow, or in fifty years. Yes."

When he finally struggled upright, I sat in his lap, holding his precious head so I could look into his eyes. "I know now; you've shown me that we can get through anything together. And more importantly, I *want* to get through it with you. I choose to do all of it with you. The good and the bad. Everything in between."

"Tuesdays?" he whispered, finally abandoning my nose to skim his thumb across my jaw.

"Every Tuesday we have left, I want to spend it with you."

He groaned when he captured my mouth with his, our tongues tangling together. He tasted like the salt from our tears and the sweet, heart-wrenching love that filled every inch of my body. "I love you."

"I love you, too."

He cupped my head to draw me closer. Eventually, our frenzied kissing calmed, and he pulled back, placing lingering, gentle pecks onto my nose, eyelids, cheeks, lips, jaw, neck.

"So…"

"So…?" I echoed, eyes fluttering at his attention. I could stay like this, in his arms, forever.

"Which one do you want?"

I blinked my eyes open, staring at him with a hazy smile on my face. "Which one?"

"Which ring, Angel?" He swept my hair back, turning us so I had an unimpeded view of the jewelry on the table. My eyes glanced from box to box.

"*I* have to pick?" Impossible. Every one of them was perfect in its own way. A different representation of our relationship—*of me*—over the years.

"They're yours."

"Are they?" I squeaked. The concept was laughable. All these gorgeous, unique declarations of love and adoration? It seemed like too much. Dylan chuckled.

"I didn't buy them for me." He toyed with the ends of my hair while I studied them all, looking from one to the other to the other.

"What happens to the ones I don't choose?"

Dylan shrugged. "We can sell them, probably. Put the money towards a down payment on a place here."

As much as I enjoyed the idea of living with Dylan again, a violent rejection surged inside me. Someone else? Wear these beautiful pieces of art Dylan had picked out just for me? The thought broke my heart.

"Tess? What are you thinking?"

It was ridiculous and sentimental and stupid, but I felt like they'd all been sitting in a box, stuffed away in the dark for so long. Just like me, they needed to get out in the fresh air. Take a breath and feel the love that surrounded them.

"Tess?"

"They're all so perfect..." Most girls only got one ring. I should just pick one and be grateful and blissfully in love.

"I'm glad you think so." Dylan tucked a stray strand of hair back behind my ear.

"Which one, um...which would you pick? If you had to pick now?" I was chickening out, but Dylan's opinion mattered. Maybe he had a favorite, and that would be that, and he would sell the rest, and I'd never have to think about how beautiful the onyx was or wonder what the solitaire would look like on my hand.

Dylan frowned as he looked down at them all. "I'm not sure."

Well, there went that idea. "I just..."

"Talk to me, Angel." Dylan's voice contained a hint of a smile, and in that moment, I knew that he *knew*.

I looked at him through my lashes. "Is it...very extra and high-main-tenance if I love all of them?"

He pretended to look shocked. "*All* of them?"

I sat up straighter. "Yes! What, you want me to reject the ring you picked out for me first? Or the one when I was going through my art déco phase? You want me to just live my life knowing there's someone out there wearing the ring you wanted to marry me with?" I flailed my hands at the gleaming metal on the table. "It's not even about the rings, Dylan! This could have been a paperclip!" I wailed, tilting my head back to the ceiling.

"I know. I'm sorry," he murmured, cradling my jaw and bringing my gaze back down to his. "It's not about the rings; it's about us."

"Yeah." I may have been pouting. Uncharacteristic, but if I was going to be spoiled rotten, I might as well act like it.

Dylan heaved a dramatic sigh, glancing at the table one last time. "I guess we'll have to keep all of them."

My heart leaped at the thought, but I shook my head. "That's too much. How will I even wear them?"

"Probably on your fingers," he teased, grabbing my hand before I could pinch his side. "It's not too much. They're yours, Tess. Bought and paid for. Wear a different one whenever you feel like it. Wear two. One on each finger, I don't care. Just..."

"Just?" I arched my eyebrow, waiting for the catch.

"At least wear your wedding band consistently. That seems like the big one."

I laughed, tipping my forehead into the cradle of his shoulder. "Deal. As long as it's a paperclip."

I felt him shrug, then lean over. He rummaged in his work bag for a few moments before pulling out a paperclip, a triumphant grin on his face. Within minutes, he pushed a too-big, sloppy metal circle onto my finger.

"All of you, Tess. The diamonds and the paperclips. I want it all."

It was perfect.

Epilogue

Dylan

A year to the day that Tess left me, I made her mine forever.

It turned out when you dated "literally for-fucking-ever," as Gracie put it, not only did a lot of people *want* to attend your wedding, but they felt obligated to travel. Even if the wedding was scheduled on a random Tuesday.

"It's thirteen years in the making, man. We wouldn't miss it for the world!" Mac had assured me, even though I'd told him he and Lexi were under no obligation to schlep their four kids and a babysitter up to Chicago for a wedding. Lexi had told me to shut up and then convinced me to upgrade their tickets to first class.

The ceremony was small, just me and Tess, my family, and some of our closest friends at the Chicago courthouse. Mac stood by me while Grant and Gracie provided a necessary buffer between my parents. Next to Tess, Vanna, Lexi, Meery, Lainey, and Jasmine wore dresses of all different colors and styles, and everyone was so happy even our stoic and seasoned officiant, Nigel, looked a little misty towards the end.

We'd kissed and laughed while everyone around us cheered loud enough that a bailiff came in to make sure everything was okay.

Later, several hundred close friends and colleagues erupted in cheers when we walked into the museum we'd rented for the reception. The caterers graciously, with very confused faces, allowed Tess to tap the keg.

In the sea of family, friends, co-workers, pottery classmates, and book club members, I never lost sight of my wife.

My wife.

"I think my feet are going to fall off," Tess moaned, tucked against me as I carried her across the threshold of our hotel suite. The next day, I'd make her hop back into my arms to do this again at the loft we were renting in Logan Park. It was bright and open, with exposed brick and original beams and enough windows that I got a little self-conscious walking through the living room in a towel, even though the landlord assured us they had a reflective privacy coating.

"Well, that's what happens when you spend nearly four hours dancing on a concrete floor," I told her, lowering her to the bed.

"I had my Chucks on. I thought that would help."

"I'm sure it did," I muttered, taking in the sight of my wife sprawled on a pristine white comforter, decked out in scuffed, bubblegum-pink Chuck Taylors and a short, lacy dress with sleeves that covered her arms. She was perfect, cheeks flushed with happiness and wine. "Surely your toes would be bleeding by now if you'd had heels on."

"What's that?"

"Hmm?" I was too busy visually tracing the hem of her dress to look where she was pointing. I'd wanted her out of that thing since I'd seen her in it this afternoon. As she wiggled to a seat, the skirt inched up further and further. It was a helluva show.

"On the cart right there?" She brushed past me to look at something in the room. I immediately mourned the loss of her thighs, but used the opportunity to unbutton my shirt. I'd lost my jacket and tie hours ago. My shoes went next.

"Look what Henry sent." She showed me a bottle of heart-stoppingly nice champagne, and the note that accompanied it.

Wish we could be there. You love birds come see us soon. - Henry & *Beth.*

"I wish they could have been here," Tess said, kneeling over me as she examined the bottle. I pulled her into my arms.

"Me too. But we'll see them in a few months." We were already planning a trip to Nashville for Gracie and Grant's fall break. My father, of all people, had suggested a family staycation. Go figure.

He wasn't winning any dad of the year prizes yet, but he was trying, and had told me twice today that he was proud of me. Us. Even Tess had thrown her arms around him when she'd overheard.

"In the meantime," I continued, gathering Tess up even closer, pressing her down to feel my growing cock. "At least he sends good gifts."

"Have we had enough champagne?" she asked, eyeing the bottle.

"Is there such a thing as enough champagne on your own wedding night?" I tilted her chin with my thumb, pressing the open bottle to her lips. "Drink up, Wife."

Her eyes sparked at the new title, and she took a sip, then another, giggling when I didn't pull it back. Bubbles spilled down her neck, and I chased them with my tongue, making her moan.

I loved seeing her like this. Loose and happy and hot. It made me remember all the sloppy-drunk college sex we'd had after football games and the scorching, could-barely-make-it-through-the-door couplings after a night out in Nashville.

The new, soul-deep, heart-pounding ways we made love now. Now that I knew every inch of her. Not just her skin, but her heart, her soul. Every corner and hidden shadowy place.

I pulled her closer. She tasted like wine. Her hips wiggled on my lap as she gasped my name.

"I'm thinking about all the times I've fucked you," I admitted, skimming teeth down her jaw as she pried the bottle out of my hands. She set it somewhere on the ground. I was too busy working her dress up over her ass to see. Or care.

"*All* the times?" Her breath hitched, and she picked back up where I'd started on my buttons, prying my belt loose shortly after. "That's too many times to remember."

"But not enough times, in general." I pulled her dress over her head. She snorted, and I grinned when it got stuck and she had to shimmy out of it. I stopped smiling very quickly at the way her tits bounced. Her bra hit the floor next. She winced as the strap slid over her wrist.

"How's it feeling today?" I asked, leaning back to allow her better access to my zipper.

"It's fine. Shut up. Kiss me," she ordered, yanking at my pants. Considering I was sitting down, they didn't budge. I caught her forearm and brought it up to my face, lightly tracing the fresh ink there. It was still a little pink on the edges.

"Probably still too early to hold you down properly," I told her, loving the way she pouted. Loving it so much that I stood and threw her onto the bed. She bounced, hair splayed all around her.

A perfect, epic sight.

Rainbow hair, a braided silver chain with five engagement rings nestled between her breasts, and the fresh tattoo on her wrist.

1. Love Dylan, always
2.

I had the same on my arm, too, but with her name instead. A reminder of our vow to keep choosing each other, and to never lose sight of ourselves ever again.

Staring at all her engagement rings on a chain, I gulped, eyes darting to her left hand where she wore the first ring I'd ever gotten her—the rainbow stones—and the last: A band of thin gold loops lovingly called "the paperclip ring" by its designer.

"I fucking love you." It didn't matter how many times I said it, it kept feeling truer. "Now take your underwear off before I rip them off."

Goosebumps erupted over her skin. She shucked her white, lacy panties while I tore the rest of my clothes away, knocking her Chucks off in the process. Within seconds, she was naked on the bed, stretched before me like an offering.

Everything lit up with bright, sparkling lust. Tess shot up at the same time I lunged for her, and we met in the middle, teeth and tongues and greedy fingers.

When I pushed up inside her, she felt like home, and like the most mind-bending pleasure I'd ever experience.

"Dylan."

"Wife."

We whispered and groaned and cried out. It was too much, but it was too short. Between the wine and the day and the sheer amount of emotion thrumming between us, she clutched me, sucking in a breath and clenching her perfect muscles around my cock faster than I would have liked. I groped around the edge of the bed while she arched and sighed around me. Finally, my fingers made contact with glass.

I braced above her as she groaned, thighs shaking around my rocking hips. Her eyes blinked open. Lightning struck. I brushed the bottle across her lower lip, watching her sip while I thrust in and out of her, so slowly an ache started building low in my belly. *Perfect.*

"Not done yet?" Tess asked, looking up at me with puffy red lips and bright blue eyes.

"Oh, Mrs. Morris, I'll never be done with you." I barely glanced at where I plopped the bottle down on the nightstand before I flipped her around, grinning, heart swimming at the sound of her laugh.

Hours later, as the sun streamed through the window, I stared at the spot on my chest where our hands tangled together. Tess's bright rainbow glitter and the plain, still-foreign gold band on my finger.

It made me think about the first time I'd ever seen her. A quiet girl with so much curiosity, it had captured my imagination. Now, a grown woman, fully aware of herself, who held my whole heart in her palm.

A lot of things could unfold over the years, but as I lay there, brushing my fingers through her multicolored hair, I knew that this, my love for her, would never change.

Also by

She's mastered the heart's anatomy, just not its emotions.

Doctor Lainey Carmichael doesn't have time for relationships. She's too focused on finishing her prestigious cardiothoracic surgery fellowship and landing her dream job. Besides, all the men she knows are doctors, and she's sworn never to date anyone from work (again). But an unexpected confession from her quiet, burly, kind-of-boss, Dr. Samuel Reese, makes her take notice of something other than her scalpel.

While Sam's covert attraction to Lainey has only grown over the years, she hardly noticed he existed. Now, as he captures her attention again and again, he might have a chance to prove he's more than just another attending.

The good news? They've got more chemistry than a pharmaceuticals lab. The bad news? Lainey, herself, might be the biggest obstacle in the way of her own happiness.

Hearts on the Table is a standalone coworkers-to-lovers romantic comedy with a dirty-talking, cinnamon roll MMC and a charming, whip-smart FMC with work-life-balance issues.

For fans of strong women who can have it all, and the men who love them. Found family, secret/forbidden relationship, and a little biting.

Acknowledgements

I could not write a book like this without my husband, who makes me understand what it's like to choose someone every day, and who makes me write when I'd rather couch rot. Houst, I will choose you a million and one times and never have a single regret.

The Romantasy Crew, who are unfailingly witty and incredible and always down for one more sprint. You are probably the main reason I tried this whole publishing thing to begin with. Your support means the entire world to me.

My editor Jessica, and illustrator/friend Rebecca, who make the technical/hard parts of this job a joy. Jessica, sorry I still don't understand commas. Rebecca, you brought my characters to life when I could hardly articulate what I needed. Sorry if I was a diva this time around.

My alpha and ARC readers, like Kim and Susannah, who give me some much-needed perspective when I'm too close to the words. (Also, Kim, bonus acknowledgement for letting me rant in your general direction for 15 minutes when I'm stuck on a chapter. Thanks for being cool about it.)

Finally, I'd be remiss if I didn't acknowledge you, the person who picked this book up and gave an indie author your time and attention. Thank you, thank you, thank you.

About the author

Romance author Julia Fisher writes about smart, relatable characters, sizzling chemistry, and life-changing love stories. She lives in Atlanta with her family, too many pets, and a massive TBR she'll never be able to work through.

Love.V2 is the second installment in the Occupational Hazards series, where all is fair in love and the workplace...as long as no one calls HR.

Scan below to join my community, find more books, and get exclusive extras!